Shakespeare High

ACT I

Tiffany L Johnson

Tiffany L Johnson

Contents

Shakespeare High: Act I

1

Juliet

The familiarity of the hall, with its garish yellow paint and pale blue tiled floors, brought a smile to Juliet's face. She gave the stubborn door of her locker a gentle kick so she could begin organizing her belongings. A new school year, but not much has changed, Juliet thought. The scent of lilacs and lavender wafted into the hallway, preceding Puck as he rounded the corner. Juliet wondered what perfume he was wearing as he approached her.

"Girl, just look at how the summer has changed you. You ended last year as a bud, and before me is a rose almost in full bloom."

Juliet rolled her eyes at his theatrics.

"How is the sexiest virgin this school has to offer?" He didn't give Juliet time to respond, but she blushed at the mixed compliment. "I know I'm gonna see you at Romeo's party Friday night, right?" Puck giggled.

Juliet smiled and playfully swatted Puck's chest. "I don't believe I've received an invitation."

Puck grabbed Juliet by the shoulders and leaned in. "Please, girl, you know these parties have an open door. Besides, I know deep in my heart that you are a closet bad girl. You want to be at this party." Juliet attempted to turn away, but Puck held firm. "The closet is a dark place, my delicate flower. Senior year is a fine time to step out of it and bloom!"

Puck gave a twirl, showing off his floral kimono, which he'd expertly paired with a plain cream-colored jumpsuit. It looked rich against his ebony skin. He continued down the hallway but shouted to Juliet as he went. "Come out Friday and dance with us devils! That's all I'm saying!"

Puck opened his arms to Ophelia, whom most regarded as the queen of the school. Juliet turned back to her locker, hoping she wouldn't be drawn into the conversation. "Now, I know you will be at Romeo's on Friday. We couldn't kick off a new school year without our favorite seductress."

Juliet pretended to gag into her locker. Sure, Ophelia was bewitching with her long red hair, green eyes, and a body with curves that other girls begged to have. All of those qualities made it easy for Ophelia to have any boy she wanted. But Juliet thought her behavior made her hideous. She didn't understand all the fuss. So everyone wanted to sleep with her, to *be* her, but did anyone truly love her? Her outer beauty wouldn't last forever. Then what would she be left with?

Juliet shook her head. She wouldn't be celebrating the beginning of senior year by attending a party with the likes of Puck and Ophelia. Friday nights were youth group nights at Messina Baptist Church. A time to gather with friends, worship, and reflect on all the blessings God had provided that week.

After neatly stacking her binders and triple reading her school schedule, Juliet walked to the auditorium for the first day welcome assembly. The room was, for the most part, empty. Most students remained in the hall greeting each other, checking out the new underclassmen, and other things that didn't interest Juliet. She searched for a seat in the center, but noticed Katharina sitting in the front left corner. *Well, the center is awful anyway,* Juliet thought as she changed her plans. Very few people would give up a prime seat to sit with Katharina, who was regarded as a shrew even on her best day, but Juliet couldn't help but like her. There was something rebellious and free about her that Juliet admired. Katharina wasn't afraid to say how she was feeling, and she didn't care who judged her.

Juliet plopped down next to her. Katharina didn't say hi, just tilted her sketchbook so Juliet could see her drawings. "I'm designing a collection and trying to get some notes down. I'm thinking glass would lend itself well," Katharina mumbled.

Juliet got lost in the geometric shapes, swirled with blue, purple and green hues that softened the sharp edges of the objects which contained them. The morning bell startled her. Within moments the auditorium filled and the lights dimmed. Mr. Caesar, Shakespeare School District's superintendent, walked onto the stage. He cleared his throat and the microphone let out a screech. Juliet cringed as her ears rang.

Katharina whispered, "Well, that's a fine way to kick off a new school year. We'll all need hearing aids by the end of this thing."

"Good morning, fine gentlemen and fair ladies." Juliet was one of the few to chuckle at the odd greeting and waited for Katharina to make a flippant remark.

Katharina did not disappoint. "It's like he hasn't met any of us."

Mr. Caesar continued, his tone becoming somber. "As many of you know, just last month we laid to rest Principal Kingsley Hamlet. I want to begin our assembly by taking a moment of silence in his honor."

The room fell mostly silent. Juliet did her best to block out the whispers of her classmates so that she could say a prayer for Principal Hamlet in earnest. Mr. Caesar's voice cut through Juliet's prayer as he moved the assembly along. "Amen," she whispered.

"We must say goodbye to Principal Hamlet, but I am so pleased that his son, Dr. Princeton Hamlet, will take his place. Dr. Hamlet has been teaching English and Creative Writing for the last ten years at Shakespeare Community College. We are honored to have him join us and are so blessed that he chose to fill his father's position. Please join me in welcoming Shakespeare High's new principal, Dr. Hamlet!"

Few in the room clapped, except a few freshmen, Juliet,

and Superintendent Caesar. She was grateful that Katharina didn't rebuke her for being lame. The feeling passed quickly as Juliet realized that her classmates were all leaning towards each other, whispering excitedly. The cheerleaders were giggling and adjusting their uniforms to show off more cleavage.

Katharina leaned toward her. "How is it possible that this guy is winking with his smile?"

"If you're trying to say our new principal is a fox, then I agree," Juliet whispered back.

"A fox? No one says that anymore."

Juliet shrugged and turned her attention back to Dr. Hamlet. Charisma oozed from his flesh where other men might sweat. Her stomach turned over whenever he glanced in her direction. His voice was so rich and velvety. She closed her eyes and took pleasure in listening to him address the student body. While her eyes were closed, she asked the Lord's forgiveness; this was not how a girl should think about her principal.

Katharina got Juliet's attention with a gentle nudge. "I bet those dimples got him everywhere in life. He probably isn't even qualified to run a school, but he smiled at the right person, and BAM, here he is."

"Shh!" Juliet wanted to hang on to Dr. Hamlet's every word.

The first-day-of-school anxiety began to wash away from Juliet when she saw Macbeth in the bandroom, shining his trumpet. She flopped down next to him.

"How is it possible that we do not have every class together? I mean, how many AP classes are being offered this semester?" Juliet felt like she was whining, but she could see Macbeth felt her sentiment.

She and Macbeth had been friends since they were in middle school. His family had moved from Acheron so that he could attend a better school. They'd shared every class together his first year. In the beginning, they were good study and project partners. Juliet always sought him out for group work because he was the smartest person in the room. He was just so soft spoken that no one else realized it. Later, when Macbeth joined the band and chose the trumpet--the instrument Juliet played-- they became closer. They'd been inseparable, as if fate had insisted they belonged in each other's lives. It was strange not seeing his face until the end of the day.

"Who am I going to study with now?" she complained, leaning her shoulder against his.

"I guess our classmates have finally started taking an interest in college," Macbeth chuckled. "We should be thankful that we'll be surrounded by fewer dullards."

"Speaking of dullards, you will never guess who has AP Latin with me!" Juliet paused for effect and fanned out her hands as if she were a game show host. "Ophelia Fisher, beauty queen and head of the cheerleading squad! Can you believe she's taking Latin?" Juliet dropped the showy demeanor and quieted her tone. "She actually spoke to me and was nice, so I suppose I should feel bad about calling her a dullard. Turns out her dad started pushing her over the summer to start taking school and her future more seriously. He spent the whole summer tutoring her. Who would have guessed that our janitor is fluent in Latin?"

"God, imagine if I worked this hard in school and became a janitor. My parents would disown me. Although, to be honest, I think I'd get more joy out of being a janitor than a doctor. So are you planning to go to the party that Puck was shouting about all morning?" Macbeth asked, catching Juliet completely off guard.

Mr. Hal tapped his baton causing all to sit up straight before Juliet could respond. She made several errors during the warm-up that did not pass the notice of Mr. Hal. He berated the brass section before suggesting a water break.

"Mr. Hal is such a diva, right? Macbeth asked. Juliet's face was on fire. "Look, don't worry about it. You can suck during warm-up and during practice, but never during a performance."

"You're right, as always. Anyway, you're joking about going to that party, right? I think you already know the answer to that. I mean, beyond my father killing me for going to a party where there may be beer or God knows what else, it's unlikely that I'd know anyone there. Besides, I don't even know Romeo!"

Macbeth shrugged his shoulders. "It's our senior year. Maybe we need to have a little fun before high school is over. Besides, you don't need to know Romeo to go to his party. He is infamous for welcoming party crashers. I heard the one he threw at the end of last year had over a hundred people! I think I might actually go this time, see what all the fuss is about."

Juliet looked at Macbeth wide-eyed. "Well, at least you wouldn't have to walk into the party alone. Lady follows you everywhere. You always have someone to talk to."

"I'm Asian. My parents arranged for me never to be alone. Trust me, it gets tiring having a shadow."

Macbeth looked toward flutes. Lady dutifully waited for Mr. Hal to return. She glanced toward them and caught Juliet's eyes.

"I don't even feel affectionate towards her. She's just there. You know that," Macbeth continued, unconcerned that Lady might hear, "but I'll make the best of it because, let's face it, I don't get a choice in who I marry."

"You know, loyalty steeped in tradition probably lasts longer and stronger than most marriages that were forged by choice. So, I'm jealous of you nonetheless," Juliet admitted.

Mr Hal returned. With his eyebrow arched high, he addressed the brass section, "I hope we can get through a few basic scales now that everyone has had a chance to regroup."

Juliet's mind wandered as practice continued. What would it be like to have an arranged marriage? Who would her parents choose for her? Probably DJ. His father was Pastor Ramos, who led the congregation at Messina Baptist, the church her family had attended since before she was born. Juliet's mother played piano there, and her father was a trustee. Marion Ramos had gotten pregnant just after Juliet's mother had found out she was pregnant. The two families had bonded even more. When DJ's mom got sick, Juliet's mom had stepped in and helped any way she could. When Marion died, she'd made Juliet's mother promise to keep DJ on a righteous path.

Juliet had loved Mrs. Ramos, and she looked up to Pastor Ramos. She always felt accepted and loved by them, so it would be easy to become a more permanent member of the Ramos family through marriage. Besides, DJ was attractive enough, with his athletic build, dark shaggy hair, and those eyes that always seemed to be shielding secrets. She had thought about asking DJ on a date many times, mostly because she knew he was one of the only boys her father would approve of. Instead, she just left hints inviting him to ask her out. While they spent time together at youth group and teen Bible study on Sundays, he never showed interest in her beyond friends. Maybe because he was a football player and she was a "marching band nerd." Maybe his reasons went deeper than that. Perhaps he was intimidated by Juliet because she was on the advanced track at school. Maybe he preferred girls with large boobs and round butts, as opposed to Juliet's petite frame which lacked even the hint of a curve. Maybe he already held affections for someone else. Probably a girl like Ophelia; those girls had it all.

After school was marching practice. "I hope your playing improves on the field." Macbeth teased, as the band walked to the football stadium.

"I better improve. Mr. Hal might recommend I spend another week at band camp." She laughed at herself. "Stop worrying. I just got in my own head thinking about parties and arranged marriages. You know I'm a daydreamer."

∞∞∞

After marching band, Macbeth walked Juliet home with Lady trailing silently behind. Juliet admired the tall sycamore trees that lined every street of her neighborhood. It was the first day of September, but a few leaves had begun to turn golden yellow, deep red, and vibrant orange. Ahead, her father's white sedan was pulling into the driveway of their modest ranch-style home.

"Juliet, this is where I bid you adieu." Macbeth bowed and added with a smirk, "Your father scares me."

He stepped back and extended his arm to Lady, who offered Juliet the same loathsome scowl she always gave her, and how could Juliet blame her?

Her father smiled at her as he exited the car. "Juliet, my shining glory. How was the first day of school?"

"We have a new principal, as I'm sure you know, but otherwise, it was the same as every other year. Well, except that Macbeth and I do not have a single class together until 4th period band! I have no idea who I'm going to partner with to study! And you won't believe this: Ophelia Fisher is in my AP Latin class! Can you imagine me studying with her?" Juliet rambled as they entered the house.

Her mother heard her and chimed into the conversation. "Juliet, I'm surprised at you. We must not judge based on past behavior. Much can change about someone in the span of a summer. Give Ophelia a chance and you may be surprised to find that you have more in common than you think."

Her father leaned toward her. "Or she may be the same empty-headed, vain beauty queen as last year. One who is lucky to have a father to advocate for her."

Juliet's mother was shocked. "Mr. Capulet! You better go and pray for forgiveness before we sit for dinner, which will be ready in an hour!" She whipped her dish towel and the two pretended to rush off to their rooms in fear.

Juliet sat down for dinner after completing her homework and changing into fresh clothes. Her mother would not tolerate her sitting at the table in the sweat-soiled clothes she had worn to marching practice. Juliet admired her mother's attention to detail. The table was always set as if an important visitor would come at any moment, and Juliet was convinced that if a speck of dust hit any surface in the house, her mom would be instantly alerted. She wondered if she would ever live up to such high homemaking standards.

Her father had other standards for her. She was to be intelligent, hard-working, and a defender of justice, like him. He was a district attorney and took immense pride in his work. He felt God had called him to punish the sinful and bring peace to the faithful. He would always tell Juliet, "You must be strong and smart to combat a world full of sin."

Now that she was a senior and on the precipice of her life, Juliet couldn't help but wonder what the point of working hard to get into college was if she was merely meant to manage a home for a husband someday. She felt pressured to do it all: get the education, find the perfect husband, manage a career, have children, and run a home. These were the goals her parents had set for her, but Juliet never stopped to think about whether or not those things would make her happy.

Clanking dishes created a chorus in the kitchen as her mother rinsed the dinnerware. Juliet helped clean off the table. Her father lounged in his recliner in the next room and zoned out in front of the TV. Juliet considered whether she would be happy if her life looked like this. Was she happy with the path her parents had put her on? Did her parents care about her happiness, or did they care about upholding their idea of a perfect life? Had she been simply acting as her parents' puppet?

She began questioning what would happen if she stepped off her current trajectory. How would it feel? How would her parents react? Was their love conditional? Maybe Macbeth felt the same way about his own parents' expectations. She now understood why he wanted to attend the party at Romeo's. Senior year seemed like the last chance they had to explore before committing to their preordained destinies.

That night as she lay in bed, she fantasized about sneaking out and going to the party. Images of groups of boys drinking alcohol, loud music, girls dancing provocatively, and teenagers skinny-dipping in a pool filled her mind. Juliet didn't even know if Romeo had a pool, but it seemed like something that might occur at a party in the absence of adult supervision. In the darkness of her room, her thoughts rose unrestricted. She imagined going with DJ. Maybe if he saw a different side of her, he would see how fun she could be. They might drink alcohol and loosen their ambitions. She dreamed of receiving her first kiss, her body shuddering as she imagined what it would feel like to have DJ's arm around her waist.

Feelings of guilt soon took the fun out of her fantasy. Lying to her parents, attending parties with alcohol, and kissing boys would just bring shame to her family, and Juliet wasn't sure she could bear that burden. She whispered a prayer, one that wasn't memorized from a book, and called out to God with a genuine yearning. "Lord, help me to do what is right for me. Show me the path that is mine to walk. Help me to find a love that sets no boundaries and has no expectations."

2

Claudio

Claudio stepped into the locker room shower. He was always first to hit the showers after a hard practice. These two-a-days kicked his butt into shape fast, but Claudio feared starting each school day smelling of dirt and sweat. He could admit that he didn't know a lot about girls, but he fully understood that a sweaty, pimple-ridden jock was not what they clamored for. His teammate, Don Pedro, never seemed to care what girls thought of his hygiene. His showers were always the shortest. Claudio was positive that he didn't even use soap. That was fine for Don Pedro, but Claudio had a girl he aimed to impress.

His mind filled with images of Hero as the lukewarm water pelted his body. He had admired her since she joined the cheerleading squad. Her blue eyes, her long champagne-colored hair, the way her thighs looked in her uniform, the way she blushed whenever she took center stage... Claudio could go on; it all drove him wild. His body started to respond to his thoughts. *Damn these hormones!* he thought.

DJ ripped open the shower curtain and Claudio quickly turned away, but his best friend saw. "Hey, lover boy. Morning bell just rang. so we have five minutes to get to class."

Claudio would feel embarrassed, but he and DJ had been friends since Claudio's family moved to town ten years ago. They lived on the same street and had become instant playmates. DJ was his first friend, and they told each other everything, even embarrassing things like discussing their wet dreams and all the changes they went through during puberty. Claudio counted himself lucky to have someone like DJ in his life.

They had English and geometry together, so they talked as they rushed to get to their first class on time. "Bro, you really need to ask her out already or just move on," DJ said as he dodged a scrawny boy, nearly spilling the boy's stack of binders. He knew all about Claudio's obsession with Hero.

"Every time I try to approach her, I choke. What am I supposed to say? 'Hi, I'm Claudio, and I think you have amazing eyes. Would you let me touch your hair?' " Claudio laughed.

"She's good friends with Benedick's girl. Maybe you should ask her for advice. She could mention your name and see how Hero responds," DJ suggested.

Claudio threw his arm around DJ. "You are a genius! I just hope Benedick and Beatrice are currently an item. You know how those two are."

Mrs. Jones stood in the doorway, arms crossed. "Gentlemen, you're late. I'll give you one free pass because I know you had practice this morning, but don't allow it to happen again. You'll need to manage your extracurriculars with your studies or face the consequences," Mrs. Jones reprimanded as they slid past her to their seats. "Don't expect me to bestow special privileges on you as some other teachers do. I do not idolize football as they do."

"I'll work on my time management," DJ responded, "but I thought you would prefer me to smell of soap rather than to stink up your classroom with my sweaty balls." Claudio laughed and immediately regretted it.

Every wrinkle on Mrs. Jones' face seemed to turn downward. "We are only three days into the school year. Would you boys like to end the first week with detention?"

Claudio wiped the smile off his face. "No, ma'am. We're sorry for our lateness and will not let it happen again."

He glared at DJ until he apologized, too. Claudio did not

want to get grounded and miss Romeo's party. Hero would be there, and perhaps this time Claudio would work up enough bravado to approach her.

∞∞∞∞

Claudio sought out Benedick after school at football practice. Benedick was refilling his water bottle at the refreshment table, which conveniently faced the cheerleaders. "Hey, Ben. Stopping to admire your girl, or just getting water?" Claudio inquired, trying to sound light and casual.

Benedick turned and did not look happy. "I guess I was checking her out, but not in admiration. More to see if she is as miserable as me. We had a fight after the first day of school. She was mad that we didn't have any classes or lunch together."

"That doesn't sound like your fault," Claudio reassured him.

His eyes wandered to Hero, who was practicing a pike. He was amazed at her athleticism and continued to listen to Benedick as he watched her perfect form.

"Well, that wasn't quite the part that pissed her off. She asked me to go see the counselor and have my schedule changed. I refused. I told her if she needed to have our schedules match so badly, she should do it herself. She got crazy angry and said that I never do anything for her, that I'm always thinking of myself, blah blah blah. I thought she would get over it by the end of the day, but she wouldn't let me give her a ride home. She walked by herself. I tried to coax her into the car, but I wasn't about to follow her home, which is apparently what I was supposed to do. She texted me later that night to say that my driving off was proof of my selfishness and that we were through."

"Damn, Ben. That sounds like an intense fight." In truth, Claudio had lost track of the details while watching Hero.

"It was. Probably the worst we've had. I feel sorry about upsetting her, but really, I'm not changing my schedule just to have classes with her. I was thinking it might be good for our relationship if we had space during the day. But of course, telling her that didn't help. And I'm not gonna go following her down the road begging her to get in my car either. We don't live in a romantic comedy. I just wish she could see that I love her without me needing to be by her side every minute of the day. I need to figure out a way to apologize and smooth things over. So far nothing has worked. I can't tell if she is milking the fight or if she is serious this time." Benedick rubbed at his stomach as if Beatrice had physically wounded him.

Don Pedro pushed his way between them. "What are we chatting about, boys? We're about to run drills."

Claudio responded first. "Just trying to brainstorm a way to get Ben back into Beatrice's good graces."

"Look, bro, you need to take lessons from me. You ever see me lose my focus over some girl? Hell, no! I need to get drafted, and no chick is going to hold me back."

"So that's why you don't shower in the mornings?" Claudio paused for the punchline. "Chick repellent? I just assumed you lacked the ability to smell."

"Exaaaactly!" Don Pedro was unoffended. "Ben, focus on the game, become a tight end for a pro team, and she will regret the day she ever let you go. She will beg you to take her back."

Coach's whistle blew, indicating it was time to run sprints. Don Pedro was right that girls could be a distraction, but Claudio found his desire for Hero improved his game. He hoped his abilities would make her take notice. He may fumble when he tried to talk to her, but he was the best wide receiver Shakespeare had had in years. Maybe she watched him play the way he watched her perform. He often fantasized about making the winning touchdown that would fill her with admiration. Then she might come to congratulate him after the game, their eyes would lock, and she wouldn't be able to stop herself from falling for him. It was silly, he knew, but his wanting made him a better player.

Claudio had felt excitement at the possibility of finding

out what Hero thought of him, if she thought of him at all. With Benedick and Beatrice entangled in an argument, he would have to find another way. It was his senior year, and he didn't want to imagine a future without Hero in it. He would have to find the courage to win her heart, or, as DJ suggested, just move on already.

3

Bianca

In a bedroom that was more suited for a child, Bianca awoke. It was well before her alarm was set to go off. She counted the little pink flowers on the wallpaper and tried to fall back asleep. Unable to quiet her mind, she found herself staring at the back of Katharina's head. Katharina kept her dark locks long, refusing to cut it when Bianca decided to donate hers. Bianca missed having long hair, but felt good about shedding a few inches of it for a good cause. The hair would grow back; besides, it didn't stop boys from trying to capture her attention. Surely Katharina was the prettier twin. Her eyes seemed to be bluer, and her cheekbones were more defined. But she chose to hide her beauty behind dark clothes; she wore a scowl at school that kept everyone at bay. Bianca wondered how her sister could choose such a lonely existence.

She rolled onto her back and started thinking about Romeo's party. This was her last year of high school, and she would be damned if she graduated without going to a single party. Plus, she knew that Romeo always had the best ones. The other girls on the squad always raved about how fun and unrestricted they were. He lived in a mansion, and his father practically encouraged him to flaunt his status. Bianca remembered hearing about a party Romeo had held over the summer. Some college students had brought ecstasy and they'd played a risqué game of Truth or Dare. She crawled out of bed and stuffed herself into

Katharina's. It was no easy task, fitting two almost-adult bodies in a single-sized bed. Katharina turned over and grumbled under her breath, "What do you want?"

"Can't I just share a bed with my sister like we used to?"

"Again, what do you want? I know you. You wouldn't be up this early and jostling me awake if you didn't want something. And--I need to say this--your breath smells awful."

Bianca defended herself. "We had garlic knots last night! No amount of brushing or swishing can wash that away! Look, I'll get to the point and then brush my teeth again. Would that make you happy?"

"You could at least turn the other direction while you speak to me."

Bianca went back to her own bed. Why did every conversation with her sister have to feel so laborious?

"I was thinking that we should go to Romeo's party." Bianca quickly continued before her sister could interject, "It's our senior year, and I have always skipped parties because of you."

Katharina glared at her, her eyes narrowed like an animal zeroing in on its prey. "You are capable of attending parties by yourself, you know. Don't blame me for your lack of a social life! While we're on the subject, you don't have to set me up with someone just so you can go on a date, either!"

Katharina turned away and Bianca hated what she felt compelled to say. It felt like stabbing her sister in the back.

"Kat, we agreed when Mom and Dad passed that we would stick together. I know we were young, but I took that promise seriously. I guess it didn't mean as much to you. I know I could date or go to parties with my friends, but I want you there. You are the one person I really trust to have my back in this world."

Have I gone too far? she worried. Katharina had a hard time in social situations. It was like she was afraid to make friends because she would then have to face the possibility of losing more people she loved. Bianca had felt that way after the car accident, as if it would be better to not love at all than to love and have fate cruelly strip it away. Then she'd realized she didn't want to be miserable her whole life; she wanted to love everything, every moment.

Crossing the threshold once more, Bianca sat on the edge of Katharina's bed and gently placed her hand on her sister's back. It felt ineffective, like trying to soothe an angry bear.

"I just want us to have fun. It's our last year of high school. I'm not asking you to go and make friends or to fall in love; I just want you to go and support me. Be there." She sighed and softened her tone. "I need you. Please? Besides, did it ever occur to you that I am just as scared of these things as you are? I just choose to handle my fears by facing them with a smile. But it does help to have you with me."

Katharina's body gently shook. She hated showing any emotion that was not some equivalent of anger. The alarm screeched. Bianca quickly turned it off and decided to take a shower, even though she'd had one the night before.

When Bianca entered the bedroom again, she was pleased to see her sister was dressed and pulled together. "Bianca..." Katharina seemed to be holding back tears. "I will go to this lame party. I am doing it because I love you. But, you should know, I refuse to have fun. It's just the way that I choose to deal with the world." She crossed the room and hugged Bianca. "You owe me the biggest favor."

"Anything you want!" Bianca couldn't contain her excitement. She began jumping on the bed and shouting, "Thank you! Thank you! Thank you!"

"Shh! Do you want to wake Grandma up!"

Bianca was grateful that their grandmother had provided a home for them after their parents died, but she wasn't an easy woman to live with. She'd given them a home, food and structure, but nothing more. The girls were to stay out of her hair and clean up their messes. Bianca always felt lucky that she had Katharina to keep her from feeling isolated.

"Can I please do your hair and makeup for this party?" Bianca gave her sister the biggest puppy eyes, knowing she might be pushing her too far, but she imagined her sister having a Cinderella moment. Katharina wanted nothing to do with the idea, but Bianca pressed on. "Think about the heart attacks everyone would have! First their hearts would stop at the fact that you came to the party, and then they would drop dead over how good you looked."

Katharina's lips were pinched, but a smile was fighting its way across her face. Bianca guessed that her sister was amused at the idea of shocking everyone. "I suppose it would show them that they don't really know me at all."

Bianca extended her hand. "Deal?" She waited a moment and Katharina shook on it. She could not conceal her excitement. She had done the impossible, moved the unmovable! "I really do owe you, but I think you'll have fun."

"I'll get you back by making you suffer through something I enjoy. Maybe drag you to a lecture on sculpting techniques." Katharina actually cracked a smile. Bianca loved her sister's smile. It was rare to see her happy. "Come on, we're going to be late."

Bianca practically skipped her way into school. She could not wait to tell Ophelia and Hero. They would never believe that she had actually convinced Katharina to attend a party.

4

DJ

DJ sat, bored on a Friday night, in the basement of Messina Baptist Church, where his father preached. As a preacher's son, it was his unspoken obligation to be involved in youth group, Bible studies, summer camps, and choir. DJ knew the role he had to play, the obedient son filled with the endless love of Jesus Christ, but sometimes he found it exhausting.

To the left of the room a group of boys gathered around a ping pong table, waiting for their turn to play against the winner. DJ found the game dull; there was not a single player in the room who offered him a challenge. Ahead of him he watched several teens eating pizza and bobbing their heads along to some Christian rock band. DJ would not be joining them; he could not get into praise music. It just didn't resonate with him like the rock bands Claudio had introduced him to. Besides, it was bad enough that he had to sing in the choir every Sunday. To his right a group of girls were playing Heads Up. Juliet was among them with the word squirrel stuck to her forehead. She looked over at him, caught his eyes, and smiled.

She left the game and joined him on the faded plaid couch, which was probably as old as the church itself. The cushions were worn in the middle, and you could feel springs poking you in the back. Juliet was one of the few people in youth group that DJ could tolerate being around. They had known each other since birth, and her mom had helped raise him after his own mother passed away. She felt like a sister to him, one who was easily tolerated. She understood DJ's predicament more than other people did. Both of their fathers were community leaders; they both bore the burden of their fathers' reputations. Juliet was far better at accepting her place in life, or at least, she made behaving perfect look easy. It didn't feel easy for DJ.

"What's bothering you? You seem off tonight," she said.

DJ sighed, "I'd rather be at Romeo's party than sitting here. Sometimes this Friday night routine feels stale."

"I actually think I'd like to go to Romeo's party, too, just to see what all of the fuss is about. I've heard some wild rumors." She seemed just as surprised as DJ by the admission. "But let's face it, my father would lock me up for life if I went to a party like that. Can you imagine what your dad would say?" She smiled and looked off into the distance.

The two sat silently for a moment, both lost in thought. DJ began devising a plan. "What if we sneak out now and go to the party? It's six. We could be back by nine. No one will notice us. If we get back late, we can tell our parents that we wanted to be alone to talk with each other, so we went for a walk along the stream. We can tell them we lost track of time, and apologize profusely for not asking approval before leaving the group." DJ smiled at his own plan and could tell that Juliet was intrigued. "You and I both know our fathers wish we would marry each other. Your dad adores me. We are each other's perfect alibi. Think about it! They will be so happy that we wanted alone time, they won't even question our absence."

"You're right about our fathers' wishes," Juliet said, then softened her voice. "Why not go to this party together and see each other in a new setting? Maybe our parents are right about us being a good match. But we'll never know if our only encounters happen under their and--" Juliet gestured towards the painting on the wall, "--Jesus' watchful eye."

The suggestion took DJ by surprise. His attractions lay elsewhere, and he didn't want to hurt Juliet by pretending for their parents' sake. He could see that she was nervously awaiting his response.

"You're right. This could be our opportunity to see each other in a new light. Maybe our parents are right about us." His stomach turned at the lie. "What are we waiting for? I'll leave my car in the parking lot so my father doesn't know we left. We can walk a block or two and I'll call one of my friends to pick us up."

∞∞∞

Don Pedro came to the rescue in his beat-up two-door Honda Civic. DJ and Juliet squeezed into the back with their legs touching as they rode. The block surrounding Romeo's mansion was already full of cars, and it was only six thirty. Don Pedro offered to drop Juliet and DJ at the front, but Juliet said she was nervous and the walk would help.

DJ laughed. "Oh, sweet, innocent Juliet."

As they exited the car, she reached for his hand. DJ held it, expecting her to drop it the moment she exited the coupe, but she didn't. Her small hand trembled in his. Was she nervous about the party, or nervous about holding his hand? DJ felt nothing for her, and felt terrible that he had agreed to make this... What was this? A first date? He felt torn inside; half of him wanted to live the lie, to please his family, and conform to the religious views he'd grown up with, just like Juliet seemed determined to do. The other half wanted to live true to his inner desires. It felt as if there were something clawing around in his insides. It wanted its freedom, and DJ could not suppress it forever.

Don Pedro looked back with a smirk on his face. "Get a look at these two love birds. Giant cornerback falls for quiet, studious beauty. I'm going to tell Puck to make that his next headline for his Puck Talks column."

DJ squeezed Juliet's hand. "Don Pedro, get a life and a girlfriend already. Perhaps Puck's next column heading should read: 'Don Pedro's inability to maintain a boner prevents him from dating.' Or 'Don Pedro's refusal to shower after practice causes his dick to contract a rare fungus.' "

Don Pedro punched DJ in the arm hard and Juliet's giggle seemed to numb the pain. He was happy his joke broke through the tension.

Once inside, Don Pedro immediately found the keg and helped himself. DJ, still holding Juliet's hand, searched the room for Claudio. His heart leapt into his throat; Claudio was in the kitchen laughing with Romeo. Juliet pulled him in the opposite direction, toward the beer pong table, and that clawing feeling strengthened. He felt as if he were being split in two. Should he stay with Juliet or go to Claudio?

As they observed the game in progress, DJ considered his predicament. He recalled the pamphlets at his father's church which suggested that people were born homosexual, that being homosexual was not a crime. It was, in fact, a gift from God. DJ had felt wonderful when reading those words, and had continued reading the pamphlet, hungry for acceptance. It had said that God gifted some individuals with a challenge that He knew he or she could overcome with His divine help. It was when homosexuals turned from the Lord and indulged in their desires that they committed a mortal sin.

His father had given a sermon on the subject once. DJ remembered his dad likening being born gay to being born with an addictive personality. DJ had chuckled at the idea of being addicted to men, and later felt the horror and the shame of being considered an addict. It happened to many, his father preached, but only the faithful could overcome the burden they were born with. He'd asked his father, later that evening, what path homosexuals were supposed to take. Why would God cause them to be born with a sinful desire? His father was firm in his belief that those individuals were meant to choose between two paths to avoid their sinful inclinations: with the help of the Lord, they would marry and raise a family in accordance with his law, or they would never marry, and therefore suppress all sexual desires.

"I think I could be good at this game." Juliet's voice broke through DJ's thoughts. "Let's find another couple to play with."

Couple? Is that what we are already? DJ wondered, and then answered Juliet, who was looking at him expectantly. "I think I know a team that would give us a challenge. I hate when the game is too easy. Wait here. I'll be right back."

Juliet smiled so widely, and once again DJ felt guilty. The person he had in mind was Claudio. He actually had no idea if Claudio was good at beer pong. DJ himself had never tried the game, so worrying that it was too easy was another blatant lie.

Claudio was no longer in the kitchen where DJ had first seen him. The kitchen was now filled with smoke; several students were taking turns with a bong. They noticed him and motioned him to join them. DJ mouthed a no thank you and moved on. The house was huge; Claudio could be anywhere. He tried to avoid stopping for conversation, but there were people everywhere. Finally, someone pointed him toward the family room. When he entered, he found a game of spin the bottle in play.

"DJ, get over here and join us." At first DJ couldn't see who had addressed him, but then saw Ophelia waving him to an empty spot.

"Later," he said. "Have you guys seen Claudio? Juliet and I were looking for some partners to play beer pong with."

"Woah, you're not talking about Juliet Capulet, are you? What would Jesus do if he knew she were here?" Everyone but DJ laughed at Ophelia's joke.

"There is more to her than you think. Now, have you seen Claudio or not?"

"So defensive." Ophelia always said everything with a sense of ease and control. "We all saw him a few moments ago when he exited the game like a chicken. He must have a real hard on for some of the girls who decided to join us."

The room once again filled with giggles. As he hastily exited the room, he heard Ophelia add that she thought Claudio had gone outside. He was pissed off that she was teasing his friend, and was now worried about Claudio.

As DJ moved through the house, looking for the door that exited toward the gardens, he ran into Puck.

"Well, look at the two of us rounding a corner in haste," Puck said. He reached out and stroked Don Jon's face, an act of intimacy DJ was not prepared for. "So, what brings you to Romeo's party? Should we find a quiet place to talk?"

DJ realized that Puck was being flirtatious. Did Puck know? Was there something about him that he could not conceal from someone who was also gay?

"Sorry, Puck, I didn't come to the party to get stuck with you." DJ pushed passed him, but felt uneasy as he walked, as if he could feel Puck watching and studying him. Was he walking in a gay way? Was that even possible?

Once outside, self-consciousness washed away and he refocused on finding Claudio. He scanned the gardens. He had to do a double take when he saw Katharina sitting by the pool. *What is she doing here?* He hated to talk to her, but it paid off.

"I saw him walk into the hedge garden a few moments ago. I imagine you can still find him there. He looks like he could use a friend, but who am I to judge? I myself am sitting alone at a party."

The Montagues' hedge garden was a massive maze. It was said that when you looked out from the third-floor balcony it resembled the family's crest, although DJ had never seen it himself. Mr. Montague was very proud of his family's name and wealth. There were rumors that he spent a quarter million every year just to maintain the gardens and exterior of the three-story mansion. DJ lived in an English-style cottage, like most of Shakespeare, and was impressed with Romeo's backyard. He started toward the hedge, and for a moment wondered if Katharina had tricked him into getting lost in the maze. It seemed like something she would do. As DJ walked deeper in, he heard crying.

"Claudio?" he called out. "It's DJ. Where are you?"

It was silent for a moment, and then Claudio whimpered,

"Here. I'm here."

Around a thick green corner DJ spotted his friend sitting against the shrubbery and drinking straight from a half-emptied bottle of bourbon.

Claudio looked up and met DJ's eyes. "Why didn't you tell me you would be here tonight? How did you get past your father?"

DJ sat next to Claudio, who offered the bottle. "No thanks. You are never going to guess who my alibi and date is." Claudio was intrigued, lifting his eyebrow. DJ continued, "Juliet Capulet." He paused for effect, taking joy in his friend's shock. "If our parents find out we left group, we'll just say we wanted time to get to know each other. It's obvious they're all waiting for us to date and for me to eventually propose to her. I think their anger would be short lived."

Claudio laughed and DJ felt like he was on top of the world. When Claudio wiped the dripping snot from his nose, DJ resisted the urge to wipe the tears from his cheeks.

"So, there is a big party going on, and you, my dear friend, are crying in a maze. What's with that?"

DJ put his hand on Claudio's shoulder for a brief moment, but wished he could pull him closer, embrace him, and offer him more love than he could ever find with a girl like Hero. DJ wondered why it was that Claudio didn't see that it was DJ alone who could brighten his world.

"I panicked and made an absolute fool of myself in front of Hero."

"I'm sure it's not as bad as you think." DJ did his best to offer consolation. "Tell me what happened."

Claudio took a long swig, gagging as he swallowed it down. "I was talking to Romeo in the kitchen when Ophelia came prancing in." Claudio stopped and took another sip before continuing. "She grabbed my arm and told me I was going to play 'spin the bottle.' You know how damn insistent she can be. She tried getting Romeo involved, but he brushed her off while I stupidly went along. At first it was a small game. The bottle kept passing me. Ophelia kissed some sophomore girl and everything was fine, but then Bianca, Hero, and Beatrice walked in. I was so afraid of what would happen if the bottle landed on Hero. I mean, you've seen what happens to me if I just think about her for too long. I could feel that I was getting all red in the face, and I just stood up and walked out. Ophelia teased me that I was going to have blue balls if I walked away now, and everyone laughed. It's as bad as if I had just stayed and risked getting a boner. I'm freaking mortified, man. How can I recover from this? Damn Ophelia!"

"Ophelia is wretched! It's like she thinks her beauty allows her to treat people however she wants."

Claudio whimpered and swallowed hard. "Why am I such a loser? I could have had a chance to kiss Hero if I stayed, but she makes me feel panicky inside. Like, what if I kissed her and it was awful and she hated it? It's embarrassing that I've never kissed a girl. What if I'm bad at it?"

DJ grabbed the bourbon from Claudio and choked down the bitter liquid. "I've never kissed a girl either. Should we practice on each other?" DJ cracked a smile and Claudio's face contorted as if he'd just stepped in dog shit. "Relax, man, I'm just trying to lighten the mood. Look, the reality is, half the school is in the same boat you're in. And Hero, I can't say what she was like in her previous school, but since she's been at Shakespeare High, she has never once had a boyfriend. For all we know, she is just as green as you are."

Claudio was silent for a moment, then lifted the bourbon to his lips and finished the bottle. His words came out in a slur. "DJ, my man. You are the best friend a guy could ask for. Did you know that?"

Claudio turned and locked eyes with him. In that moment, the clawing inside DJ felt like it would break through his skin. Those claws would grab Claudio and reveal the truth to him. Trying to be just Claudio's best friend wasn't enough, and it was getting harder to smother it, to lock it all away. Claudio leaned toward him, and for a moment, he thought Claudio was

27

feeling the same yearning. His heart was beating out of his chest.

Claudio began talking again as his body rocked gently. "I'm too wasted to get up. My world is spinning. Help me, please."

With that, Claudio fell headfirst into DJ's lap. At first he panicked that his friend had passed out. *Is this a blackout?* DJ wondered. He repositioned Claudio and could hear his gentle snoring, so he decided not to run for help.

"My world is spinning, too," DJ whispered. "It's spiraling out of my control, and I don't know where to turn."

Claudio snored and DJ did something that he hoped he would not live to regret. He ran his fingers through Claudio's sun-streaked hair, then leaned down and kissed his friend on the lips. DJ felt terrified but truly alive. He attempted to reach for his cellphone to check the time and tell Juliet that he was sorry. He knew she would be worried. He'd been gone far longer than it took to find a beer pong partner. The phone was trapped in the pocket under Claudio's head, and DJ didn't want to disturb his friend and have this moment end. So he leaned into the hedge and savored it. His eyes closed and listened to Claudio's breathing, enjoying the warmth their bodies made together. He would make it up to Juliet. Coming to this party was his idea, and he had abandoned her. He wasn't sure how he would make it up to her, but he owed her more than just an apology.

5

Hamlet

It was 6:45. The school was quiet except for the sound of a mop sliding across the floor and the occasional screech as it was wrung out in an old bucket. Dr. Hamlet was just finalizing his calendar for the following week when he looked up at the clock. Damn, he thought, I'm going to be late for dinner, and mother is sure to be miffed. He reached for his phone. Three unread message alerts popped up when he unlocked the screen. They were from Arabella, his ex-girlfriend. At least, he'd assumed their relationship was through. After all, he had left their apartment without notice two months prior. He felt terrible for not answering any of her calls or messages, but the situation was delicate. Saying the wrong thing would be reputational suicide.

He swiped the notifications away and proceeded to dial his mother. He could hear the irritation in her voice when she answered, so the lecture he got was not surprising. His response was even toned. "I understand, Mother. I lost track of time. I'm going to let Polonius know that I'm leaving and then I'll be on my way."

After hanging up, the atmosphere in his office changed from comfortable to frigid. He pulled the brown suit jacket off the back of his chair, put it on, and wrapped his arms around his waist. *I suppose I have yet another thing to add to Polonius's list,* Hamlet thought. He stopped at his closet before leaving to check himself in the mirror. The image caused Hamlet to stumble backwards, falling against his desk. In the same moment the mirror fell to the floor. Hamlet was thankful that it stayed intact. He tried to calm himself; his heart seemed to be beating ten times its normal speed.

"Don't be silly," He whispered to himself. "It has been a stressful time, and grief is playing with your mind. Get up and carry on."

Grief could be a long and strange process. Any psychologist might say it was not surprising that Hamlet should imagine his father. He was now in his father's old office, filling his old role, and his mind was overcome by the stress of the first full week of school. He wished his father could really be here, to guide him and tell him he was doing well. He choked back the tears that welled up. There was no time for crying.

Hamlet gathered his thoughts and followed the lone light shining in hallway A. The door to room 106 was open and Polonius was inside, mopping. Hamlet waited for him to look up before speaking. He didn't want to startle the janitor.

"Polonius, I'm closing up my office and heading home. I can't thank you enough for all of your help this week." Hamlet extended his hand, but Polonius put his own hand up to refuse.

"Sorry, dirty hands." The janitor slid them into his pockets before continuing. "You needn't thank me. Any way that I can help the school, you can bet I'll do it. My kids go here, and that's all the motivation I need to keep things in good repair." He chuckled at himself.

"Well, nonetheless, I really couldn't have gotten through the week without you, *that* I know for sure." Hamlet smiled warmly, his words sincere. "Please let me invite you and your family over to dinner as a thank you." Polonius was about to protest, so Hamlet said, "It's really the least I can do for all of the extra hours you put in because of me." He put his hands up to stop Polonius from declining. "Don't say no. Besides, I can tell you're the best ally a man could have. My father always spoke so highly of you. We can use the dinner to honor my late father and you can tell me more about the ins and outs of Shakespeare

High."

Polonius seemed surprised, as if no one had ever stopped to appreciate his work before, and how could he refuse such an earnest offer? "I... I..."

"Please, let me do this simple thing. It's been a stressful transition for us both. Some food and a drink outside of these walls is needed. How about next Saturday?"

Hamlet knew he was pushing, but he wanted the relationship his father had had with Polonius. His father had praised the man as his secret weapon in creating a top-notch school. He'd told Hamlet that the man was full of potential, and that had proven true.

"I'd love to meet your family. Besides, I'm a lonely bachelor in need of some company during this tough time. What do you say?"

"OK," Polonius agreed. "How can I say no? At least let me bring dessert. My daughter, Ophelia, is an amazing baker."

"Excellent! How about pot roast? It's one of the few dishes I know my way around. I'll hide the take-out containers before you arrive." Hamlet laughed at his own joke and Polonius smiled.

"That's a meal I know my family will like."

"How many are you?" Hamlet inquired.

"It's just myself and my two children, Ophelia and Laertes. My wife left us a few years ago."

"I'm sorry to hear about your wife."

Hamlet hoped he hadn't brought up bad memories for the man. Polonius was not much older than Hamlet, maybe ten years his senior. Hamlet had never married, nor did he have children. He couldn't imagine having to manage children by himself; he could barely manage a long-term relationship.

"Don't apologize. She never was cut out for the life I had to offer. My wife had a wild spirit, and I was her fool. Ophelia is the spitting image of her mother, and just as free spirited." Polonius seemed lost in thought.

"Well, I look forward to meeting your family. Now to deal

with my own. I'm already thirty minutes late to a dinner with Ol' Gerty. If you've ever met her, then you know I'm in for a verbal lashing!"

Polonius laughed. "I've met her. You'd better run to your car and drive at least five miles over the speed limit. And because I've met her, I'll be sure to keep the fact that you just called her 'Ol' Gerty' a secret."

Hamlet laughed deeply, and it felt good to end his first week this way. "So, you have met her!"

He turned and began walking toward the exit, then stopped as he neared the main office. He'd forgotten to ask Polonius to check the thermostat. *Never mind. The poor man is as late getting home as I am, and he has children to care for. This can be dealt with on Monday, as well as getting that mirror secured in place,* Hamlet thought, and then he finally left the building.

Hamlet passed the Montague Mansion, as it was called in town, on his way to his childhood home. The Hamlet, Montague, and Augustus families all lived close to one another. They were the founding families of the town, "old money," as some would say. There were an excessive number of cars parked around the mansion, and several students were walking toward the house. *I guess young Montague has the house to himself tonight,* Hamlet thought. *I envy the antics the young can get away with.*

Gertrude opened the door, greeting Hamlet with a scowl. All the wrinkles around her mouth helped emphasize her irritation. "JR, you are impossibly late. I sent Rosaline home an hour ago. I hope you weren't expecting me to let my food grow cold on your account!"

He followed his mother towards the dining room as she continued to chastise him.

"Rosaline left you a plate in the fridge. You can heat it up yourself."

His mother's heels clicked on the tile when she was angry, her heavy steps an extension of her emotions.

She spoke over her shoulder. "I'm having a pinot noir. Will you have a glass?"

Hamlet was surprised to find his uncle sitting at the dining table as they entered the room. "Uncle Claude! I wasn't expecting you to come to dinner tonight." Hamlet shook his uncle's hand before responding to his mother's question. "Yes, I'll have a glass. Thank you, Mother."

Gertrude just looked at him as if he had lost his mind and sharply responded, "JR, I am not the maid. She's gone home. Or have you forgotten already? You will pour your own wine and heat your own plate. Claude and I will enjoy our wine and wait for you here." She raised her glass to her lips and sipped.

Hamlet bit his tongue. He should have known better than to expect his mother to make even the smallest gesture of maternal affection. It seemed that grief had not softened Gertrude as Hamlet had imagined it would. *Silly of me to think that my father's death would gift me with a mother,* Hamlet reasoned as he skulked to the kitchen, feeling like a child whose rump had been smacked.

Hamlet let out a shout when he entered the kitchen. Before him stood his father, his face pained and pale.

"What am I seeing? An apparition?" he wondered aloud.

He gripped the counter and looked into his father's face. He seemed to be saying something, but Hamlet couldn't hear him. Claude entered behind him and put his arm on Hamlet's shoulder, making his skin crawl. His father disappeared.

"Everything OK? I thought I heard you call out." Claude was even toned, but his face showed concern.

Hamlet took the bottle of wine and began pouring. The wine splashed on the counter.

"Hamlet," Claude insisted. "Talk to me. Your hands are shaking. What on earth is going on with you?"

Hamlet was not ready to admit that, for the second time that night, he had seen his father.

"I'm sorry to have upset you, Uncle. I just stubbed my toe." He turned and let his exhaustion show. "It's been a long week and I'm tired."

"Well, you'd better clean up this mess before Gertrude sees and once again reminds you that the maid has gone home." Claude rolled his eyes and Hamlet shared the sentiment.

They rejoined Gertrude in the dining room. "What was all the fuss about?" she asked.

"Apparently the boy stubbed his toe and has been overly stressed."

Hamlet hated when his uncle referred to him as a boy; he was thirty-eight, but knew he needn't remind Uncle Claude of his age.

"Stressed." The word dripped from his mother's mouth like venom. "Stress was what you placed on your father and me when you got yourself fired. Stress was what Claude had to deal with trying to cover up your scandals and working to ensure that you would qualify for your father's position." His mother pounded her fist on the table. The wine glasses shook on impact. "So you will be grateful for the stresses of that job. Your father died so you could have that job."

Claude placed his hand on top of Gertrude's, and she turned her hand to interlace her fingers with his.

"Mother, you make it seem as if I killed my father in order to take his job. He had a heart attack! Besides, I'm sure I would have been able to secure a teaching job eventually. I am grateful for Uncle Claude's help regardless."

Gertrude emptied her glass and Claude rose to fill it again. He offered the bottle to Hamlet, though his glass still sat untouched.

"No, I should leave before I upset my mother further. Uncle Claude, will you be leaving soon? I could walk you to your car."

"You haven't even touched your dinner," Uncle Claude guffawed. "No, I will not be leaving. Your mother shouldn't be alone. She needs someone with her during this time."

34

"Don't baby him." Hamlet's mother took a sip of wine and then looked Hamlet sternly in the eyes. "Claude has been staying here the last few days. He has been a great help and comfort to me. He may stay on permanently."

Hamlet felt his chest tighten. He was confused by her admission, and he now questioned the affection he had seen between the two a few moments ago. His father had been in the grave for such a short time. Was his mother now sleeping with his uncle? Hamlet pushed his food around his plate, his appetite completely gone.

Claude once again reached for Gertrude's hand. "Hamlet, when your father passed away..." He seemed to search for words. "Well, suddenly I felt it was my duty to be with your mother during her time of grief. A loyal brother cares for the family in his brother's absence. Although, it turns out I needed her just as much as she needed me. Maybe I needed her more. We have both helped each other grieve."

Hamlet stared blankly at his plate. For him, his father had been his world, while his mother had always been a distant universe. Had his mother ever loved his father, or had she just been waiting for him to die so she could jump in bed with Claude? Now that Hamlet thought about it, his mother and uncle had always had a special bond. Hamlet thought back to all of the family holidays and how Gertrude and Claude could often be found sitting apart from the group having a private laugh. Once, on New Year's when Hamlet was a boy, he'd gone into the basement while playing hide and seek. When he'd gotten to the bottom of the stairs, he'd seen his mother sitting on the pool table and his uncle standing in front of her. His uncle had said he was helping his mother because her pantyhose had gotten twisted. Hamlet had been so young, he hadn't thought anything of it. But the image came to him now, as if his mind had buried it and saved it for this very moment.

"Oh, don't act so stunned. Think of this like a levirate marriage," his mother casually suggested.

Her cool demeanor agitated Hamlet. "I have no words for

this situation, and quite frankly, I'm too tired to process this." With that, he stood to leave. His food sat untouched, becoming cold once again.

His uncle stood and followed him to the door. "Don't be so cross with her. We all grieve differently, and we have been a great comfort to each other."

Hamlet turned to face his uncle. "It just seems to me that the two of you might have been grieving long before my father died."

Claude looked as if he had been slapped.

Hamlet turned to open the door, but Claude caught his arm and pulled him in. "Son, I have done a lot for you these past few weeks. Surely you are indebted to me for your job security."

Hamlet could smell the alcohol on Claude's breath, and knew it was the wrong time to try to have a rational discussion with him.

"Your father's death was sudden and tragic, but we all must look for the gifts. You have a job, and your mother and I have fallen in love."

There was something about hearing his father's death referred to as a "gift," and the word "love" so soon after that made his stomach churn. He spit on his uncle, who gripped his arm tighter. "I will forgive you because I know you are grieving, but trust me, you do not want to make an enemy of me."

Fury filled Hamlet. He felt it from the pulsing in his head to the tingling sensation in his toes. When he finally got to his car, the keys shook in his hands as he tried to place them in the ignition. He gave up his fumbling and decided to collect himself before driving home. His attention turned across the street. The party at the Montagues' house had tripled in size. There were teens all over the front lawn, sitting in large groups, some making out, and most holding a plastic cup that Hamlet was sure was filled with alcohol. Watching the clusters of youths both calmed and distracted him.

He supposed Roman's son was unafraid of the cops breaking up the party; Roman Montague would probably just buy off the sheriff's department. Hamlet had known Roman when he was in high school, though Roman had been three years ahead. He'd been head of the debate team, prom king, a legendary long-distance runner, and very popular. He'd given Hamlet a ride home once. During the brief drive, he'd told Hamlet that he should look at the world like a candy dish, one where he could help himself whenever he wanted. Their families' money bought them that right.

Hamlet's father had instilled a different set of values than those the Montagues held. He'd taught Hamlet that they should use the wealth they were born with to help elevate others, that education was a worthy investment, and it had motivated Hamlet to become a teacher himself. His father had been so proud the day Hamlet had graduated with his doctorate. Had the stress of Hamlet's actions really caused his father's heart attack? He'd been so disappointed when Hamlet was fired, and had died soon after.

Guilt for the anguish he'd caused his father turned to guilt over running away from Arabella. If he were really a man, he would give her the answers and closure that she deserved. Instead, he just ignored her calls. Better to say nothing than to lie. The truth was not possible.

Hamlet replayed the incident that had gotten him fired from Shakespeare Community College. Chrysantha had captivated him from the moment she'd entered his scriptwriting class. She was beautiful and witty, so Hamlet had begun showing her favoritism. It was his habit with beautiful girls, to shower them with attention, then give one of their essays a poor grade. Often this game would pay off. The student would come to his office for help with the assignment, or beg for a retake, and Hamlet would take advantage of their vulnerability. Chrysantha was different. Hamlet's favoritism wore thin when she'd started dating another student in the class. She'd finally come to his office when she'd noticed her grades were slipping. She'd been upset, but not enough to entertain Hamlet's hints at an exchange of favors. Rejection had caused a temporary madness in him. He hadn't realized how much desire had built up inside him, nor how angry he was that Chysantha wasn't like all of the other girls he'd selected, willing to unfold herself for a better grade.

When she'd outright accused Hamlet of giving her poor grades because she hadn't returned his "obvious" affections, he'd lashed out, pushing her against the wall of his office and telling her she was a liar. His desire to assert his power had caused a madness he'd never felt. Groping at her breasts, he'd told her that if he wanted her, he would have her. She'd been too weak to fend him off. He'd let his hands reach to the buttons on her pants. He'd told her that if she cared about her grade, she would be a more willing participant in his lessons. He'd pressed himself against her and tried to pull her shirt up. To his torment, she had not conceded, just kept pushing back. When she'd tried to bite him, he'd realized how far things had gone. She'd run out of his office in the middle of the day, clothing disheveled, crying.

There were, of course, witnesses who saw her leave. He'd half expected the campus police to show up. Afraid to go back to his apartment, he'd gone to a hotel. The next day he hadn't shown, and the dean had called to inform him he was fired. Chrysantha had gone to the dean's office instead of the police, and Hamlet counted himself lucky. The school had promised her a full scholarship and Hamlet's removal from staff in exchange for her silence. He'd tried to paint her as a liar who was unhappy with her grades, but too many of his colleagues had heard the shouting and had seen Chrysantha leave his office in tears. The phone call he'd made to his father later that day was one of the worst he'd ever made. His father had tried so hard to remain supportive, but it was obvious that he was disheartened. That same night his family donated money to the college in order to ensure that the whole matter would be kept under wraps.

Hamlet realized he had been sitting in his car for almost an hour. His hands were steady enough to start the car. He thought about the new bottle of tequila he would open once he got home. This day was far more than he could handle sober.

6

Don Pedro

The half keg of cheap beer was nearly tapped, empty bottles of vodka littered the kitchen counter, and the Montague Mansion was filled with the odor of marijuana. Don Pedro, feeling a step beyond tipsy, wished he could commandeer a bowl of chips during his quest to find a corner or empty room to lounge in. Parties were not really his thing, but he had nothing better to do on a Friday night, and his parents couldn't care less where he was. Plus, free food and drink were things Don Pedro was all too happy to partake in.

Sometimes he envied his peers whose parents gave them curfews and grounded them for poor grades. His parents were too busy fighting with each other to remember that, at one point, they had birthed a child. Don Pedro refused to be like them. They were high school sweethearts and had loved each other in the beginning. Then the reality of life had set in and they had never really prepared for it; they'd been more concerned with being popular than having a life plan. You can't pay the bills with likability. That would not be Don Pedro's path. He refused to fall in love or get distracted before he had a successful career with the NFL. There would be no unwanted and unloved children, no careless spending and stacks of unpaid bills, and definitely no fighting to maintain a marriage that had become more about survival than love.

After flipping through several cabinets for food, Don

Pedro settled on a box of Wheaties. He ate it straight from the box, not wanting to add milk to the mix of alcohol floating in his stomach. The search for a quiet place to keep the spins at bay led him to the great room. Benedick grabbed his arm from behind before he made it to the couch and all hope of solitude was vanquished.

"Donny, I'm so glad I found you. You will never guess what happened tonight." The excitement in Ben's voice did not in the least intrigue him.

Don Pedro didn't even pretend to think. "I'm going to guess that you and Beatrice got back together, you popped her cherry upstairs but sucked at it, so she broke up with you again."

"Dude, that's so harsh. When Beatrice and I make love, it's going to be magic, man. Magic."

"Magic? How high are you right now? When I start seeing magic on the field, I'll believe you to be capable of magic elsewhere."

"Don't distract me with your insults. I'm trying to tell you that I kissed Bianca while playing spin the bottle and she looked like she enjoyed it, man."

"Oh, wow. I'm surprised Bianca got out of the house without Katharina. What about Beatrice?"

"Well, that's the thing, and it's where you come in, I think I can use this to get Beatrice back."

Don Pedro cut Benedick off. "What's the thing? You know what? No, I don't care what the thing is or what the plan is. My answer is no. Now, leave me and my box of cereal alone."

"Come on. At least hear me out," Benedick begged.

"Fine. Though I've already said no, and if this cereal doesn't start absorbing alcohol, I may throw up on you. So talk away. You've been fully warned."

Benedick smiled and Don Pedro knew he was going to get wrapped up in some idiotic plan to help his friend get his girl back. Couldn't Benedick see that he was fighting for a relationship that was doomed for failure? As far as Don Pedro was concerned, Benedick and Beatrice would probably have a baby young. Everyone would be so happy for the young sweethearts. Benedick would take a nine to five job that he would grow to hate to support his wife and child. He would put in overtime to pay for the big house that he would've bought just to please Beatrice. Soon the two would start fighting over money and they would be exactly where Don Pedro's parents were now.

"So, I noticed Beatrice looked super annoyed that I was playing spin the bottle. She sat down, but left after two rounds. After I kissed Bianca, it dawned on me that I could use Beatrice's jealousy to my advantage. If I could make her think I was going to move on, she would lose her mind and beg to have me back. Bianca, Beatrice, and a few of the other cheerleaders are on the patio dancing. I figure I could dance with Bianca in front of Beatrice and let her jealousy do the rest. I predict she will be pushing Bianca aside and grinding up on me after one song." Benedick looked quite pleased with himself.

"First of all, that sounds like a stupid plan. Second of all, why does this involve me? And third, I just need to reiterate, the plan sounds stupid."

"No, dude. Beatrice is going to be begging to be on my arm once she feels threatened with losing me for good. I know her. This will work." Ben was so glued to his plan he couldn't see all the cracks in it.

"It's your funeral. How am I to play a role in your demise?"

"Well, the problem I'm having is that Katharina is sitting by the pool, and you know she is not going to trust me around her sister. Your role is to distract her. Just talk with her or whatever so she doesn't intervene with my plan."

Don Pedro held his cereal up like a shield in front of his chest. "OK. You want to bury yourself, fine. But you want me to talk the devil out of sending you to Hell? Not going to flipping happen! Talking with Katharina is like shaving your face with a bar of soap and a dull razor! I don't feel like getting verbally cut down so you can play mind games with Beatrice and Bianca. It's just cruel to everyone involved."

Benedick reached in his pocket and counted out a wad of

money. "I've got a hundred and thirteen dollars in my pocket, and it's yours if you can sit with Katharina."

The choice seemed simple once money became involved. Don Pedro thought about all of the dinners that money would buy. His mom had stopped preparing family meals years ago, and in doing so had stopped really caring about feeding anyone but herself. The refrigerator often contained a few yogurts, a jug of milk, and some eggs, but those things didn't get replenished until his parents had a fight about it. He'd tried to talk to his father about it, and his response was to start leaving a twenty on Don Pedro's nightstand on Sunday mornings. Don Pedro made it stretch as much as he could, but when his mom stopped paying the cafeteria bill at school, things became harder. Cheap noodles couldn't provide the nutrients a football player needed to be at the top of his game. Don Pedro would never admit it to his friends, but he often went to the cafeteria at the end of the day to ask if there were any fruits or vegetables that would be trashed. The head cook had begun saving a grocery bag for him to take home each week. He was the only one of his friends who worked. He stocked shelves at the local grocery store, but was determined to put all of that money toward college expenses.

He snatched the money. "Lead the way. Let's get this over with."

Katharina was sitting cross-legged by the edge of the pool, just as Benedick said she would be. Her back was to the group dancing. Don Pedro stopped to roll his jeans up before dropping next to her and plunging his feet in the water, which was warmer than he'd expected. *Of course the Montagues have a heated pool,* he thought. Once the water settled, he was struck by how pale Katharina's reflection looked next to his coffee-colored one.

"Sorry, I hope I didn't splash you," he said, hoping to start a conversation. She started to get up, but Don Pedro put his hand on her leg. "I promise I am not here to ruin your moment of gazing into the depths of this pool. I just want to cool off and eat my cereal."

He tilted the box toward her. She pulled her skirt up to her knees and placed her legs in the water, then reached for a handful of cereal.

"Wheaties? Really? This tastes like cardboard. I bet there is not one Olympian who has ever attributed their athletic success to a daily breakfast of Wheaties, and yet there they are on the box anyway. Money really can buy you anything." She was quiet for a moment. "Unless, that is, *you* attribute your athleticism to Wheaties. In which case, I'm dumbfounded."

Don Pedro wasn't sure if he'd received a compliment. That's how it went with Katharina, he supposed. "When it comes to fuel, I take what I can get. Better to run on Wheaties and alcohol than alcohol alone, I say."

"Fair enough, but you could have forgone the alcohol altogether and saved your stomach the trouble."

"Ah, but peer pressure is the greatest pressure of them all." Don Pedro let out a soft chuckle. "Besides, how could anyone survive one of these parties without the influence of alcohol? The fact that you are sitting here sober makes me question your sanity." He saw her lips curl up to a half smile and felt proud that he had done what so few of his classmates could do. "And I must say, the fact that you are sitting here at all is making me question my own sanity. I mean, I didn't think I was that drunk, and yet here I am and here you are."

They both laughed and Don Pedro was surprised at how beautiful Katharina was when she smiled. He had always thought Bianca to be pretty, but her smile seemed forced. Katharina's smile seemed to be the most genuine emotion he'd ever witnessed. They sat silently for what felt like forever. He stole glances at her every chance he got. Something was different about the way she looked tonight, but he couldn't tell what. Maybe it was the moonlight on her porcelain skin, or the fact that she had her hair pulled out of her face.

The music had stopped playing on the patio and it became even quieter. It was beginning to make Don Pedro uncomfortable, and he wondered if Katharina felt the same. He wasn't sure if he should just get up and walk away. Surely the dancing had ended with the music, so his duty to Benedick had been fulfilled.

He decided to break the silence. "Your hair looks different."

She touched the edges of her updo. "For that, you can credit Bianca. In fact, my being here is all her doing. This isn't my scene, as you've obviously guessed. I would much rather be home sculpting clay, carving wood, twisting metal..." She paused and exhaled audibly. "I'm sure you get the point." She seemed to be studying his reflection in the water, then spoke again. "Perhaps you're right about needing alcohol to enjoy a gathering like this. I still can't believe I let Bianca drag me here."

"Ah, but tonight you get to be the artwork," Don Pedro mused. "Bianca has manipulated, twisted, and shaped you into what she considers beautiful, and here you sit on display, at the gallery of her choosing."

Katharina turned toward him wide-eyed. Quite frankly, he was shocked at himself for saying it. She nudged him. "You're pretty deep for a football player."

"And you're pretty nice for a shrew," he retorted with immediate regret. "Sorry, it was a bad joke. I'm kind of known for making ill-timed jokes. Um... What am I saying? Ah, yes. What I'm trying to say is there is a lot more to me than I let on. More to me than being an athlete. I imagine there is more to you than the reputation you carry, too. I just had a very rude way of saying it." He looked up at the stars. "So, I hope you accept my apology. It's genuine. I meant no harm."

"There you go, getting all philosophical again." She leaned her shoulder against his but did not linger there. "I guess you're right. I have preconceived notions about football players, just like everyone has made up their minds about who I am."

They sat silently again, staring into the water. Don Pedro closed his eyes and steadied his breath. The alcohol and cereal had been churning in his stomach, and the gentle motion of the water was not helping to soothe it. He needed to focus on keeping it down. He looked toward the hedge maze. At least that was unmoving. How funny it was that he was sitting with Katharina and wasn't hating every minute of it. In fact, if he had to admit it, he was truly enjoying her company. Perhaps she came off as bitter because she was driven to make a better life for herself, like he was.

"Do you want more? I might start dumping the bag into my mouth if you don't stop me." He offered her the bag of cereal, which he'd removed from the box.

"Why are you actually here talking to me?" she asked, catching him off guard. "Oh, don't act surprised. There is not a single person at this party who would willingly sit next to me. So, did you lose a bet? Did my sister beg you to try to make me have a good time?"

"Are you having a good time?" He was surprised by how much it mattered to him.

"I don't hate sitting here with you. You say little, and you brought snacks, so I can't complain. But I know you cannot be here by choice, and that bothers me."

Don Pedro contemplated how to respond. Maybe he didn't have to. He could leave any time he wanted and never give her an explanation. Instead, he danced around the truth because he found himself wanting to stay with her.

"I won't lie to you, Katharina, because that's not my way. I did sit down at the request of a friend, but I've stayed because I don't hate sitting here with you either."

Instinctively he slid his hand closer to hers so that their pinkies touched. *It must be the alcohol*, he mused. Katharina's hand did not move away.

"But why? Why did you have to sit next to me?"

"My friend--who is the definition of an idiot--wanted to dance with your sister and was afraid of you. He asked me to sit with you and keep you occupied. I told him he was an idiot and I didn't want to, but he paid me."

Katharina moved her hand into her lap and Don Pedro

saw in her reflection that she was chewing her lip. He wished that he'd left that last detail out. She must be feeling hurt. Who wouldn't be? He felt awful that he was the source of her pain.

"How much must one be paid before they are willing to tolerate me?" she asked.

"Probably the same amount that someone would need to be paid to sit next to me after a morning football practice," Don Pedro joked, but he got no smile from her. "Look, I sat down for all the wrong reasons, and I'm sorry that it hurt you." He reached over and turned her face towards him. He wanted to look her in the eyes when he spoke. "The important thing in all of this is that I stayed. I stayed when I could have gotten up, gone back to the plush couch I had my eyes on, and eaten my crappy cereal alone. I chose to stay here because I like your company. So, no one is paying me to tolerate you anymore. I've been off the clock for a while now."

Don Pedro searched her face and tried to gauge how she was feeling. Her eyes seemed watery, but she held his gaze. God, she looked beautiful tonight. He felt his stomach turn over.

"I can't tell if I'm going to throw up or if I want to kiss you." His body swayed, leaning closer to her.

"That's simultaneously the most disgusting thing and the nicest thing a boy has said to me." With that she cracked a smile. He felt awkward until she said, "I don't know why I care if you like me or not. Especially now that I know you were paid to keep me entertained. Which is kind of gross, if I'm being honest. Like, does this make you a gigolo?" Her smile faded. "I guess for a brief moment I let myself think that I was connecting with you. And then I was reminded that there are very few people in the world worth trusting."

He took her hand. "I'm going to tell you something because I think you, of all people, will understand. No one knows what I'm like beyond what I let them see. I'm not close with a single one of my football teammates. I just hang out with them because they're my team, and I can't reach my goals without them. But they don't have my back. Not really. So, I'm just like you, in a way. I'm just better at hiding it. I guess I care what you think of me, too, because you might be the only one who can truly see through all the bullcrap."

Don Pedro's heart was racing. His brain screamed, *WHAT THE HELL ARE YOU DOING!*

The buzzing of a phone broke the moment. He was thankful. If he'd held Katharina's gaze another moment, he might have kissed her, and he was afraid of where that would take him. He felt a tightness in his chest, an emotion he couldn't yet label.

Katharina looked at her phone. "Looks like your friend's plan was to create drama with my sister. She said she's waiting out front and ready to leave. Whatever happened must have been bad. She included a crying emoji." She stood up, looking angry. "I came tonight to protect her if she needed it, and I failed. I'm embarrassed that I got distracted from my duty. I suppose congratulations are in order. You did your job well. Well played, Don Pedro."

She didn't say goodbye, just tucked her phone back in her pocket and jogged to the door. Don Pedro pulled his feet out of the water and tried to stand up. He was spinning. He wished he could chase her and apologize again, but he was in no shape to do that. Instead, he flopped into a lounge chair and tried to focus on the garden. His eyes felt heavy, but, just as he felt ready to let them rest, he saw two figures walking out of the hedge maze. He used his arms to push himself forward as he strained to see who it was. That was a mistake. He found himself puking into the now empty cereal bag, and he was still unsure who he'd seen walking out of the maze.

7

Romeo

The deep mahogany grandfather clock in the library let Romeo know that it was now nine. He placed the old worn journal on the side table, stood, and stretched. His great grandfather's journals were engrossing, telling how his family had come to the United States from Italy and settled. But it was time to make another appearance at his party.

He always threw large parties when his father was out of town to meet with a client, or to take his stepmother on some exotic weekend away. He felt expected to. His cousins, Benvolio and Mercutio, always began the rumor that the mansion would be empty and ready for a party long before Romeo consented to hosting one. His father seemed to encourage it, too. He wanted Romeo to be popular in school like he had been. Romeo always wanted to argue that his father should not be representing the worst criminals if he cared about popularity, but he already knew what his father's response would be. He would say, "Romeo, when you have money, you can buy whatever reputation you want."

The irony was that these parties didn't really make Romeo popular. Sure, the party was always a hit, and most of the school came, but no one came to spend time with Romeo. They were just using him, his house, and his money to have a good time. Whenever there was a party, he would make his appearances, but mostly kept to himself.

Romeo stopped and looked at his reflection in the glass case where the rare antique books were kept. It always surprised him how much he looked like his father: The same thick black hair, green eyes, and even a small mole on his right cheek. He might look like his father, but he was more like his mother, and would leave the first chance he got, just like she had.

Romeo's father forbade him from seeing his mother, and had used his wealth to gain full custody when Romeo was eleven, but his mother was persistent. She would leave little notes for him at the playground, taped on the underside of the slide where she and Romeo used to pretend they were in a tee-pee. As Romeo grew up, the letters slowed, but he still checked the slide from time to time. He was thankful. His father tried to paint his mother as a lunatic, but Romeo always knew the truth. Money had continued to corrupt his father, and his mother could no longer respect him. She was full of compassion, empathy, and love. The more criminals his father represented, the more fights his parents had. She never cared about the money.

Romeo stepped into the hall and made his way past a guest room, where he could hear giggling. He assumed someone was making it to second base. Two rooms down was his bedroom. Smoke curled out from under the door. The skunky odor told him that his bong was in use. He went downstairs. To his left he could hear chatter in the piano room and someone picking at the keys. He turned toward the kitchen, which was empty. A cup was placed over the keg tap. The sounds of arcade games came from the direction of the entertainment room, but he decided to walk towards the garage. His cousins could often be found lurking there with a few friends.

Along the way he passed the mudroom and heard soft crying. When he looked in, he saw a petite blonde leaning against the wall. She was a pitiful but beautiful sight. She looked up and saw Romeo standing in the doorway.

"Oh, no. You're Romeo, aren't you? And here I am crying in your coat room like a complete fool. I'm sorry," she said, wiping her tears. "This is so embarrassing."

Romeo entered the room and sat on the storage bench. "Don't be embarrassed. You'd be amazed at how many people end up leaving these parties in tears." He cracked a smile and hoped she would smile back. Her lip just quivered. "So, let me guess. Did your boyfriend get drunk and hit on someone else?"

She wiped at her damp cheeks and gave him a half smile. "This is your party. You don't want to be sitting here listening to my problems."

"Trust me, being here with you will be the highlight of this whole night. So, tell me, why is a beautiful girl like you crying alone, and why have I never seen you before tonight?" Her porcelain skin turned a deep shade of red. "Oh, come on. You must hear that you're beautiful all the time."

"I've never been told that I'm beautiful by someone other than my parents." She was twirling a lock of hair around her finger nervously. "Unfortunately, you are kind of right about why I'm crying. The guy I came with--the one who was supposed to make sure I got home--ditched me. He said he was going to find us beer pong partners and never came back. Now I don't know how I'm getting home without my father finding out and I didn't even get to play!"

Romeo was captivated, not by the story, but everything else about her. The way her mouth moved when she spoke. The way her irises shone against the now reddened whites of her eyes. The way every word sounded like it was being sung. The goodness that seemed to radiate from her. Romeo found it difficult, but tried to focus on what she was saying.

"You probably already know this," she said, "but I have a reputation of being a pious nerd. I've never felt bad about what others say because I know there's more to me than that. I guess I came here to prove to myself that I can let loose. Instead, I just feel like a bigger loser."

"I'm sorry, but I can't say if I've heard that about you because I still don't know your name. Besides, it seems to me that the only loser in this situation is the guy who ditched you."

Romeo was disgusted by how cliché he sounded, and

could tell that she wasn't a girl who would be easily impressed by empty pick-up lines and chatter. He liked the innocence about her.

"Besides, I don't pay much attention to the gossip and rumors that people spread around school. I bet my reputation is that of a party hound. But I'll let you in on a secret: I spent most of the night in the library upstairs reading old family journals. And I hope you can keep this to yourself: I've never played beer pong. It seems that I might be more of a loser than you are." She raised her eyebrow and he placed his hands over his heart. "True story. Look, why don't we start over? I'm Romeo. What's your name?"

A smile crossed her face and she offered her hand. "Juliet."

"Your name is as beautiful as you are." He kissed her hand before releasing it.

He felt like gazing upon her was awakening a piece of his soul that had been lying dormant his whole life. When she looked at him, it felt as if his soul was soaring in a million directions. Chaos filled him, but he tried to keep his cool.

"Tell me, how can I banish those tears and make this night a happy one?"

Juliet wiped the tears from her face. "You listening to me has already helped me calm down and gather my wits. Thank you for being so kind to me. I shouldn't keep you from the fun any longer."

"I wasn't joking when I told you I was reading in the library. You are not keeping me away from fun. I really do hate these big events and all of the immature fools who show up. Not that you're an immature fool. Look, now I'm tripping over my words and my foot will, no doubt, end up in my mouth." She laughed. "So, how can I help?"

"I just really need to find a way home. I'm sure it won't be long until my father realizes I'm missing. There's no telling what he will do when he finds out I lied and snuck away."

Romeo stood. "Surely your father isn't as harsh as you describe. Your date may have left you without a way home, but I can fix that. Let me take you."

Juliet's laugh sounded nervous. "You clearly don't know who my father is. After tonight, he'll probably build a tall tower and lock me away until he can find a nunnery willing to take me. Besides, I can't take you away from your party."

Romeo took her hand. Electricity pulsed through him at her touch. Something about Juliet had put him under a spell which he could not break. "Come on. I'll take you home, and if your father builds a tower and locks you up, I'll stand beneath it every night when he's gone to sleep and keep you company."

Juliet's skin became rosy once again. "If you knew my dad, you would reconsider taking me home. Even my best friend avoids him."

Romeo brushed off her warning. "I think before we face your father, we both need to do something we've never done before."

Her face went blank. "What?"

He grabbed her hand and she resisted at first, but then followed. He led her back to the beer pong table, hoping the room and game were still abandoned. To his delight it was. "I challenge you," he said, handing her a ping pong ball. "Ladies first, of course."

She was radiant and full of laughter as they played, neither one taking a drink, but it didn't matter. A small group of people passed through the room mid-game, seeming to be in a heated argument, but Romeo didn't care. This was the most fun he'd had in ages. It was a close game, but Romeo cleared the last cup.

She put out her hand. "Romeo, it was a pleasure. You have a natural talent for sinking ping pong balls in plastic cups."

He loved her banter. "The pleasure is all mine."

He moved his hand from hers and placed it on the small of her back. She stepped back as he moved even closer, her bottom coming to a rest on the beer pong table. He was surprised at how well he was keeping his cool. Juliet had him captivated, and he wanted to impress her more than any girl he'd ever met.

He looked her in the eyes and she trembled in his arms.

"There is just something about you, Juliet. You seem more honest, purer than the other girls I talk to." He wanted to kiss her, but wasn't sure if she would be receptive. Usually girls just threw themselves at him because of his money, but somehow he'd known from the moment he'd seen her that she would be different. Juliet broke his gaze and turned out of his embrace.

"Thank you for the game, but I really need to get home." She shyly looked down at her feet. "You've been so kind to me. I hate the idea of you getting tangled up in my troubles. But if your offer stands, I'll take the ride."

Romeo wanted to tell her that he would be happy to be tangled up in her any way that she would allow, but he knew he shouldn't say that aloud. Instead, he walked her to the garage and opened his car door for her.

"Don't you need to tell anyone that you're leaving?" she asked.

He shrugged. "Most of the people at this party are too self-absorbed to notice one way or the other."

He held her hand between shifting gears, and it filled him with euphoria that she didn't push him away. He found it so endearing that her palms were sweaty. She was so beautiful; he stole glances at every stop sign and his heart truly skipped a beat when she glanced back. When they entered her neighborhood, she asked him not to drop her off in front of her house. Romeo parked three houses down. He still wanted to be a gentleman and see her safely to the door, even if it had to be from his car.

The lights were on in every room of Juliet's house, proof her parents were waiting the way she had feared they would be. Romeo wanted badly to kiss her, but she was out the door the moment he parked. He watched her walk away and prayed that he would be alone with her again, if only to hold her hand and make her smile.

When the door opened and Juliet's father came into view, he held his breath. From where he sat, he had no chance of eavesdropping, but he could see Juliet looking down and her body shaking as her father spoke. Romeo knew she was crying. How could anyone be so cruel to someone so pure?

As Romeo sat by helplessly watching, he was struck by how familiar Juliet's father looked. He realized he had never asked her last name. Juliet's father grabbed her by the arm and pulled her inside. Romeo's fists clenched so tightly that his nails dug into his palms. He wanted to run to the door and offer himself up for any punishment Juliet was to receive, but knew it could make things worse.

When he got home, he turned the car off and sat in the garage. He considered whether or not fate was real. If it was, it had brought him the most beautiful gift. What if he had stayed in the library longer, or turned toward the billiards? Would Juliet have left with someone else? What if he had met her earlier in the night? Would she have been so open and vulnerable with him? It seemed there were thousands of possibilities, but ultimately tonight the stars had aligned and brought them together.

Just as Romeo was beginning to feel the elation that comes with new love, a crushing realization came to him. He knew why Juliet's dad looked so familiar. If fate were real, it was crueler than Romeo could have ever imagined. He wondered if Juliet had come to his home knowing who his father was. He finally understood the term "lovesick," and the feeling was awful.

8

Juliet

Juliet stared at her puffy eyes in the compact mirror she kept in her purse. She wished her mother allowed her to wear makeup. She desperately needed a mask to hide behind. Juliet had all the time in the world to think of a way to tell the truth, since her father had confined her to her room. But she'd made a pact with DJ. He may have abandoned her, but she wouldn't go low on his account.

Her father and mother had not spoken to her since she'd come home late Friday night. They were angrier than Juliet had ever thought them capable. She had never disappointed them, and it was new territory. Now it was Sunday, and she didn't know if her lies would be brought to light, nor what the outcome would be for her night out.

The door to the teen Sunday school room opened and DJ walked in. He immediately grabbed a metal folding chair, sat next to Juliet, and grabbed her hands in his.

"Juliet, I'm so sorry. Did I get you in a lot of trouble?"

She didn't respond. She placed her finger on her lips and nodded towards Rosie, who had been sitting in the corner playing games on her phone since Juliet arrived.

"Hey, Rosie, could you please give me a moment alone with Juliet?"

Rosie got up and looked annoyed. "Haven't the two of you had enough time alone?"

Juliet sighed. "Great, the whole church knows about us sneaking out."

After Rosie left, DJ turned back to her. "Let me explain what happened."

"We don't have time for that. Deacon Williams will be here any moment to start class. I need to know that you stuck to the plan. Everything rests on this." She could see that he was surprised by her focus. "My dad is talking to yours this morning and you know how he is. If even the slightest detail in our stories doesn't match, we'll be caught. So, did you keep to our alibi, or did you abandon that the way you abandoned me?"

She could tell that her last comment struck a necessary blow. She didn't feel bad. It was DJ who had convinced her of this plan, and it was he who'd left her stranded.

"I stuck with our story." He stuck his hands in his pockets and leaned back in his chair. "I was thinking that we should start dating. I mean, at least until this all blows over."

Juliet was immediately annoyed by the suggestion. DJ had only considered dating her to go to a party, where he'd ditched her for God only knew what, and now she was good enough to date simply to get him out of trouble. Her hands sat tightly on her lap. She knew he was right, though. They would have to sell their lie to their parents, and dating might just be their ticket out of a much larger punishment.

"Fine. But you should know that I met someone else. I really like him and don't want him thinking we're together. We can pretend at church, but don't expect me to keep the charade up while we're at school."

His eyes widened. Not only did he think she wasn't worthy of him, but he was shocked that anyone would want to date her at all. If they weren't in a sacred space, she thought she might enjoy hitting him a few times.

"Juliet." DJ didn't get a chance to finish. Deacon Williams walked in with his son, George. Rosie trailed behind.

Deacon Williams cleared his throat. "I hope I'm not interrupting something. Rosie told me you asked her to leave the room."

Juliet cursed Rosie under her breath and shot her an angry glare before addressing Deacon Williams. "No, sir. We're ready to begin class."

Deacon Williams' Sunday school message was about keeping your mind and body pure. Juliet felt the lesson was being directed at her. She supposed she was meant to feel shame and remorse for her behavior the last two days, but she didn't. Something had changed inside her, as if meeting Romeo had shaken her core values and liberated the desires that had been smothered by them. She reflected on how she had only prayed once since coming home on Friday, to ask that she not be found out, and that she would be alone with Romeo again. It was the kind of prayer one made with the devil, not with the God she had been raised to believe in. There was an eerie discord unfolding inside her, rising in her throat like a scream.

∞∞∞

Juliet and DJ entered the sanctuary side by side, and she could feel the glares and hear the judgmental whispers. Was it not enough that she was being punished by her parents? Did the whole congregation need to show their disapproval as well? Isn't this what everyone secretly hoped for anyway, that the pastor's son and the district attorney's daughter would fall in love and marry in holy matrimony? DJ whispered that everything would be OK, and Juliet hoped he was right.

She sat next to her father in the pew and he put his arm around her as he always did. Juliet did not relax into it. Not knowing how the conversation between her father and Pastor Ramos had gone kept her on edge. When Pastor Ramos invited everyone to greet one another, she slipped off to the bathroom; her palms were sweating. She dried her hands twice and wiped her brow before returning.

The words of Pastor Ramos's sermon, which normally

brought her joy, entered her mind and slipped away as quickly as they came. She was thinking about what DJ had been going to say before Deacon Williams had walked in. He owed her a major apology, and now she was supposed to act like his girlfriend. If she weren't entangled in this lie, she would probably stop talking to him. Their families spent a lot of time together, but that didn't obligate them to be friends. After Friday night's events, she wasn't sure he'd ever been a true friend.

As she replayed the night of the party, it occurred to her that maybe he was supposed to leave her so that she could meet Romeo. Maybe this all had to happen so that she could let go of the idea of some great romance happening between them. Perhaps there was a divine purpose to the choices made by everyone at the party that night. Something about Romeo finding her, the way her body responded and yearned for him, felt like it was meant to be.

Juliet's family did not stay for the coffee social after church like they usually did. She gave DJ a pleading look as she left the sanctuary. The silence on the drive home made her nauseated; she had never disappointed her parents or lied to them. She'd spent her whole life trying to please them. Even as a child, she'd been careful to pick up her toys, to wear the clothes her mother chose for her, to only engage in the activities her parents selected. This was the first time she'd done something of her own accord, and in doing so she'd met someone who made her heart soar. She wondered what her life would be like if she'd always made her own choices.

Her father pulled into the driveway. "Juliet, I'm dropping your mother off and I'd like you to sit in the passenger seat. We need to talk, and I thought we would go for a drive while we do it."

Juliet's stomach churned. "Sure, Daddy."

Her mother patted her shoulder before heading inside. If it was meant to bring her comfort, it did the opposite. There was no doubt in her mind that she had been caught.

As they pulled out of the driveway, her father began to

speak. "We haven't spoken much about what happened on Friday. I didn't want to have this talk with you until after Pastor Ramos and I were able to pray together. I have to admit that I was very angry with the choice you made to leave youth group with DJ. You chose to defy my rules, you broke curfew, and my heart along with it. Your mother and I have always been able to trust you to make the right decisions. This is new territory for me. I wasn't expecting to have this feeling of betrayal from my own daughter."

Juliet and her father both stared at the road ahead. "Pastor Ramos was able to remind me that I was young once, too. I was not always the perfect son, and I, too, went through a change when I fell in love with your mother. I really needed that reminder, and it changed my anger to thankfulness. Sneaking out with DJ was wrong, no doubt about it. But I couldn't have chosen a better match for you. I just wish you would have told me or your mother that you were having feelings for him, that you desired alone time with him. There are so many tricky emotions that come up during this time, this age, this transition..." Her father seemed to be searching for the right words. "Your mother and I want you to know that you can come to us with anything. We are happy to allow you and DJ to date, but please, you must tell us where you are going and abide by our curfew. I also hope you know that your body is sacred. I trust that DJ shares your morals, but the excitement of new love can be blinding. Don't let yourself be tempted. You must stay strong until marriage, as God has directed us. Your mother and I were married right after high school ourselves, and I'm proud that we waited for each other."

Juliet could hardly process everything he'd said. The lie had worked. He was waiting for some kind of response, but she didn't want to continue lying to him. Silence seemed a better choice.

"I hope I haven't made you feel uncomfortable," her father said in a soft voice. He took one hand off the wheel and reached for hers. "I think the important thing is that your mother and I want to be able to give you more freedom and trust that you will make the right choices. Pastor Ramos reminded me that you will be eighteen in a few months and your choices will be out of my control. That can be a hard pill for a father to swallow. I want to protect you with every fiber of my being. I know all too well how cruel this world can be, and the evils that exist around every corner. Some of them can seem inviting, but I hope that all I have taught you over the years will be a guide for you." He squeezed her hand and invited her to join the conversation. "I hope you can understand that I only want the best for you."

"I understand." It was the only thing she could think to say, but it was a half-truth. She understood his sentiment, but couldn't decide if her father wanted what was best for her, or what was best for *him*, and she lacked the courage to ask.

She kept her eyes on the road and noticed that they were turning onto the street where Romeo lived. Her stomach began a gymnastics routine that moved to her chest as they got closer. As they passed by the large estate, she spotted him outside with a hoodie pulled over his head, cleaning garbage off his lawn.

"Absolutely disgusting. I imagine that young man threw a party last night. Do you know him?" Her father did not give her time to respond. He seemed to be starting one of his rants, the kind where his face turned red and beads of sweat formed around his temples. He got this way whenever he spoke of a criminal he was in the process of prosecuting. "His father is Roman Montague. That man is one of the lowest creatures to walk the earth. Worse than the pond scum that chokes the life out of all that lives in the pond. Mr. Montague is a criminal defender, and is good at his job."

Her father dropped her hand and slapped it against the steering wheel. "I can't fault the man for being good at his job. It's just, well, what I find so repulsive is that he affords his largess by representing the worst criminals this district has to offer." Her father waved his left hand as if fending off a demon. "This family has been on the payroll of mob families like the Shylocks since before they arrived on American soil. The corruption runs so deep. I would love nothing more than to be the one to bring the Shylocks and Montagues down."

Juliet felt lightheaded and was trying hard to suppress the acid that was rising into the back of her throat.

"Remember that case I had a few years ago with the father who killed his family and burned his house down to cover it up? We had a mountain of evidence to show that the act was pre-meditated, even proof that the toddler was smothered with a pillow and not smoke. Well, Roman Montague dug up some bar fight that one of the detectives had with the defendant while they were in their early twenties. He used it to suggest that there was a grudge between the men and convinced the jury that some of the evidence was influenced and manufactured by the detective. It was absurd, and yet Montague spun the tale in such a way that the jury felt uncomfortable sending the man to prison for life. Instead, this child and mother killer will spend a few years in a mental hospital and then will likely return to the public under supervision of a mental health provider. And that poor detective was demoted to traffic cop! How is that for justice?! It makes me sick, absolutely sick. Juliet, you steer clear of anyone with the last name of Montague. That family is entangled with the devil himself."

The drive finally ended as Juliet's father turned into their driveway and parked. She unbuckled her seatbelt and quickly opened the door, then immediately fell to her knees and threw up.

Her father rushed to her side. "Lord, please tell me this isn't some form of morning sickness. You and DJ didn't sin, did you? Juliet, speak to me!"

Juliet wiped her mouth but remained on her knees. "No, Daddy. I'm still a virgin. I just got sick hearing the story you were telling me."

She'd felt so alive when she'd talked to Romeo and held his hand on the way home. She wondered how she could have lived in Shakespeare her entire life without ever meeting him or connecting his father to the defender that had so often fueled her father's rage. Would she have gone to that party had she known? Her head and heart began a war that seemed to have no peaceful ending.

9

Laertes

The soft sound of water rippling over rocks woke Laertes. For the second time he hit the snooze button, but he could already hear repetitive pop music blaring from Ophelia's room. It was her way of making sure he and their father were awake and getting ready. Laertes often lay in bed contemplating taking the bus rather than going to school an hour early just so that he could ride with his dad, Polonius, who was the head custodian at Shakespeare High. The early hours never seemed to bother Ophelia, but Laertes wondered if she was just putting on a show in order to please their father. What teenager could possibly enjoy waking up at five a.m.?

"Happy Monday," Laertes said to the ceiling, throwing the bed sheets off.

He dragged his feet into the kitchen and began his daily chore of assembling lunches for everyone. The fridge was getting baren, and the options were slim. He decided to use the jar of sundried tomatoes and cream cheese to make sandwiches. If Ophelia complained that it was disgusting, he would just remind her that she was supposed to shop on Saturdays, not spend them resting on a vomit-covered toilet seat.

By the time the sandwiches were made and tucked in brown paper bags, Laertes had changed his mind about snapping at Ophelia. His sister had carried the burden of their mother's absence even more than he did. She'd stepped up and helped do things that no other children were expected to do. She folded laundry, shopped, balanced the budget, and cooked dinner when most of her peers were out rollerblading or having sleepovers. It often seemed to Laertes that everyone in the house was still trying to catch their breath after his mom sucker punched them.

Laertes ran upstairs to grab a quick shower. He spent a few extra minutes looking in the mirror, debating whether or not to shave the few stubbly hairs that had popped up on his face and chest. They were bright red and stood out. He was late to hit puberty and it made him feel self-conscious, especially when he hung out with Ophelia and her friends. He simply could not decide if the sprouts of hair made him look more or less manly. Ultimately, he decided to shave. An online article he'd read had suggested that shaving frequently actually stimulated hair growth, but he'd never looked into it further to discover if it were true or not. Either way, the hair would grow back, so he supposed it was a worthy experiment.

Once at school, Laertes headed toward the newsroom. It had been his second home since he'd started high school and joined the paper. He wrote student and faculty features for *The Shakespeare Chronicle*. Each week a different person was highlighted for their role or achievements at the school. He found the interviews fun, but the part he enjoyed most was taking the person's portrait.

Laertes loved photography in general, but taking a portrait was so intimate. He learned the most about a person from their picture, not the interview. He could tell by their eyes if they held back secrets, by the way they smiled if they were outgoing, by the way they positioned their body if they craved power. They could use their words to attempt to paint themselves in a certain light, but the camera always revealed the truth.

He had taken a picture of his mother when he'd received his very first camera. He'd been six years old, and the disposable was a gift from Ophelia. He'd run around asking everyone to model for him. At the time the photos were printed, he'd been too young to see the signs. But now when he looked at the picture of his mother, he could see the wildfire burning behind her eyes. She'd always meant to leave, but it hadn't made her going hurt any less.

He plugged his USB flash drive into the computer and began flipping through the snapshots he'd taken at Romeo's party. He normally didn't take candid pictures like this, but Puck had approached him Friday before school was out. He was in charge of the gossip column, "Puck Talks," for the school paper, which was the only reason most students bothered buying the *Chronicle*. The party was supposed to be massive, and Puck needed the extra set of eyes to capture all the drama. Laertes couldn't say no. He'd tried, but Puck could be insistent, to put it kindly.

Capture drama was exactly what Laertes did that night, and he wondered which photos Puck would end up using. One of the first photos he'd snapped was of Hero. She seemed to be admiring the backside of a certain football player. There was one of Don Pedro sitting poolside next to Katharina, the school spitfire. Laertes had spotted them from an upstairs window and was able to get a shot of the two; they were holding hands. Laertes didn't want his name on the project if Puck chose that picture. Katharina was a force to be reckoned with. Seeing her reminded him of the photo he'd snagged of her twin sister, Bianca, as she'd played spin the bottle. He was able to get a picture of her kissing Benedick before his sister, Ophelia, had kicked him out of the room. Laertes cringed at the hurt it might cause Beatrice to see that photo go to print.

A few slides later was the picture of the track team having beers on the front lawn. Laertes doubted Puck would put that in the paper. It would be sure to get some of those students kicked off the team, and while Puck loved drama, he did his best to maintain beneficial relationships. Outing the track team would keep him from attending any of Romeo's parties in the future.

The next photo was one that Laertes felt ashamed to have

taken. It was of Juliet sitting alone near the beer pong table, looking like the world had started caving in on her. He could see the pain in her face and had known she was holding back a world of emotion when he'd taken the photo. Right after the flash, she'd gotten up and walked off. Laertes was sure that she'd found a room to lock herself in.

He'd written an article on her last year, which had highlighted her volunteerism in the community and school. He remembered how optimistic and innocent she'd looked in the portrait he'd taken, like she knew she could save the world. That portrait was a stark contrast to the one on the screen now. He debated deleting the photo when Puck came into the room.

"Now *that* is a photo to behold! I need to know the backstory. Who brought 'Our Lady of Virginity' to the party? Why was she alone looking like a fat child whose cake had been taken away? Who did she leave with? Does her father know about this?!" Puck grabbed Laertes' shoulders and gave a gentle but excited shake. "This photo leaves me with so many questions! Perhaps I should just skip the digging, print the picture, and let the rumors unfold. This straight A princess is sure to cause a stir among readers."

"Puck, this photo is nothing." Laertes felt protective. "There are way better options for you to stir the pot." He hoped Puck would take the bait and forget about Juliet.

"Oh, damn, you have a crush on her, don't you?"

Laertes went red. It wasn't that. Maybe it was a little. He knew Juliet's father would never have let her go to a party like that; printing the photo would bring a load of pain to someone who had been nothing but the definition of kindness.

"OK, sweetie, I'll let her go this time." Puck nudged him. "Move over and let me see these pot-stirring options."

He could smell the lilac of Puck's perfume as he scooted closer to share the computer screen. Puck began flipping through the photos and stopped on the picture of Hero looking at Claudio. "Well, well, well. It looks like you caught this girl sizing up Claudio, and she looks pleased. You know, I heard a rumor that Claudio ran away from spin the bottle when a group of cheerleaders walked in. I bet Hero was among them. I could post this photo and caption it, 'The Homecoming King and Queen You Never Saw Coming.'"

Laertes breathed a sigh of relief. "Hero was part of the game when I snapped a picture. My sister seemed to be leading it. I could ask her for the details, if you want."

"Puh-lease! Digging for dirt is my favorite activity. I'll find Ophelia and get all the juicy details." Puck turned and put his hand on Laertes' leg. "This is *so* exciting. I feel like I'm playing a game of love connection." Puck wrapped his arms around himself. "I just love *love*! Maybe I should ask Macbeth if we can turn this into a regular column. We can call it 'Not-So secret Admirer' or 'Secret Desires of Shakespeare High.' Oh, I like the sound of that one. I could use my insider knowledge to help students connect with their crushes. Macbeth would get on board just to sell the paper each week!"

"I don't know, Puck." Laertes tried to insert some sense into Puck's excitement. "Love is often unrequited. It could end up causing more pain and embarrassment than intended."

"You are such a wet rag! I'm gonna go find Ophelia. I bet she'll love this match-making idea."

Laertes watched Puck leave, his signature silk kimono and the scent of lilacs flowing behind him. He turned back to the photos and decided to delete the photograph of Juliet in case Puck changed his mind.

Now that his meeting with Puck was over, he could turn his attention to the feature he planned to write about the new principal. His father had informed him the night before that they would be having dinner with Dr. Hamlet. He was supposed to submit his article to Macbeth for review by Friday, but submitting before getting a behind-the-scenes look at Dr. Hamlet's house would be a missed opportunity. The students had been abuzz after the introduction of the new principal, and Laertes' article was sure to draw many readers to *The Shakespeare Chronicle.*

He opened his school email account and wrote a quick message to Macbeth. "Macbeth, I'd like to turn in my article on Sunday evening. I know this will leave you less time to edit, but my family has been invited to dinner at Dr. Hamlet's house. This could be an opportunity to really get to know the new leader of our school. Could lead to a sales boost for this week's edition."

Laertes didn't wait for Macbeth's response before sending his next email; Macbeth would do anything to ensure the paper made its sales quota. "Good Morning Dr, Hamlet. As you know, you have been chosen as this month's Student/Faculty Feature. I was wondering if you would be open to doing the interview and portrait at your house. My father informed us last night of your invitation, and I thought it would be a wonderful opportunity for the students of Shakespeare High to get to know our new principal on a more personal level. As with our prior interview arrangement, I will send you questions a day prior for review. Please let me know if this is possible so that I may prepare to bring my portrait lighting and camera to Saturday's dinner. Regards, Laertes."

By the time Laertes hit send, Macbeth had already responded. "Does Macbeth ever stop working?!" Laertes both admired and felt sorry for the paper's editor. Macbeth was involved in more extracurriculars than anyone else in the school, and still managed to keep his grades impeccable. He often wondered how Macbeth juggled it all without burning out. It seemed like a stressful life.

Laertes opened the email and read, "Laertes, This is a HUGE ask. You know I like to have the paper formatted and ready for print by Friday evening. So here is what I will do. If you think this feature is going to be such a seller--and I agree with you that it will draw readers--we will make it the front page. I will format the rest of the paper on Friday, leaving only enough room for eight hundred words and a three by five photo. Since you will be here early Monday morning, I will allow you to add the article and photo without my edit. I'm trusting you to get this right. ~Mac."

Laertes felt excitement and pressure. He would have to dig deeper with the interview than he'd originally planned in order to nail this opportunity. His student and staff features never made the front page. He opened up his interview document and began adjusting questions. Instead of asking, "How does your experience as a professor influence your decision-making as a principal?" he decided to ask, "Why leave a college teaching post to become a principal? Do you feel like this is a step down or step forward?" He added more intimate questions, too, including ones about Hamlet's family history. "Your family is considered old money in this town, and your father left quite a legacy. Does this add any pressure to your position? How do you plan to leave your mark on the family name?"

This interview had the potential to be the feature that helped him truly begin building a portfolio. Maybe it would earn him some more respect with his peers at *The Shakespeare Chronicle*, and he could use the momentum to fill Macbeth's shoes as next year's editor. He was letting the success fantasy run away from him; it wasn't like the *New York Times* would be calling him up after the article went to print.

"Laertes, your sister is a wealth of knowledge!" Puck's voice startled Laertes out of his daydream. "I'm going to need a little more of your paparazzi action to nail this match-making column."

Laertes groaned and pulled his hood over his head. Snapping photos at Romeo's party had made him feel dirty. He could try to say no, but Puck wouldn't drop it until he said yes. *Ugh! Leave me to my own work!* He wanted to scream, but when he opened his mouth, he found agreement coming out instead. He felt more uncomfortable as Puck filled him in on the plan. It seemed wrong to meddle in someone's love life. He hoped the article wouldn't backfire and have negative results for Hero and Claudio.

10

Beatrice

On Thursday morning, Beatrice was still stewing over the kiss between Benedick and Bianca. She had forgiven Bianca the next morning after receiving a lengthy text. Bianca had explained that the kiss was nothing more than part of a game for her, and that she had rejected Benedick when he'd attempted to come on to her later that night. Bianca had apologized and said she'd never meant to hurt Beatrice.

Beatrice had checked with Hero, whom she trusted more than any other friend, and Bianca's story checked out. Hero even said that Bianca had left the party crying because Benedick wouldn't leave her alone. Beatrice still felt jealousy when she saw her, but it wasn't her fault. The jealousy rolled in with the anger she felt toward Benedick, becoming a ball of fire in her chest. He should have known better than to join a game that would compromise their relationship, even if they were taking a break. If he really wanted her back the way he claimed, he would have sought her out at the party rather than trying to replace her with someone else.

She continued to ignore his attempts to speak with her. He tried to text her several times, but she stayed strong and deleted every text as they came. She couldn't help but smile at the irony that Benedick was now skipping his third period class to try to see her at lunch. Had he changed his schedule in the first place, none of this would have been an issue. He always took her for granted, as if she would stay by his side without receiving anything in return. This time he wasn't going to win her back easily, even if she did miss him all the time.

Spin the bottle had likely been a way for him to make her jealous. Ophelia had heard from several sources that Benedick was desperate to have her back. According to Ophelia, he was lovesick. *Well, prepare to hurt*, Beatrice thought. *Your silly games are down a player.*

It was her turn to make *him* jealous. When she was through with her plan, she would have every guy in school begging for a date. She got out of bed and began dressing in the clothes she'd picked out the night before, starting with the red push-up bra that would highlight her cleavage under the tight V-neck T-shirt she planned to wear.

She stood in front of the mirror and admired how flat her stomach looked. She had barely eaten since Friday's party, and when she did, she purged it. She was going to take control of her body. No more pudgy, insecure Beatrice. No more being the girl with the pretty face. She was going to have the body that every girl dreamed of. If she controlled her calorie intake, she would get there in no time, and Benedick would know once and for all what he'd lost.

Beatrice went downstairs, where her mother was preparing to toast bagels to go along with the bacon she'd fried. The smell filled the kitchen with an aroma that made Beatrice's mouth water and her stomach ache.

So far she had been able to avoid eating with her mom, but this morning she scrambled for an excuse. "Good morning. It smells heavenly in here. I wish I had time to eat with you, but Hero and I need to study for our biology exam."

Her mom looked up in surprise from spreading cream cheese. "Beatrice, you are too busy lately. You've barely sat down with me this week. I was hoping we could at least have breakfast before you ran off."

Beatrice kissed her mother on the head and tried to soothe the tension. "I know, Mom. It's always hard in the beginning of the year for me to balance all the classwork and cheer-leading. Let's have dinner tomorrow. I won't make any plans, I promise."

Her mom seemed satisfied. "I just miss spending time with you, Beatrice. Next year you'll head off to college and I'll see you even less." She looked past Beatrice. "I must admit, the thought of that has been weighing heavily on me. I'm not ready to be alone all the time."

"Oh, Mom, I haven't even decided on a school yet. Besides, I promise we'll facetime and get together as much as possible. You won't be lonely." She gave her mom a quick hug before starting toward the door.

"Wait. At least give me a moment to wrap a bagel to go." Her mother sounded rejected.

She did miss morning breakfast with her mom, but she didn't like to start her day by having to purge a meal. It always left an acidic taste in her mouth, and then she worried that her breath smelled bad. Sacrifices would have to be made in order to get the body she wanted. "Push through, stay strong, it's worth it." This became her daily mantra. As she walked to school, she fantasized about all the calories the walk would burn, how thin she would become, and how badly Benedick would want her back.

When she arrived at school, she tossed the bagel into a waste basket. The student council was already hanging home-coming posters, and she wondered if she and Benedick would make up in time to put their names on the ballot for king and queen. She approached Juliet, who was standing back and guiding her fellow council members on poster placement. "I didn't realize it was that time of year already," Beatrice commented.

"It's sort of sad to think that it's our last homecoming as students at Shakespeare High," Juliet said. "After this, we return as alumni. I want the game, ceremonies, and dance to be perfect."

"Well, if there is one thing you're good at, it's being perfect. Don't worry about it too much. Have you put out sign-up sheets for homecoming king and queen? Benedick and I are on a break right now, but I still want that crown, even if it's with a different king by my side." Beatrice felt her chest squeeze as she said it.

The moment the words left her mouth, she knew it wasn't true. Benedick was the only king she wanted by her side. She wanted to punish him for kissing Bianca, but she still couldn't imagine a future without him. She didn't want to let her mind go down the rabbit hole of winning and having someone else, like Claudio or Macbeth, wear the crown next to her.

"Sign-up sheets will be in the cafeteria starting on Monday. More information will be given on the morning announcements today, and Macbeth will have information posted in *The Chronicle*." Juliet directed Bianca to straighten a poster and whispered to Beatrice, "She doesn't have the spatial awareness Katharina has. It's amazing how different they are."

As the girls talked, Romeo entered the school and they both took notice.

"Weird," Beatrice said, "Morning bell doesn't ring for ten more minutes, and Romeo Montague is already here. Have we entered *The Twilight Zone*?" She was joking, but she noticed the way Juliet's body stiffened and the way she looked at Romeo.

"Is it odd for him to come to school early?" Juliet asked. "I don't really know him. It's funny how our town is so small and yet it's still possible for someone to be anonymous if they wish."

"Oh, that boy hasn't tried to stay anonymous. But I suppose you've kept your circle small."

"Well, perhaps this will be the year I widen it." Juliet blushed and Beatrice wondered if she had a crush on Romeo. She'd heard rumors that Juliet had shown up to the party last week.

No way those two could end up as an item, Beatrice thought. *The school's good girl and filthy rich bad boy? No. That only happens in the movies.*

11

Hero

"Why is your brother following me this week?" Hero asked Ophelia as they crossed the field to cheer practice. "I swear he must have a crush on me, because he keeps taking pictures of me."

Ophelia just smirked and shrugged.

"Woah, woah, woah! What are you up to? I know you, and your body language screams that you're up to something!"

"Trust me when I say that whatever I'm up to is in your best interest. Really, you will thank me in the end," Ophelia said. With that she swung her amber ponytail and skipped toward the other cheerleaders, who were warming up.

Hero scowled and decided to fill her water bottle before practice began. She felt uncomfortable that Ophelia was keeping secrets at her expense. Hero might be a cheerleader, but she didn't enjoy the spotlight. Being a cheerleader was just something that was expected of her. Her mother had enrolled her in gymnastics and dance from the moment she could walk. Sometimes it felt like her mother's love was conditional on her becoming a cheerleader and being popular. Her mom often made comments that expressed her disappointment that Hero had gone through high school without once becoming squad leader, as she had once been. Hero never admitted that the reason she hadn't become squad leader was because she never asked for the position.

She saw some football players approaching, Claudio among them. From the corner of her eye, she saw the flash of Laertes' camera. She turned and flipped him off. "Take a picture of that," she said under her breath. She turned back to the water jug and began filling her bottle.

"What's your beef with Laertes?" The familiar voice instantly filled her stomach with butterflies.

She tried not to blush, but she could feel heat rising from her chest to her neck. "I think he's following me. He's taking a lot of pictures of me. I asked Ophelia about it and they are definitely up to something."

She noticed the way Claudio rolled his shoulders back and stood taller before replying. "If he's bothering you, let me know. I can talk to him and make sure he stops."

She met his eyes for a brief moment before he looked back at his water.

One of the other players, an underclassmen Hero didn't know, chimed in. "Look at you, playing knight in shining armor."

Claudio shot the player a scowl.

"It's OK," she said. She struggled to find something more to say.

Benedick ran over and threw his arm around Hero before she could walk away. She could see the disappointment in Claudio's eyes.

"Hey, Hero." Benedick was catching his breath as he spoke. He was already sweaty.

Hero pushed his damp arm off of her. "Do you really think it's a good idea to put your arm around me? You've already hurt Beatrice enough."

"Look, it was a stupid game. You know that. Could you talk to Beatrice for me? Is she still mad?"

"I don't want to get in the middle of your drama. Ask her yourself." She had seen how much this had weighed on Beatrice. Her friend had seemed tired and distracted ever since the party, and Hero was feeling protective.

Benedick grabbed her wrist to once again stop her retreat. "Come on, Hero, just tell me if I have a shot of getting her back or not."

Claudio intervened, to Hero's relief. He grabbed Benedick by the shoulder and pulled him back. "Don't put your hands on Hero like that, man. She said she didn't want to get involved. What part of that don't you understand?"

"OK, bro, no need to get all hostile." Benedick shrugged Claudio off and headed back towards the field.

Hero nodded to Claudio before walking back to her squad. Laertes was in the stands snapping photos as she walked. *Well, that is not how I imagined my first conversation with Claudio would go,* she thought. *At least the awkwardness is over with.*

She'd taken notice of him many times. He had an attractive athletic build, a warm smile, and he seemed kind to everyone. Some football players could be such bullies toward those they felt were below them. Claudio's demeanor was different, like all he wanted was for everyone to be happy and have fun. He seemed like he was able to diffuse any situation. Hero wondered if he'd offered to talk to Laertes because he was just being his usual kind self, or if he thought about her the way she thought about him. She hoped it was the latter.

12

Ophelia

Ophelia spent most of Friday bragging to her friends. She would be going to their very handsome principal's house, an opportunity most of her female classmates could only fantasize about. Half the girls would relish the opportunity just to be called into his office so they could smell the musk of his cologne. The boys made fun of the new principal, but Ophelia knew it was out of jealousy. They were just boys. How could they compete with a man like that? Hamlet was the kind of man who attracted women just by existing, and Ophelia could tell he knew it by the way he carried himself through the halls of Shakespeare High.

Now, she sat soaking in her bathtub, thinking about how bored she was by the boys her age. She had dated, by her own estimation, at least a third of the boys in her school. Some of them had been upperclassmen, and the others were considered handsome among her friends. She hadn't cared for a single one of them; she just wanted to make her friends green with envy. Most of her relationships--if she could call them that--only lasted until she grew bored. Most of the boys cried when she broke up with them and tried to convince her to stay, but Ophelia was always focused on the next challenge.

She called to mind an old boyfriend, Gremio. He'd been so obsessed with Bianca, always bringing her flowers and gifts. But Bianca wouldn't date without Katharina's approval. Everyone knew Katharina would never approve of her sister dating a senior when they were mere freshman, but Gremio hadn't given up. Ophelia had gotten tired of watching their cat and mouse game and decided to see how long it would take to turn Gremio's desires to her. It didn't take much. Ophelia had offered a shoulder for him to cry on. She'd wiped his tears and planted doubt in his ears about Bianca's true reasons for turning down his dates. Soon he'd been bringing *her* the flowers. The relationship had only lasted a week. Gremio had cried and groveled when it ended, at first to Ophelia and then to Bianca, with no success. After accepting that neither girl would be his, he became mute, retreating from all his social circles. Ophelia had known it was her fault, but the guilt had turned to awe at her own ability to turn a lavish man pitiful.

Dr. Hamlet would be an exciting conquest, Ophelia thought as she dried herself off. It would certainly be proof that she was a force to be reckoned with, that she could gain power over any heart she desired. Wasn't that the essence of most relationships, one person overpowering the other, making them weak of heart? Ophelia felt more powerful with every heart she broke. She imagined how accomplished she would feel to entice a man who was in an actual position of power, like her principal.

She selected a form-fitting dress from her closet, then stood in front of her mirror combing her long, ginger hair. It would be best to pull the top half of her hair up in order to show off her decolletage. Most girls her age didn't understand how sexy men found this area. She spritzed her mother's favorite perfume behind her ears. It always made Ophelia feel beautiful, as if she embodied her mother.

She should be angry with her mom for abandoning the family, but she wasn't. She understood there was nothing in this town that could capture her mother's spirit. Her mother was far too ambitious. It was amazing she'd ever married her father. Once, Ophelia had asked her mother what she'd seen in her dad. The answer had stuck with Ophelia.

"You father was the burst of kindness that I needed after

being with a cruel man," her mother had answered. "That man thought he could control me, but once I regained my courage, I left him puppetless. Love can make you so weak. Best to avoid it. Just pretend to love in order to get what you want in life. Your father gave me kindness when I needed it and put a roof over my head. He is a good man. I will always be grateful for his love, but he will never have my love in return. I think he knows that."

"What about us?" Ophelia had asked, referring to herself and her brother.

"You and Laertes are the gifts I gave your father for being such a good man to me. He wanted a family, so I gave him one. He loves you unconditionally."

"Does loving us make Daddy weak?" Ophelia had asked.

Her mother had smiled. "Your father has a huge weak spot for you and Laertes. If you want to test his love, cry out and see if he will come running."

Later, Ophelia had tried it. She'd gone out to ride her bike and pretended to fall. Her dad had come running, like her mother had said. He'd scooped her up in his arms and carried her inside, even though Ophelia knew she was too heavy and her father would be sore from doing so.

Though Ophelia had not yet been a teenager when her mom had told her these things, she'd understood the lessons and kept them locked in her heart. Love was a weakness; attach yourself to a man who can give you what you want, and when he isn't able, move on. Ophelia was only in high school. There was nothing the boys could offer other than a higher status among her friends. So she used each boyfriend as a learning experience. She studied their behaviors, learned what made them tick, and used it to manipulate them. Perhaps Hamlet would be the test of how skilled she had become.

The bedroom door swung open and Laertes startled Ophelia from her thoughts as he flopped onto her bed. "What do you want?" she asked.

"I was hoping you would listen to the questions I was planning to ask tonight," Laertes said. "Macbeth is giving me the

front page of *The Chronicle*, so this could be pretty big for me."
Laertes looked up at the ceiling, his head cradled in his hands.
"I want to ask questions that are edgy and provocative. That's
more your thing. So, will you help me?"

Ophelia sat on the bed next to him.

"Are you wearing mom's perfume?" he asked as he sat up
and looked her over. "And what are you wearing? You realize
this is dinner at our principal's, not a date, right?"

Ophelia smirked. "Can't a girl want to feel beautiful?" She
grabbed the leather-bound journal out of Laertes' hands.

It failed to work. "A girl could want to feel beautiful, yes,"
he argued, "but with you, there is always a bigger plot at hand.
So, are you going to fill me in?"

She pushed his comments aside and read over the page.
Laertes suddenly put his hand on Ophelia's arm.

"Nooooo." His voice dropped to just above a whisper.
"You are not going to try to sleep with Dr. Hamlet." Ophelia's
eyebrows pinched as she focused more intently on the journal.
"Oh. My. God. You are." His voice raised once more. "Ophelia,
this is too much, even for you."

The journal smacked against Laertes' chest a little harder
than she intended as she tossed it his way. "It seems you would
rather meddle in my affairs than worry about this big interview
of yours. So tell me, why would this be too much for me?"

He met her glare. "If you were anyone else, I would assume
this was a joke, but I see the way you toy with the guys at school.
Are they not enough for you anymore?"

"They're boring. They have nothing to offer other than
their virginity, and taking someone's virginity isn't as magical
as everyone makes it seem. You boys are rather pathetic when
you start out." Laertes rolled his eyes. "But Hamlet is a man
with confidence, experience, money, and a position of power.
Think about how easy the rest of my school year would be if
I gained the principal's affection. Having that attention is like
being the teacher's pet, but on steroids."

"You realize it would be illegal for you to date him. He's

not going to take the bait because he won't want to face the downfall."

"I'm seventeen, and will be eighteen before the end of the school year. The only thing stopping him is his position of leadership. People will say he groomed me and that he was a sexual predator, but I will be the one grooming and preparing him." Ophelia ignored the twisted look on her brother's face. "Besides, I find that the brain's ability to reason shuts down once sexual desire takes over."

Laertes threw his hands in the air. "Ophelia! This is too much! You are shooting well above your rank and it's not going to work!" She showed no signs of wavering. "You seem determined, so I guess all I can do is sit back and watch you fail. I suppose it will be refreshing to see one of your games backfire for once."

"Ophy," her father's voice echoed down the hall. "Laer, are you ready to go?" Ophelia cringed at being called "Ophy." It was like her father refused to recognize the woman she was becoming. "I'm going to put the berry crumble in the car. I'd like to leave in five minutes."

Both Laertes and Ophelia stood to leave. "Don't forget your charm, Ophelia. You're going to need it," Laertes taunted. His lack of faith didn't faze her. Instead, it filled her with indignation. She would show him how capable she was. She could have anything she wanted.

∞∞∞∞

Dr. Hamlet greeted the family at the door. Ophelia was taken in by his warm, dimpled smile, and she returned it with a soft smile that she hoped was just as alluring.

"Can I take that from you, Ophelia?" Dr. Hamlet asked, gesturing toward the dessert in her hands. She passed him the dish. "Do I need to refrigerate this? You must forgive me, I know very little about cooking and baking," he said, making casual conversation.

Ophelia noticed how at ease Hamlet was; he didn't trip over his words the way her peers did. This was the confidence that came with being a grown man, and Ophelia was ready to engage in some banter. "Depends on whether you like your berries cold or warm, although I imagine a man like yourself prefers things hot." Hamlet cracked a smile. Her father turned towards her wide-eyed, but didn't reprimand her.

Ophelia's father changed the subject. "I'm glad you decided to invite us over. We never seem to have much time to talk about our plans for school upkeep, or any new projects you have in mind."

"Oh, no, we shouldn't talk business! Come, join me in the great room. I've set up some drinks and light nibbles. Let's get to know each other more while we wait for the roast. I just took it out of the oven." Dr. Hamlet smiled and turned his attention toward Laertes. "Laertes, perhaps you'd like to ask me a few questions before we eat?"

Ophelia cut in front of her father and stood close to Hamlet. "Lead the way."

She noticed all the masculine decor in Hamlet's home. He even had a bear skin rug in front of the fireplace. *Tacky,* she thought, *but I'll use it to play upon his fantasies.* She browsed the appetizers, choosing shrimp toast and sparkling water. Hamlet left the room to take the crumble to the kitchen and Ophelia perched herself on the rug, leaning on her arm, her long, bare legs draped to her side. She knew this would highlight the small of her waist and the curve of her hip.

"Ophelia!" her father said through gritted teeth. "Stop this right now! This is my boss and your principal's house, not a brothel! Your behavior is embarrassing!"

"Father, do relax. I'm just making myself at home."

Hamlet returned.

"Please excuse my daughter's manners. She makes herself comfortable wherever we go." Her father attempted a chuckle, but it came out strained.

Hamlet didn't seem to notice her father's unease. His eyes were locked with Ophelia's, and she felt she may have sparked his interest. How cliché it was for a man to imagine making love to a beautiful girl on a fur rug in front of a fire. He must be thinking about it. Men were so predictable.

"I'm glad she feels at ease," Hamlet responded. He sat down in a brown leather armchair and turned his attention toward Laertes. "How about those hard-hitting questions? Or shall we start with the portrait? Perhaps it would be best to capture me before I stuff myself with meat and starch."

Laertes agreed that they should start with the portrait and Hamlet suggested they go to his office. To Ophelia's annoyance, she was stuck with her father and his judgments. He sat there silently while Ophelia studied his face. He didn't look angry, but hurt, which surprised her. She got off the rug--it was pointless to remain there--and sat opposite her father on the couch.

Without turning toward her, her father spoke in a hushed voice. "Ophelia, one day these games you play with men will get you hurt. I've seen the way you behave at school and with your friends. I'm not oblivious, but I know I can't stop you. You don't understand the consequences. You must consider how your behavior impacts others. Your mother walked through life causing destruction. She used her pain as an excuse to become numb to the way she hurt others. I had hoped you would choose a different path, develop honest friendships and find true love."

Ophelia bit her lip rather than engage in an argument. How could her father speak of "honest friendships" and "true love?" What did he know of those things? The woman he loved had left him with two children and not a note of regret. When you loved someone, they took what they wanted and then hurt you, just like her mother had said. She was thankful to hear footsteps coming toward the room.

"Well, Polonius," Hamlet said as he entered the great room, "I hope your son captured my good side. He only took three shots!"

84

Ophelia answered for her father. "I'm not surprised. I'm convinced you don't have a bad side, Dr. Hamlet. You are very photogenic."

His eyes swept over her. Men loved to have their egos stroked. She was slowly chipping away at his defenses. If Hamlet were a peer, she would have him begging to touch her by the end of the night, but she knew it would take more time and effort to weaken a man.

All throughout dinner and dessert, Laertes asked his interview questions. Ophelia kept Hamlet's attention with her witty remarks and by acting fascinated with his life. She could tell that he was enjoying her attention and that her father was growing more displeased. After dessert, her father quickly shuffled them towards the door. Ophelia was perfectly happy to be rushed to the car, because she knew the remains of the berry cobbler sat on Hamlet's counter. It would be her reason to see him again, and when she did, she would have him all to herself.

13

Romeo

Romeo passed through the kitchen without acknowledging his father or stepmother, who were sitting at the marble island enjoying the breakfast their cook, Juanita, had prepared. They didn't acknowledge him either, or ask him to join them, and Romeo was glad they were both so self-absorbed. With his mind not fully made up, Romeo headed straight for the garage. Once in the car, he hesitated to put the key in the ignition. Would he really do this? Was she worth it?

The drive would give him more time to think. He had heard the rumors at Monday's track practice that Juliet was dating DJ. Everyone was saying how the pastor's son and the "church mouse" were perfect for each other. The news was hard for Romeo to wrap his head around. In order to remove himself from the gossip and chatter, he did what he did best. He ran. He'd run ahead of his team the entire practice. His coach had said it was his best time. Could it really be that the electricity he had felt with Juliet was one-sided? How could she be with a guy like DJ after he'd left her alone and crying without a ride home?

Monday night had been rough. Romeo had tossed and turned, constantly thinking about holding her hand, the way she'd smiled at him, the way she laughed, how badly he wanted more of her. He had to approach DJ at school; he needed answers. To Romeo's relief, DJ had admitted it was all a deception to keep their parents from knowing they had snuck off to the party. Knowing who Juliet's father was, and how harsh he'd been towards her when he'd greeted her at the door on Friday night, Romeo understood the need for deception.

After discovering the truth, he tried a few different ways to meet her at school. He wished he had gotten her phone number, or at least knew her class schedule. They didn't have the same lunch, and he didn't even know her locker number, or where to begin looking for her. He didn't want to get anyone else involved, so he went to DJ for help. At least he knew how to find *him*.

DJ had suggested that he come to school early on Thursday. Juliet was on student council and he could pull her aside. That plan hadn't gone the way Romeo had wanted at all. Beatrice had been there. He wouldn't risk Beatrice saying anything to the gossiping cheer squad. The emotions he felt for Juliet were delicate, and he had a strong instinct that it needed protection. It was DJ who had come to the rescue with a new plan.

So here Romeo was, driving to church on a Sunday morning. In his entire life, he had never stepped foot in a church; he wasn't sure he was welcome. He wondered if he was dressed appropriately in his jeans and pale blue, untucked, button-up shirt. This plan wasn't foolproof; it made him sick to his stomach. But how else could he see her? He could only hope that her father didn't yet know who he was.

Romeo pulled into the parking lot. If he were religious, he might have said a prayer. Instead, he opened the glove box and pulled out an old stuffed animal that his mother had given him. "I know you would love her," he whispered as he squeezed the ratty old tiger before tucking it back into hiding. He wished his mother were with him during these times. He longed for her guidance; talking to his father wasn't possible. He imagined his father would encourage him to pursue Juliet only to piss her father off, to take her virginity and move on.

After one last look in the mirror, Romeo willed himself to enter the small white church. An elderly man stood at the door, handing out pamphlets with the church announcements.

"Hello, son. I've not seen you before. Welcome." The man embraced Romeo.

"Thank you," he responded, quickly making his way to the sanctuary before the man had a chance to ask his name. Romeo felt it was best to avoid conversations when possible. Less chance of Juliet's father figuring out who he was.

Romeo had often felt the shame of his father's work. There was always a trace of discomfort when he uttered his last name, and a look of knowing always crossed the other person's face. He knew, from his grandfather's journals, that Montague wealth was deeply tied with the Shylock family's organized crime syndicate, and though it wasn't his choice to be born into this family, he bore the shame of it. The Montague name came with privileges, too, but Romeo knew there would be no special treatment in the sanctuary of God.

The small sanctuary felt cramped, with nearly every pew filled. Romeo scanned the room and quickly spotted DJ and Juliet sitting together. Romeo choked back the jealousy at seeing them together, shoulders touching. He had to remind himself that it was all a facade. If DJ was right, Juliet was pining for him, too.

Romeo made his way toward the pair and sat next to DJ. Juliet's parents were sitting in the pew behind them, and Romeo recognized Mr. Capulet right away. This made the situation all the more difficult. "Hi, DJ." Romeo tried his best to sound casual. "Thanks for inviting me." Nodding toward Juliet he added, "Is this the girl you can't stop talking about?"

Juliet looked pale, as if she'd seen a ghost. DJ must not have told her. Romeo thought that was a good idea, since he might not have followed through with coming. He stood, shifting his weight from foot to foot, unsure if he should sit down or flee.

DJ eased the discomfort of the moment. "Hey, man, so glad you decided to come." He stood and hugged Romeo, then gestured toward Juliet. "This is my girlfriend, Juliet."

She looked mortified, but she stood and reached her hand

toward him. "Nice to meet you. I'm sorry, DJ didn't say your name."

Romeo held onto her trembling hand while he spoke. "Romeo. Pleasure to meet you, Juliet."

He didn't want to drop her hand or her gaze, but knew her father might take notice if he lingered too long. He sat in the pew and silently cursed DJ for being between him and Juliet. The service began with a hymn and Romeo mouthed the words. Then the pastor invited everyone to greet one another. The congregation got up, shaking hands and hugging each other.

Romeo took advantage of the commotion and slid past DJ to Juliet. "Should we greet each other with a hug?" She smiled, stood, and pressed into his embrace. While he hugged her, he whispered, "I will drive by your house tonight around midnight. Will you open your window so we can talk?"

She nodded. The color had returned to her cheeks. "I should go make my usual greetings."

Romeo wondered if she already knew about his father. It was bad enough trying to work around the ridiculous scheme she and DJ had made in order to attend his party. This whole situation was damned, and Romeo knew it. He should probably walk away and count his losses, but he couldn't stop the feelings he had for her. He couldn't foresee the future or what fate had in store. All he knew was that he needed to be with Juliet. He felt it in his bones. Romeo kept his eyes on her as she made her way back to the pew.

The congregation remained standing and sang another hymn. Romeo found the church service robotic, not a ceremony that could awaken one to God. But he could hear Juliet's voice rise above the monotone crowd whenever they stood to sing. That was something that could move his spirit. She sounded like the most beautiful songbird God had ever created.

The sermon was about the church of Ephesus, but Romeo didn't pay attention to a word of it. Instead, he sat wishing that he could reach over and touch Juliet, just to feel her energy run through him. She was his key to unlocking the mysteries of the universe. He didn't stay for the refreshments after service.

"Midnight?" he mouthed to her before leaving.

She glanced toward her parents and nodded. Yes. Romeo left the church feeling like a saved man.

∞∞∞

"Romeo." His stepmother's voice always sounded so high-pitched and whiny. "Where have you been all morning? What kind of trouble are you getting yourself into these days?" She placed her hand on Romeo's shoulder as he filled his glass with orange juice.

The way Destiny acted and spoke always left him feeling disgusted. She was not his mother, not his friend, not anything. She was the bimbo his father was currently sleeping with. It was almost sad that she didn't realize that the moment the Botox stopped working, she would be kicked to the curb. Romeo rolled his shoulder and pulled away from her.

"Where's dad?" he asked. "I assume he's getting into some trouble of his own."

Destiny sighed. "He's been in his office since we finished breakfast. He's got a new client and case to work on. You know how that goes."

"What kind of criminal is he defending this time?"

"Oh, I think he mentioned grand theft auto and the death of a child. One of the guys who works for Shylock's used auto parts shop wasn't careful on his grab."

"Wonderful. I can only assume there is a huge payout." Romeo's words were empty.

He drank his juice and left the cup in the sink. He was feeling more disgusted with his father's work than usual.

"Well, you know how it is. Yes, the man stole the car, but he didn't know about the baby. I mean, who leaves their baby in the car? That mother is really at fault." She perched on the counter and continued. "It's complicated. I'm sure your father will

90

get him a brief stay behind bars, or maybe a fine and community service." She attempted to shift the subject. "Anyway, would you like to watch a movie with me?"

Romeo couldn't get past how easily she could talk about the case. His mother used to weep over the injustices his father helped serve.

Romeo was already leaving the room when he responded, "No. I don't think our tastes are the same."

Destiny always made attempts to spend time with him, but what was the point? She wasn't his first stepmom, and she wouldn't be his last. He wondered why his father bothered to marry these women, and why they would marry him with the prenuptial hoops they had to jump through. He imagined that every woman who tied themselves to his father thought they would be the one to break the mold. Romeo could only assume his father thought of women like a car: he never leased, always owned, and upgraded often.

Once in his room, Romeo decided to flip through old year-books. He found Juliet being recognized for scholarly awards, on committee pages, and in extracurricular features. She was everywhere; he wondered how she had escaped his notice until now. *It doesn't matter,* he thought. *We've found each other, and I know in the depths of my soul that we should never be apart.*

Time seemed to be moving slowly, and Juliet consumed his every thought. It occurred to him that they should leave town, like his mother had. Surely her father would keep them apart, and his father would only repulse Juliet, the way his mother had been repulsed. Maybe they could find his mother. Maybe she could offer them shelter while they figured out the next steps. He was thinking too far ahead, but he couldn't help but try to find ways for them to be together. Juanita spoke over the intercom, signaling that it was time for dinner. Afterwards, he would go for a drive. Sitting in his room was driving him mad.

∞∞∞∞

Romeo drove around town and past Juliet's house four times before midnight. He could see through the sheer curtains into her family room. He saw her family sitting together watching television on the first pass. How wonderful it must be to have a family you wanted to spend time with. He drove by later and saw the lights in the main rooms were turned off and the bedroom lights were on. He hoped that her father was a heavy sleeper. Finally, on his third pass, all the lights were off. *Almost midnight,* he thought as he drove through town once more.

After parking around the corner from the Capulet house, Romeo picked up his phone. He had gotten her phone number on Friday from DJ. He'd wanted to text her a million times, but never knew what to say.

Now he began typing. "Juliet, beautiful Juliet, won't you come to the window so I can admire you?" He hit send. His heart raced while he waited, watching the windows.

A small light turned on at the corner of the house; Romeo looked for the best way to approach her window unseen. Softly he closed his car door, even though he'd parked far enough away. He was so worried her parents would wake up and their time together would be cut short.

Juliet lifted the window and leaned slightly out as he approached. Her blue eyes were even more beautiful when the moonlight shone upon them. In one bold move he placed his hand under her chin and kissed her the way he'd wanted to the night of his party. He wanted to stay connected to her as long as he could, and Juliet lingered on the kiss, too. He moved his hand to the back of her neck and he felt her lips relax. As his tongue tasted her, Romeo couldn't help imagining the taste and feel of her whole body. He decided to pull back just as she moved her hand onto his chest; he would not be able to control his desire if he let things continue.

"I thought you came to talk." She had the coyest smile on her lips.

"I did, but you are an enchantress, and I am your fool."

"Any man who comes to my house in the dead of night is indeed a fool! Do you know who my father is?"

Romeo's smile dropped. "The bigger question may be, do you know who *my* father is?"

Romeo wished they could go back to kissing, but knew this conversation needed to be had.

Juliet grabbed his hand before responding. "Unfortunately, I know. It's made me quite sick knowing. Not because I think you're bad because of who your father is. But that's how my father will view things." She pulled her hands over her face. "I'm so embarrassed of my behavior these last few days: lying to my family, pretending to date DJ, trying to avoid you out of fear of my dad."

Romeo pulled one of her hands away from her face and stroked the back of it. "Don't beat yourself up."

"But my parents have me married to DJ in their heads. My father has said numerous times what a wonderful pair we are and how we have his blessing. I don't know how to come clean about all of the lies I've told lately. I never anticipated meeting you. I just wanted to know what it would be like to go to a party. Now all of this--"

"Juliet, I want to be with you; I can't get you out of my mind. I've never felt this way. I will walk through hell to have you, or spend my life in a living hell knowing I didn't do all I could. I will forsake my father for you, but I need to know..." His heart felt like it was in his throat as he spoke. "Do you feel the same? Are you willing to face the oncoming storm that being with me will cause?"

Romeo was surprised when she leaned closer and kissed him. When she leaned back and nodded a yes, there were tears in her eyes. "I suppose the fact that I'm leaning out of my window in the middle of the night is proof that I'm willing to risk the consequences of being with you."

"Are you scared?" he asked.

She nodded and a tear slipped down her cheek. Romeo was fast to wipe it away and kiss the places it had touched.

"I am, too," he said. "I'm scared to lose the one thing that has ever made me feel alive."

"You talk as if you love me," she replied.

"I'm not sure I know what love means, but if it feels like a clamp is squeezing your heart when the other isn't around, and when you're with the person it feels like you're weightless, well then, Juliet, I think I do, because that is exactly how I feel."

Romeo wanted to crawl through her window and give himself to her. Instead, he grabbed both sides of her head and tried to convey all of his desire with his kiss. She kissed him back and he felt her intensity match his. This was all he needed to know that she felt the same.

Romeo slicked his hair back, feeling a tingling at the back of his neck. He hoped they weren't being watched.

"Look, I would love to stay on your lawn all night or crawl in through your window, but I'm afraid the longer I stay, the more at risk we are of getting caught before we're ready to handle the consequences. Can you meet me under the bleachers after school on Wednesday? I'll skip track practice. I recently discovered you're in the marching band. You could skip your practice and be with me."

"You're right, you should go. I'll meet you, and will be restless until I see you again."

He kissed her lightly and stepped back so she could close her window. Romeo made sure no one was watching before running back to his car. He held his breath as he started the engine. He knew that he and Juliet needed a plan before their parents knew about them. Everything felt so delicate, like one wrong move could crush their chances of ever being together.

"I won't let them keep us apart." Romeo repeated that to himself the whole ride home.

His father was standing on the lawn with a highball glass in his hand. Romeo parked in the driveway rather than pulling into the garage and approached him.

"Enjoying the stars?" he quipped.

"Destiny is in a mood. I had to escape. Why must women be so needy?" He paused and looked Romeo over. "Were you out with a girl yourself? You seem intoxicated lately, like you've got a woman on your mind." He didn't give Romeo time to respond, but had a knowing look in his eyes. "I tell you, Romeo, you can't let them get the upper hand. A woman can break you. Look at your mother. She had me wrapped around her finger and then just walked away from us."

Romeo's fists tightened at the mention of his mom. His father always tried to demonize her.

"I'll not have a woman do that again, and you should learn to maintain your power," his father continued. "Avoid the pitfalls I had to go through. Besides, when you have the money we do, you can have any woman you want. When they get too mouthy, remind them that they are expendable. You know what I'm saying, son?"

"I know that I'm tired," Romeo said.

He wanted to tell his father that his obsession with wealth and power had pushed his mother away. It wasn't his mother who had weakened his father. It was his own infatuation with status. His father put more enthusiasm into work than he did his marriages. Perhaps he should feel sad that work was his father's true love. Romeo would never treat Juliet like she came second to wealth. She was the gold Romeo so desperately sought.

14

Macbeth

Macbeth awoke tangled in sweat-soaked sheets. His breathing was spasmodic and his chest burned. He tore off the top sheet and fumbled through the items on his nightstand. His inhaler was always close by, though Macbeth had gone many months without needing it. This attack had been triggered by the nightmare. The dream had felt so real, even his muscles burned.

It had taken place in a forested area cloaked with heavy fog. It had felt familiar, perhaps along the edge of Shakespeare Park. The moon had offered him a spotlight as he'd methodically hacked away at a nude female body. Whose, Macbeth couldn't tell. Her pale skin had shone in the moonlight, and her hair had been golden blonde. She'd reminded him of his best friend, Juliet. With each blow of the ax, the blood had obscured the girl's porcelain skin in crimson, making her less identifiable.

Recalling the sound of the chopping, his own tenacity at breaking the body down, the bones breaking with each whack of the ax, sent shivers down Mac's spine. Somehow he'd known, within his dream state, that the girl was standing in the way, preventing him from reaching his highest potential. If he hadn't disposed of her, she would've brought nothing but ruin and shame upon his family. Perhaps all the pressure of senior year and getting into college was wearing on him.

Macbeth stood and looked in the mirror above his dresser. "Nothing is standing in my way," he reassured himself. "I am at the top of my class, and I excel in several areas. No one is above me."

Macbeth walked to his bathroom and ran the shower, waiting for the water to turn warm. His mind continued to turn the phrase "no one is above me" over and over. He needed to wash the violence of his dream off. He felt as if the sweat he was covered in was really the girl's blood, blood that was staining his skin the longer he left it unwashed. His palms ached. Looking down at them, he noticed small curved red marks in them. It was as if he really had been holding an ax and chopping all night. Macbeth felt relief the moment he stepped under the stream of water. The pressure beating against his skin continued to calm him. Dreams could be so powerful.

Stepping out of the shower, Macbeth saw that he was running late. The dream had distracted him. He heard his father's footsteps and then came the familiar three taps on the door. It was his father's way of expressing disappointment with Macbeth's loss of time. His father had stopped lecturing him about time when he'd turned thirteen, but Macbeth heard the lecture in his head every time his father came tapping. Maybe that's why his father had said, "Today, son, is the last time I tell you how important it is to keep a strict schedule with your daily activities. You must be disciplined if you want to achieve greatness. Your mother and I came all this way, half of our journey spent on a patched-up innertube. Sharks were circling us when a small fishing boat rescued us, and we did this because you were inside your mother's belly. We did this so you could have the opportunities we were not afforded in Korea."

Macbeth punched himself in the chest; his father didn't need to punish him or lecture him anymore. The shame and guilt were self-produced now, and Macbeth could inflict his own punishment as he saw fit.

In the car his father asked about his chances at being valedictorian. "Dad, it's way too soon to know who valedictorian will be. We haven't finished first semester."

"No, it's not too early. You must secure your position in a

race early on and then have the stamina to hold the lead."

"I'm sure I'll get it. Other students don't seem to care about academics or their future. They're more consumed with their hormones than their grades." Macbeth tried to brush the conversation aside, but his father didn't let it go.

"You should go to the counselor or principal and see where you stand. Maybe your friend Juliet has overtaken you? Have you considered her? She is not your friend. She is the competition. You must think this way if you want to achieve greatness."

Macbeth was taken aback by his father's suggestion that Juliet--his one true friend and the only girl he had ever had a genuine affection for--was an enemy. It reminded him of the dream and his stomach churned with discomfort. They pulled into the parking lot in front of the school and Macbeth instantly became nervous. What was his father up to? He usually kept the car running and dropped Macbeth at the curb. "Macbeth," his father said while unclipping his own seatbelt. "For my peace of mind, I am coming in to see the principal about your standings."

"What! Dad, you need an appointment!"

"Serious, powerful people do not need appointments. What I lack in money and power, I make up for in seriousness." His dad smiled. "Don't worry, I know you have to get the newspaper on the stands. You don't have to accompany me. I can find my way."

"Please, Dad, we have a new principal. He may not take kindly to you showing up like this," Macbeth replied, but his dad ignored him and kept walking toward the school.

Macbeth didn't have time for this. His dad was right. He needed to get down to the copy room and make sure everything was going smoothly. He didn't have the mental space to worry about his father's obsessions right now. So, he accepted that his father would probably cause him some embarrassment and annoy Dr. Hamlet, but there was nothing he could do about it.

$$\infty\infty\infty$$

When he arrived at the copy room, Laertes was already folding freshly printed copies of *The Shakespeare Chronicle*. Macbeth loved the smell of paper "hot off the press." He greeted Laertes with a nod and began folding copies, too. He had great respect for Laertes. He was one of the few students who contributed articles to the paper, and also saw the process through from beginning to end.

As the two quietly worked to prepare *The Chronicle*, Macbeth allowed his mind to float back to his father's comments. How could he view Juliet as competition, as his father suggested? He admired her dedication and excitement for learning. That's what made her such a great friend. It was thanks to Juliet's tutoring that Macbeth had gotten through Early American History 101, and she was the one who'd made marching band practice bearable. If it weren't for his parents' insistence on carrying on the tradition of arranged marriages, he liked to think that she'd be his girlfriend.

"You seem happy this morning," Lady said as she entered the copy room.

Macbeth hadn't realized that he was smiling, but it began to fade at the sound of her voice. Some might describe it as soft and melodic, but to Mac, it was like nails on a chalkboard. He much preferred her to be silent, but he knew that would be a cruel thing to ask. She was stuck in this pairing just as much as he.

"Actually, I had a terrible morning," he replied.

Laertes grabbed a cartload of newspapers and made his exit. "I'll get these set up in the front lobby. You can take the rest to the cafeteria?"

"Thanks," Macbeth said. "Oh, and Laertes, great portrait of Dr. Hamlet. I'm glad I gave you the front cover. I think it will sell out!"

Lady placed her hand on Macbeth's arm, wanting to draw his attention back to her. "Tell me about this terrible morning."

Her face remained unchanged as Macbeth described the gruesome dream, and then his father's comments on being the top of his class.

"Perhaps it is connected," she said. "You had a premonition. Your father will find that someone has eclipsed you academically. Your mind is showing you that you must eliminate this person. It is important to your family and to me that you are successful."

Macbeth hadn't considered how much Lady depended on his success in life as well. He hadn't told her about his father's comments regarding Juliet, so what she said next sent chills down his spine. "And if it is Juliet who has taken your place, you must be prepared to do whatever it takes."

"What are you saying? Do whatever it takes? I already stay up late each night studying. I cannot try any harder than I already am. If Juliet has better test scores than me, there is nothing I can do about it."

Her voice seemed to deepen and she sounded more controlled than he had ever heard her. "Listen to me." She grabbed his chin and met his eyes. "I know you have feelings for her. I am not the stupid girl you assume I am. But you must put those feelings aside. It is me that you are to marry, and our children that you will support. So, if it is Juliet, then you will do what it takes for our future."

"Come off it! You and my father make it sound as if I will not get a good job if I do not make valedictorian. I've already applied to several Ivy League colleges, and will be accepted regardless of my class standing. What is with everyone's obsession with me becoming valedictorian?"

"Don't be selfish!" Lady chided him, and Macbeth couldn't believe her tenacity. "Your family came far, starting out with very little in order to provide you with opportunities. It is your obligation to do everything you can to excel and make their struggle worth it. My parents uprooted me from my life in Korea to bring me to you. Do you think I wanted to leave my friends and the boy I loved to be here with you? But here I am, and you must show that you are worthy of all the sacrifices made in your name."

She didn't look to him for a response. She simply moved a stack of folded papers from the table to a cart and pushed them out of the room.

Macbeth had never seen her so emotional. Having to please his parents was pressure enough, but now Lady demanded he be at the top as well. Could the world not see that he hadn't asked for any of this? He'd had the dreams and demands of others placed upon him since the day he left the womb. Could no one see the expectations were more than he could live up to? Macbeth became more aggressive as he folded the papers.

"Did anyone consider the fact that maybe I just want to be a ski lift operator or a grocery store clerk?" he said through gritted teeth. "Maybe I just want to be ordinary and have the ability to determine whom I will spend my life with. Maybe I would rather be homeless than work myself to insanity for others."

"Macbeth, are you talking to yourself?" Juliet's voice startled him. She placed her hand on his back and rubbed gently. He sighed. She knew how to soothe him.

"I am. I think I'm losing my grip on reality."

"Oh, no! I can't have that happening!" She smiled and Macbeth couldn't help but feel lighter because of it. "I really have so much to tell you," she said excitedly. "When will my best friend be available for milkshakes and trivial talk? Like the good old days, before we were seniors and being forced to grow up?"

"You don't know how badly I need milkshakes and trivial talk right now. This day has been so terrible that even Lady has yelled and stormed out on me."

"So you've lost your shadow? Quick, maybe we should try to keep ahead of her so she never returns!" Juliet laughed and it was infectious.

She always knew just how to change his mood for the better. How Macbeth wished that she were the one he was destined to marry. She wouldn't care what he chose to do with his life. She, too, had parents who tried to direct her decisions. Maybe they could both skip college and travel the country in a van, gathering money doing small odd jobs along the way. Macbeth smiled at the thought. The morning bell rang and the sound of students opening lockers filled the halls. "Seriously, Macbeth, I miss you, and I need my best friend. I hate that we don't have any classes together! We don't get enough time together."

"Me, too. Look, I'll text you tonight. We'll plan our milk-shake escape, I promise."

Juliet grabbed a paper. "Do you mind? This looks like a good read." He nodded and watched her turn and walk toward the C Hallway.

Puck strolled in a moment later and grabbed a stack of folded papers. "You're late," Macbeth reprimanded. "Being part of *The Chronicle* is about more than writing gossip. If you can't participate fully in this club, then perhaps you shouldn't participate at all."

Puck cut Macbeth off. "Please, sweetie. You and I know that you, Laertes, and Lady are the only ones who show up early on a Monday morning. You'd have to lose half your writers over partial participation." Puck whipped the hair of his purple wig as he walked out of the room. He called back to Macbeth, "Plus, you know my column is good!"

Macbeth scoffed and opened the paper to Puck's column. Maybe making love connections would sell more papers. He just hoped the feature wouldn't cause too much embarrassment for Hero and Claudio.

15

Hamlet

Hamlet leaned back in his chair and played his voice messages. He tuned most of them out. These parents will find anything to complain about, he thought. He was still decompressing from the abrasive meeting he'd had with Macbeth's father. It was still September; no one had enough academic data to even begin ranking students. He'd promised to inform Macbeth of his standings before the first report cards were sent home. Mr. Bak had seemed satisfied with that.

A familiar voice brought Hamlet's attention back to the messages. "I finally found you, although it shouldn't have taken me this long. You've run back to your hometown without giving me an explanation. How could you? You know what it reminded me of? The first time I came to your office to discuss a bad grade. You admitted you'd given me that grade in the hope that you could get me alone."

Hamlet quickly deleted the message without letting it continue. His palms were sweating. He stood as the next message started, a parent complaining that parents were not invited to join the homecoming committee. She wanted to have her say in the festivities. Hamlet opened his closet to look at his tired eyes and remembered the mirror. He made a mental note to ask Polonius to fix it. After the mom stopped rambling about how she wanted to see homecoming done, Arabella's voice returned. This time Hamlet could tell she'd been crying.

"Damn it, Hamlet. Call me back. I deserve better than you disappearing like this. You made me feel special, but now I don't know. Now I feel like a stupid little girl who was seduced by her professor. I feel like you were trying to woo Chrysantha the way you did me. What I really want to know is, was she the only one? Was I foolishly devoted to you while you were sleeping with as many students as possible? Did you ever really love me? You better call me before I start digging around campus. I deserve--"

Once again Hamlet cut the call short. He couldn't risk someone walking into his office while it was playing. Leaning back in his leather desk chair, he closed his eyes and took deep breaths. He focused on his heartbeat, willing it to slow with each inhale. A gentle tap at the door stopped him from reaching the calm he so desired.

"Come in," he said with as much authority as he could muster. Polonius's daughter appeared in the doorway. "Ophelia. This is a surprise." He couldn't imagine what she might need from him. "I heard the morning bell ring a bit ago. Shouldn't you be in class?"

Ophelia smiled as she slid herself into a chair. She had such a lovely smile. Hamlet immediately noticed that she was not wearing a bra under her tight-fitting tee.

"Do you like my spirit wear?" she said coyly, and Hamlet knew he had been caught looking at her chest.

"It's always a pleasure to see a student who's enthusiastic about school." He did his best to sound even. "Is there something I can help you with, Ophelia?"

"I just wanted to make sure you had a copy of *The Chronicle*. After all, you're the main feature. Besides, I have study hall first period, so I'm not missing my academics. Ms. Snyder was lovely enough to allow me to take a walk and provide you with this copy. She knows I keep up with my studies at home." Ophelia smiled and slid the paper across the desk. Hamlet looked down at himself.

"Your brother did a great job with the portrait. He's a skilled photographer. I'll have to find him today and extend my compliments." Hamlet tried to keep the conversation focused and his eyes off her nipples, which had hardened in the chill of his office. He sensed she had more intentions than simply bringing him *The Chronicle*, and he did not want to entertain her ulterior motives. "Well, thank you for thinking of me this morning--"

"Oh, I've thought about you more than just this morning."

Hamlet found her confidence both arousing and unsettling. Who had the power here? He was used to shy academic beauties, the girls who didn't know how beautiful they really were. Ophelia was a different thing entirely, and Hamlet wasn't up for the cat and mouse game she was trying to play. Underneath the desk, he dug his fingernails into the flesh of his palms. High school girls were more dangerous than his usual college conquests.

He was reminded that he was sitting in his father's old office, and the stress of what had happened with Chrysantha might have been what led to his fatal heart attack. He had to be a better man now, to honor his father. "Thanks again. I don't mean to push you out, but is there anything else? I have a district phone conference that I need to prepare for." Hamlet smiled at Ophelia and hoped it didn't look too forced.

She stood and turned towards the door. "Oh, there is one more thing." She flashed that confident smile. "I left the cobbler pan at your house. Shall I stop by this evening and pick it up?"

"No, that won't be necessary. I actually remembered to wash it and bring it to school. I gave it to your father this morning. Thank you again for bringing it. It was one of the best cobblers I've ever had. You've got a lot of talent."

"More than you know, Dr. Hamlet."

With that, Ophelia left and he breathed a sigh of relief. Thank God he'd remembered to bring the dish back to school. Hamlet wasn't sure he could resist her charms if she came to his home unattended. She was putting out all the signals, and he knew that at the end of the day, he would weaken.

His mind drifted back to Arabella. He missed her body

and her devotion. He wondered if someone like Ophelia could match the innocent, tender lover Arabella was. It was clear that he had taken Arabella's virginity. She'd trembled beneath him and cried after their first time. She'd become his student in every sense.

But Ophelia was clearly not looking for a teacher. She wanted someone who could match her power. He wondered what it would feel like, to be with a woman who was as confident as him, who knew what she wanted. Ophelia was not a woman yet, a fact Hamlet needed to keep at the forefront of his thoughts.

∞∞∞∞

Hamlet read the article Laertes had written. The boy really knew how to write in a way that captured interest. Hamlet felt bad that he'd refused to answer some of Laertes' questions, especially regarding his family's wealth. It wasn't that Hamlet was trying to hide family secrets; he'd honestly never questioned where the money came from. They had money, and Hamlet had never worried. That was all that ever mattered to him.

He skimmed the other headlines as he ate lunch, making a note to speak to Puck and Macbeth about the matchmaking feature, when he felt a chill sweep over the room. It felt as if a spider was crawling down his spine. He froze when a hand squeezed his shoulder. His muscles burned as they tried to obey his mind's commands to flee.

Hamlet felt the warmth of breath against his ear and his father's voice grated into his consciousness. "Hamlet." His father seemed to howl now. "You must avenge my murder. You must avenge my murder. Hamlet, do you hear me? You must--"

Hamlet felt as if he were being choked. He couldn't respond; his body wouldn't obey him. His muscles twitched, but wouldn't move. His phone began to ring, yet he couldn't make his arm pick up the phone. He listened to all three rings, and with each sound the hand on his shoulder loosened and the bellowing faded.

His secretary, Ms. Hultz, entered the room a moment after the call ended, and she jumped backwards at the sight of him. "Oh! Dr. Hamlet, you startled me. I thought you were out of office. I just sent a call through to you."

Hamlet grabbed the trash can from under his desk and proceeded to vomit.

Ms. Hultz was quickly by his side. "Oh, my God! Are you OK? Shall I call the nurse?" Hamlet threw his hand up to indicate a no and Ms. Hultz stepped back.

He breathed heavily. It took a moment for him to compose himself. "I'm so sorry." He swallowed. "I seem to have come down with something."

"Let me get you some water." Ms. Hultz left his office and quickly returned with a paper cup full of cool water. "I've called Polonius to empty your trash."

Hamlet managed to rasp out, "Thank you."

"I'm not surprised you're sick. These schools are germ breeding grounds. I was out sick so many times my first year on the job. But don't worry, you'll build a strong immune system." Ms. Hultz chuckled. "I was going to put this Post-it note on your desk. You received a call from someone named Arabella. She said it was urgent that she speak with you, but left no return number."

"Everything OK in here?" Polonius interrupted.

"No. I seem to have caught a stomach bug." Hamlet weakly pushed the trash towards Polonius.

"Well, extra points for getting it all in the trash." Polonius laughed at himself. "Easiest clean up I've had. I don't even need kitty litter for this one."

Hamlet managed a smile. "I think it best I take the rest of the day off. I am in no state to run this school."

"Of course," Ms. Hultz replied. "I will reschedule your meeting with the science department."

Hamlet was unsteady as he rose from his chair. Polonius grabbed him by the elbow. "Would you like me to walk you to your car?"

"No, I just need a moment to get my bearings. Ms. Hultz, could you cancel my appointments for tomorrow as well? I think I'll take some time to recuperate." She nodded and headed back to her desk.

As Hamlet walked toward his car, his stomach flipped, and it had cause to. Parked next to him was a familiar yellow Volkswagen Beetle. Arabella was more persistent than Hamlet had anticipated.

∞∞∞

Convincing Arabella not to cause a scene in front of the school was not easy, but he was relieved that she agreed to follow him home. Now here she was, in his newly furnished estate, the one his grandmother used to live in. He showed her into the courtyard and they sat underneath an umbrella.

"So, tell me," she began, "how does one go from living in a modest apartment to living in this...this villa?" She was clearly agitated. "Typical, that a man tries to rape a girl and gets rewarded for his efforts with a new home, new life, and money."

Hamlet rubbed his temples. "Please, Arabella, there is much to explain, and this has been a trying day."

"A trying day? Let me describe a 'trying day.' A trying day is waking up next to the person you love, attending class, and learning that there are rumors that a professor assaulted a student. Then coming home to find internet chat rooms alleging the sexual predator was your boyfriend. Then waiting all night for him to come home so he can tell you it wasn't true, that it wasn't him." Her voice was shaking as she spoke. Hamlet couldn't tell if she was holding herself back from screaming or crying. "And when he doesn't come home, you call and call and call, but each of your calls are sent to voicemail, and you have no way to find out what really happened, so you have to fill in the blanks yourself."

"Arabella, I'm--"

"No, Hamlet, you will let me finish. Those were dark days. I would have defended you and stood by your side had you not left. But the longer your absence, the angrier I got, and the more guilty you became in my mind. And it was frustrating that you had just disappeared! Then, finally, a break: a small article about Shakespeare High School's new principal. You had been so close this entire time. I still held a sliver of hope that you would answer your phone, feel remorse, beg for my forgiveness. But you didn't. So I finally accepted that you were guilty of all the horrible things they accused you of."

Hamlet reached for her hand. She pulled it away.

"I know. I'm a coward. But I didn't..." He searched for the right words. He didn't want to admit full guilt, yet he knew he needed to accept it. "It didn't happen the way everyone assumes. I wanted to reach out to you a million times, but I thought you would hear the story and take her side. Having you not believe me..." Hamlet paused, trying to convey a sense of inner agony. "If you had taken her side, it would've been a weight that I simply couldn't bear. So, rather than face that possibility, I ran away."

He got up and knelt before her, reaching for her hands again. She didn't move them, but she didn't push them away, either.

"You are right about that, and it was inconsiderate of your feelings. I didn't give you the opportunity to show your loyalty. I just expected the worst and hid in shame."

Hamlet met her eyes and tried to be as convincing as possible. He willed tears to well up, a trick he'd used when caught breaking the rules as a boy.

"Arabella, I love you. I haven't stopped loving you. I thought you would hate me, and I never gave you the benefit of the doubt. You didn't deserve the way I handled things, but please, you're here now, so give me the opportunity to make things right." Hamlet saw the way her shoulders relaxed and knew he could still have control over the situation.

She looked toward the horizon. "So tell me your point of view. I'm not sure I'm capable of listening with the love and sympathy I once had." Her tone of voice felt like venom, but he knew how to weaken her defenses.

Still on his knees, he pulled her hands toward his lips. She tightened them into fists and he kissed her knuckles. When she pulled away, he didn't retreat. He rested his head on her lap and caressed the outer edges of her thighs. She softened beneath him.

"I'm sorry. Oh, Arabella, I'm so sorry." He whimpered. "I've just missed you so much, and you giving me this chance to explain myself means so much. Darling, I'm on my knees before you. I'm putty in your hands. I'll tell you anything you want to know. I'll answer any questions you have, but please, *please*... I've missed you. I know the distance is my own fault and my own weakness."

He lifted his head to meet her steely gaze as he slid his hand onto her bare leg. She didn't resist, but he knew the battle was not yet won. He needed to tread carefully to win her over.

"Ask me anything, Bella. Anything."

"Am I the only one?

"Bella..." He knew she loved when he called her that. "You are one in a million. God, that sounds too cliché. I don't mean to be. Let me be straightforward." She relaxed as he continued to touch the parts of her legs exposed by her dress.

"You are special. It was love the moment you stepped into my classroom and sat in the front row. You were radiant and brilliant. I didn't know how to navigate the emotions you made me feel." She let out the slightest sigh and he choked back a smile.

"I don't even want to talk about this girl and her claims," he continued. "They are false. She was angry about her grades when she came to my office. When I told her she could redo the assignment to raise it a few more points, she lost it. She threatened to destroy me. I tried to grab her by the arm to calm her and she jerked back. She slapped me and her blouse started coming undone. Then she ran out. I knew how it looked."

He decided to change the subject. He didn't want to be caught in his lies. "I thought she destroyed us, but here you are, giving me a chance." He let a tear fall and Arabella placed her hand on his cheek. Hamlet knew he had gained a sliver of trust.

∞∞∞

Hamlet watched Arabella sleeping in his bed. It was well past midnight, but he couldn't sleep. There was too much on his mind. He lay in bed staring at the shadows dancing across his ceiling. The moon was almost in full, and it seemed so bright tonight.

What to do about Arabella? he wondered. He'd never really loved her, but she wasn't going to go away easily. Besides, he needed her as an ally to keep Chrysantha's story from spreading.

Chrysantha... She was the one who'd caused all of his troubles. Why had she rejected him? Why did she insist on making such a scene over the whole ordeal?

Hamlet slowly got out of bed and went downstairs. The couch seemed a better place to rest than next to Arabella. He succumbed to sleep. In his dreams, his father returned and sat next to him on the couch.

His father's voice was as clear as the last time they'd spoken. "Hamlet, you must avenge my murder! Do not trust those around you. You must stay safe, or they will kill you, too."

Disoriented, Hamlet woke up and looked at the clock. It felt like he had only fallen asleep for a moment, but it was already five in the morning and the sun was shining through his window. He heard movement above and remembered Arabella. He wished he'd had more time with his father, more time to understand who was a danger to him.

His father had said, "Avenge my murder." He couldn't

wrap his head around it. His father had died of a heart attack. He wasn't murdered. Hamlet rubbed at his temples as a migraine began to creep in. Could it be possible? Could his father have been poisoned? Had his death been made to look like a heart attack? Hamlet rolled away from the sun. It was a dream, and maybe that was all it was, but Hamlet had a nagging feeling. His father had appeared to him three times now. Perhaps this wasn't his mind playing tricks.

16

Katharina

Katharina normally spent Tuesdays after school in the art room. Her teacher allowed her to spin clay at the wheel, paint, or draw while her sister practiced with the squad. She found it calming to have the room all to herself; the quiet helped her think clearly. She was able to tap into her creativity without the noise of her sister. But this Tuesday, she found herself sitting in the bleachers watching cheer and football practice, hoping Don Pedro would take notice.

She felt childish. She didn't know how to navigate the feelings she'd been having since sitting poolside with him at Romeo's party. Half of her was afraid to acknowledge the desire that was now rooted in her. What would Bianca think? Would it be OK for Katharina to fall in love? Would Bianca approve of Don Pedro? The other half of Katharina was afraid not to lean into these emotions. She hadn't felt this need for a man's attention since she was a little girl waiting for Bianca to crawl out of their father's lap so that she could have a turn enjoying his embrace while he read a story.

Katharina was sure Don Pedro wanted to see her again, too. They had only seen each other in passing between classes, but he'd been in the D hallway often, and considering that he wasn't enrolled in any art classes, she felt it was safe to assume he was there to see her. Still, they hadn't had an actual conversation since Romeo's party. It was always a "Hey" or a silent nod between them as they passed to their next class.

Katharina opened her drawing book as the football team ran onto the field to begin running drills. She didn't want it to be obvious that she was there to watch. Perhaps she could design something to contribute to homecoming. But what? She closed her eyes and started humming. This was the only way she could block out the "noise," as her art teacher called it, and allow inspiration to enter her mind. The process might have worked had she been allowed a few more moments.

"Did you actually come to watch Bianca practice, or is there someone else you want to watch?" asked Beatrice.

Katharina hadn't heard Beatrice walk up the steps of the bleachers. When she opened her eyes, she was shocked at how different Beatrice looked. Her full rosy cheeks seemed gaunt.

"Why aren't you practicing with the squad? Are you sick?" Katharina was genuinely concerned.

"Eh," Beatrice sighed. "I feel like I'm not needed down there right now. I've memorized the routine, and besides, I'm sick of hearing about Claudio and Hero's new relationship. I still can't believe a few manipulated photos were able to cultivate an actual romance."

Katharina took the bait and didn't press Beatrice about how sickly thin she looked. "Seems like the whole school is buzzing about that. Who would have thought Puck would make an adept matchmaker! I read the article and thought it was meant to be comedic."

"Well, I think it would've been just another one of Puck's gossip columns had it not been for Ophelia. She's the real match-maker, and of course she can't stop bragging about it. It's starting to grate on my nerves. Speak of the devil, here comes our gossiping mascot now." Beatrice nodded toward the giant foam satyr walking up the steps towards them.

Katharina found it amusing, but could have sworn she'd seen Puck hitching a ride home with a friend. He never dressed up for practice. Not much practice went into being a mascot.

"Please tell me he's not coming to talk to us. I blame you,

Beatrice. Lord knows he isn't going to squeeze any gossip for his column out of me." Katharina was beginning to feel annoyed with the whole situation, and wished now that she had stayed in the art room. "Well, so much for tapping into my creativity today." She closed her notebook and slid her pen into her pocket.

"Ladies, what an odd pairing you are. What*ever* could you be talking about? I hope it's something I can use for my next column."

"I'd tell you to wipe that dumb smile off your face, but you can't," Beatrice retorted. "How about taking that mask off and cutting to the chase? What do you want from us?"

"I came to check a rumor with you. I heard you and Benedick are getting back together just in time to be homecoming king and queen. Any truth to the story?"

Katharina realized it wasn't Puck behind the mask, and it didn't take a rocket scientist to figure out who it really was. Beatrice's lips pinched into a thin line and her eyes were on the verge of tears.

She didn't answer right away, so Katharina cut in. "Buzz off. Can't you see she isn't feeling well?"

Beatrice shot Katharina a look. Why was it that even her attempts to help came off all wrong!

Katharina could tell by the change in Benedick's voice that he'd forgotten he was supposed to be playing Puck. "Are you sick? I can let Benedick know. I'm sure he would do whatever it took to make things better, and he would care for your every need. Would you like me to do that?"

Beatrice's words came out like bullets. "I don't need you to relay anything to Benedick. Not only can I take care of myself, but I'm sure I could find a more suitable man to care for my pain." She paused, letting her words do their work. "A better man to care for my pleasure, too. So, I suppose you have your answer. I am not getting back together with Benedick."

"Everything OK up here? I didn't realize people actually hung out on top of the bleachers," Don Pedro chuckled and Katharina questioned whether he'd come to see her or at the request of Benedick.

He sat and leaned back, steadying his hands on the back of the bench. His forearm pressed lightly against Katharina's back, seeming to answer her question. She wished he would just put his arm around her.

Beatrice stood up. "Everything is fine. I'm just telling our friend 'Puck' that the rumors about Benedick and me are false. He would have to crawl across the field kissing my feet and begging for me to take him back before I would wear a crown by his side." With that, she walked away.

"Benedick, I don't think you'll be advancing to kingship at homecoming, but if you'd like, we could crown you as the royal jackass," Katharina stated, not caring if she came off as a shrew.

"Damn. How did you know it was me?"

Don Pedro said, "I told you it was a stupid plan. Now you're out fifty bucks and Beatrice probably knew it was you as well. On the bright side, I made a few bets with the guys that she would beat you up verbally. It looks like I have more money coming my way."

"What the hell was your plan, anyway?" Katharina had to know.

"I thought if I pretended to be Puck, I could drop hints that I still love her and see how she feels about me."

"Can't you tell she's not herself lately?" Katharina asked, irritated.

"What are you talking about?" Benedick asked, caught off guard. "She looks the best she's ever looked."

"Maybe you should try looking beyond her chest and waistline, you twit. She's clearly sick over this break up and what you did at the party. You men are so oblivious!"

"Don't act like you're her best friend. You don't even have friends," Benedick shot back.

Don Pedro put his hand on Katharina's arm. She wasn't sure if he was preventing her from leaving or punching Benedick in the throat. She leaned back and let Don Pedro take Benedick's foolery on.

"Look, Ben, this charade has taught us two things. One, you are going to have to crawl across that field, because Beatrice is clearly upset. And two, you are an idiot. I suggest you hit the locker room and get out of that costume. Water break is ending, and Coach isn't going to tolerate your lack of focus."

"Whatever," Benedick mumbled. He got up and walked away.

Don Pedro slid his hand down and placed it over Katharina's. "I hope Coach can tolerate *my* lack of focus." He smiled and leaned closer. "There's been something very distracting on the bleachers today."

She felt her face turn red but couldn't help but smile wider than she had in a long time.

She pretended to look around. "I don't see anything. Perhaps I've been watching the field too closely."

"What brings you out here, anyway? Are you trying to learn the ins and outs of football?"

Flirting with Don Pedro felt so natural. She leaned closer, their noses almost touching. "I'm especially interested in learning about wide receivers." The whistle blew.

"Shoot!" Don Pedro pulled away and started walking down the benches. "I'm glad you came. I hope you're impressed by what you see."

"It's pretty enlightening so far," she shouted back and immediately wished she had said something else, something cleverer.

While she watched Don Pedro on the field, she imagined being homecoming queen with Don Pedro as her king. She laughed at the idea of anyone voting for her. That was when it hit her: she could design crowns, something her classmates would actually want to wear. As she reached for her pen, she silently thanked Don Pedro for being her inspiration.

17

Juliet

The pain in Juliet's stomach had begun the night before. She'd pushed her breakfast around her plate with her fork. Jitters, that's what her mom would call this feeling. She'd never lied or snuck around like she had been lately. Now, it was Wednesday, and she was going to skip marching band practice to meet Romeo under the bleachers. Skipping practice was anxiety-producing enough, but not knowing what Romeo had planned made her feel restless.

The only comfort Juliet felt came from knowing that she'd made plans to meet Macbeth afterwards. She missed her best friend and desperately needed someone to confide in. Of course, DJ knew about the situation, but it would be a while before Juliet felt she could trust him again. DJ had earned some favor back by inviting Romeo to church, but her eyes were wide open to the fact that he'd never cared for her. Even with her feelings for Romeo, it still stung and made her feel used.

The school day seemed to drag. Every time Juliet checked the clock, only five minutes had passed. She didn't know if she was grateful for the delay or if she found the anticipation painful. Would Romeo try to touch her? Would she stop him if he did, or would she give in to her deepest desires? She recalled Romeo's visit and the way he'd kissed her, how easy it had been to melt into him and return his affection. *No, he isn't like that,* Juliet concluded. *He has always treated me with respect.*

The familiar three chimes that marked the end of second period brought Juliet back to the present.

"Juliet, could you stay a moment?" Ms. Godshall asked.

Juliet stood by her desk waiting for the last student to leave. Ms. Godshall sat on the desk and studied her.

"I don't want to intrude, but I can't help but notice you've practically chewed your pencil in half. Is there something bothering you?"

Juliet hadn't realized it, but her pencil was covered in teeth marks and the yellow paint was chipping away. She wasn't sure how to respond; she'd never done that.

Ms. Godshall continued, "You weren't participating in class today, either." She gave a knowing smile. "This is my third year having you in one of my history courses, and it isn't like you."

Juliet realized she was still studying the indentations on the pencil. She met Ms. Godshall's eyes. "I'm sorry for my distraction today."

"I'm not looking for an apology. I guess I want you to know I'm here for you if there is something on your mind. Senior year can come with all sorts of stressors." Ms. Godshall stood and started writing a late pass as she spoke. "It wasn't that long ago that I was a senior in high school. I understand all of the academic and social pressures that arise."

Ms. Godshall was right, she was under a lot of pressure. But she didn't think Ms. Godshall could really understand what it was like to maintain the perfection her parents demanded, or what it felt like to know your first love was doomed before it ever bloomed.

"OK. Thank you," Juliet said.

Ms. Godshall gave her the late pass and Juliet tossed her gnarled pencil in the trash on the way out the door. She would be sure to keep her focus in class. The last thing she needed was a teacher calling her parents to express concern.

Juliet caught up with Macbeth as he was walking to the field for marching practice. "Mac, you walk so fast!" She grabbed his arm to slow him down.

"I can't help that my legs are longer than yours. Besides, you could have just met me on the field. No need to get all out of breath on my account." He shot her a devious smile.

She kept hold of his arm and stood rooted. "Actually, I won't be hitting the field today."

His smile faded as quickly as his eyebrows furrowed. Juliet couldn't tell if he was angry or concerned.

"Are you sick?" he asked. "Are we still getting milkshakes?" He grabbed Juliet's shoulders and gently shook her. "Tell me we're still getting milkshakes!"

Juliet placed her hands over his. "Yes, we are still on for milkshakes."

He released her from his grasp and placed his hands on the sides of his face, a move Juliet was familiar with. Macbeth always did this when he was having trouble understanding something. It was like he needed to physically support his brain.

"So," he began, "tell me then. Why are you missing practice?"

Juliet's voice began to shake. "I am meeting Romeo under the bleachers instead." Macbeth went blank, concealing his reaction, so Juliet continued talking, "I know. This is crazy to me too! There is so much I have to fill you in on."

Macbeth's hands fell from his face to his sides. "You're not going to do stuff with him under the bleachers, are you? I mean, last I heard, Romeo gave you a ride home and was really nice to you. Now you're heading for the bleachers with this--"

Juliet playfully pushed him. "Mac, don't be gross. It's still me." He said nothing. "Look, meet me here after practice and we'll discuss it all over milkshakes. If you play your cards right,

I might even buy us fries."

Macbeth's mouth twisted into a half smile. "How could I refuse you when you've added French fries into the mix? I'll meet you back here after practice, but please be careful. I can't protect you unless you're by my side, on the field, where you belong."

Juliet smiled and turned toward the bleachers. It was really sweet that he felt protective of her. She wondered if Macbeth meant that she belonged on the field or by his side. It didn't matter. She felt a sense of peace knowing that no matter what, she would always have Mac.

The stony path between the bleachers and chain fencing that wrapped around the field was littered with food wrappers, spent cigarettes, and empty cups. Juliet was grossed out, both by the trash and how lazy her classmates could be.

Going under the bleachers felt like entering a seedy underground club. It was dark, with slim beams of light entering between the rows. The light illuminated graffiti and even a used condom. She tried to be careful; one misstep and she would have to burn her shoes. There were other students under the bleachers, leaning up against support beams, but she didn't see Romeo.

As she moved closer to the center, she heard DJ's voice. Looking up, she saw that if she were but a few inches taller, she could grab his ankles. She smiled at how frightened he would be, and then even more alarmed at seeing her below the bleachers. She considered trying to jump up and grab them, but the fear of being noticed stopped her.

It took Juliet a moment to figure out who DJ was talking to--it was Puck. She wasn't one to eavesdrop, but DJ was not one to hang out with Puck. She stood on her tippy toes and strained to hear what was being said.

Puck said, "I'm glad you're finally admitting what I already knew, and you're lucky that I would never betray the community. But what you're asking is low, even for me."

"You promised that if I admitted it out loud that you

would help me. So, are you a man of your word or not? I said what you wanted."

Juliet was surprised by the edge in DJ's voice. Whatever she was listening in on was meant to stay private.

"Well, I'm not a *man* of my word, but lucky for you, I am a *woman* of my word. But I'm warning you, something like this is bound to have huge consequences, and I'm washing my hands of them all. We never had this conversation."

Juliet's heart raced. It sounded like DJ was about to get into something bad, but what on earth could Puck help him get into? Drugs? Stealing? Part of her wanted to run to him and stop him from doing whatever it was he intended to do.

Before she could decide anything, two arms wrapped around her and a kiss was planted on her neck. She felt relief that Romeo was finally with her, but she couldn't shake the dread over what she'd overheard. *I'll pray on this later and make no rash decisions,* she thought before turning around and facing Romeo.

He kept his hands around her waist as she turned to face him. She could feel the warmth of his groin pressed up against hers, and for a moment she felt a quiver of panic run down her spine. What if she was wrong about Romeo's intentions in asking her to come here?

Her voice cracked when she spoke. "You sure know how to greet a girl, but not how to treat one. It's disgusting down here! I narrowly avoided stepping on a used condom."

Romeo kept his hand on the small of her back as he guided her to an empty space. "I know this isn't a proper first date, and it's certainly not a place worthy of a girl like you. I'd love to take you out, to proudly have you by my side, but you know it's not possible yet."

"Yet?" She raised her eyebrow. "I wonder if we'll ever get beyond our parents' hatred for each other." She put her forehead on Romeo's chest. "Romeo, are we doomed from the start? I'm not afraid to admit that I want to be with you, but maybe this isn't meant to be. Maybe we should stop before the heartache is harder to get over."

He looked at her with such intensity that she was prepared to believe anything he said.

"I'm not afraid, Juliet. I am willing to risk the heartache because I'm sure that what I'm feeling for you is love. We aren't doomed. We're fated to be together."

Juliet's eyes began to leak tears as if it were beyond her power to hold them in. *Ugh, why am I always crying around him?* she wondered as Romeo lifted her chin so their lips came together.

He kept his hand on her chin as he continued, "I know this may seem crazy, but I've never felt like this about anyone, and I want to be with you." He paused and put his hands in his pockets. "I did have a reason for bringing you here beyond just wanting to spend time with you. I wanted to ask you something."

"Well, you have me here, so don't hold back now. Ask me anything."

Romeo seemed to shrug off his nerves. "I want you to be my date for homecoming."

Juliet wanted badly to say yes. "How could we do that? My dad will attend the game and expect me to go to the dance with DJ. He's supposed to be my boyfriend, remember?"

Romeo looked annoyed at the reminder. "Look, I've thought a lot about this. Maybe we aren't giving our parents the benefit of the doubt. What's the worst that could happen? They'll be angry with us, no doubt, but what is worse, living a lie, or living our truth? I want to be honest about how I feel about you. Damn it, I want to stand at the top of the bleachers and announce it to the whole school! I want to take you on real dates."

This time it was Juliet who initiated the kiss, just to keep him from actually shouting. She leaned into him. It felt so good to be in his arms, like it was safe, like she belonged there.

"You're right," she conceded, "Living with this lie is just as painful as dealing with the consequences of coming clean to my dad." She took a deep breath. "Homecoming is in two weeks.

I can have a fight with DJ. Then we won't have to totally come clean. I can't imagine what my father would do if he found out DJ and I made up this whole thing just to go to a party."

"OK, if you think that would be easier." He didn't look convinced of his own words.

"I think I need a way to explain how I met you, how I came to like you without knowing your family history. I have an idea, too."

"What is it? I'm not totally sure we should start our relationship with more lies. Don't make it too complicated."

"I could tell my father that it's a blind date, that Macbeth was feeling bad about DJ and me breaking up. He felt bad that I would have to attend my senior homecoming alone, so he found a date I wouldn't meet until the dance."

"Are you sure it will hold up? What if Macbeth isn't comfortable going along with it?" Romeo asked.

"He's my best friend. I'm sure he'll want to help us. Then after the dance, I'll tell my dad that I had an amazing time with you and that I want to see you again. I'll act shocked if he tells me that you're a Montague, like I had no idea."

"I just hope this plan works better than the one that brought you to my house in the first place."

Her phone buzzed in her pocket. "I have to go. I promised Macbeth we would go to the diner."

Romeo tried to keep her in his arms. "When can I see you again?"

"I'll text you later." With that she turned away, but Romeo grabbed her hand.

"One more kiss, sweet Juliet. I need one more," he said, pulling her close again.

Juliet immersed herself in the moment. Before she left, she couldn't help but say one more thing. "Romeo, no matter what happens, I want you to know that..." She paused to gather her nerve. "I think I love you too." She didn't give him time to respond. It would lead to more kissing, and Macbeth would be growing angrier with her by the second. As she walked away, she felt powerful. The love that she had for Romeo was completely her own, not something produced from the expectations of her friends or parents. It was hers even if she didn't understand the whys or hows of it all. It was simply hers.

18

Ophelia

Three. That was how many days Dr. Hamlet had been absent from school. Ophelia's father had told her all about how Dr. Hamlet had become sick and gone home. She had planned to schedule a meeting with him under the guise of creating a memorial to his father at the homecoming game. Forced to change strategies, she decided that if he did not return on Thursday, she would go to his house with a get well basket.

Currently, she was walking the aisles of the market looking for natural remedies: candied ginger, spearmint tea, and Epsom salts had made it into the basket already. As she entered the soup aisle, she found Don Pedro stocking shelves.

"Donny," she smirked. "Don't think I haven't noticed the little flirtation you've been having with Katharina, and I've heard you've been texting each other late at night." Droplets of sweat formed on his neck at the mention of Katharina; Ophelia loved watching boys squirm. "Tell me how you've managed to tame the little shrew."

The can in Don Pedro's hand clanked onto the metal shelf. "Jealous? I'm one of the few guys in school you haven't slept with. Perhaps you're wondering why I'd go after someone like Katharina when your legs are so obviously open."

Though other girls would take offense to Don Pedro's insults, Ophelia took them with pleasure. She had gotten under his skin and plucked upon his nerves like they were guitar strings.

"Oh, Donny, I've got bigger fish to catch. Besides, we all know your true love is football. Although, I imagine touching Katharina will be quite similar to touching that lifeless and rigid pig skin you love so much."

He grabbed her arm and she was surprised by the violence that sparked in his eyes.

"Perhaps that explains your attraction to her." She would not be intimidated easily.

His teeth were clenched and he leaned closer. "Don't talk about her that way."

"Oh, my! Don't get your panties in a twist. I hear it's bad for the sperm count."

Ophelia kept her composure and pulled her arm back. Before walking away, she added, "You know, I helped Puck set up Hero and Claudio. We could help you and Katharina go public with your love as well."

Don Pedro dropped a case of canned spaghetti, the cans rolling off in every direction. He cursed and got to work cleaning them up while Ophelia walked away, knowing he would probably be angry with her for weeks. It was worth it, though. In a way, she was helping him. It had always been clear to her that Don Pedro was like her mother. He had dreams that went beyond the small town of Shakespeare. If he weren't careful, he would blow it all, and Katharina would be his demise.

∞∞∞

Ophelia pulled into Dr. Hamlet's driveway and was surprised to see a yellow Volkswagen Beetle parked in front of his garage. *Who could this be?* she wondered while the fall breeze tossed her hair about. Before ringing the doorbell, she smoothed her hair and adjusted her top to expose more cleavage. Using her camera, she took a quick selfie. She wouldn't let this outfit go to waste.

On the front steps, she rang the doorbell and waited. The stained-glass windows that framed the door were nearly impossible to see through, but she could see the shape of someone coming down the stairs.

Hamlet's mouth opened nearly as wide as the door at the site of her. He was in nothing but a towel. She could cry. His body looked just as good as she'd imagined, but the tattoo of his family crest on his chest suggested an edge that she hadn't expected.

"Well, Dr. Hamlet. You sure know how to greet a girl. Had I known this was all it took to get your clothes off, I would have surprised you with a visit days ago."

His hand swept over his face as if he could wash his reaction away, but she saw the hint of a smile.

"Please forgive my lack of attire. I was expecting my mother. Otherwise, I would have dressed before coming down."

"Do you often greet your mother nude? I mean, I've heard many rumors about your family, but truly, this is a first," Ophelia jested.

"Oh, God, it does come off that way!" Hamlet cracked a smile and Ophelia was relieved that he'd taken her words without offense. "I was getting out of the shower when I heard the doorbell, and my mother is not a person to be kept waiting. Though I did think it was odd she was early. She has a way of being exactly on time. Really, I don't know how she does it." He stood aside for her to come in. "It's chilly, and quite frankly, I don't want anyone driving by and seeing us like this."

Ophelia leaned down to pick up the basket. She hoped her shirt was draped enough to show the fullness of her breasts. "I must admit that I feel silly. I presumed you were home sick, but you seem in good health to me. It also appears you have a visitor, and now I know there are more to come. I just thought I'd bring you a few things to help boost your immune system. I hope it's OK that my father told me about your incident."

Hamlet closed the door and chuckled. "You've made me a get well basket? How thoughtful."

He took the basket from her and set it on a decorative chest. That was when Ophelia saw her, coming down the stairs in a delicate silk blouse and a pencil skirt. She was lovely, with coffee-colored hair in a long bob and thick dark lashes. *So, this is my competition.*

"Who is this? One of your students?" the woman asked. Ophelia noted the tension in her voice and wondered if the woman also saw her as a rival.

"Arabella, this is Ophelia. Ophelia, Arabella."

Ophelia did not extend her hand, but Arabella crossed her arms and gave a tight-lipped nod. "Well, I should be leaving," Ophelia said. "I do hope you're feeling better. I miss seeing you." She placed her hand on the door, but Arabella pushed passed her.

Arabella looked back and stared down Ophelia while addressing Hamlet. "You will call me tonight and we will discuss this." She waved her hand as if she were blending Hamlet and Ophelia together.

Hamlet sat on the bench in his foyer and looked weary. He was still in his towel, but didn't seem self-conscious about his body in the least. "Please forgive Arabella's rudeness. We had an awful fight this morning, and I'm afraid the feelings are mixed about where we stand. You being here gives more fuel to her fire, but I will enjoy stealing her thunder when I explain the truth." He looked up and smiled.

Ophelia sat next to him and contemplated whether or not it was time for bold action. She hoped he didn't notice her nerves. "I suppose we should have sent *her* off with the get well basket."

Hamlet's chest heaved with laughter; the sound was so scrumptious.

"You seem trustworthy. Can I trust you?" He looked her in the eyes as if studying whether or not her response would be truthful.

She simply nodded and returned his stare. She felt shaky on the inside, a feeling she did not often have.

"Arabella was once a student of mine. We waited to date

until after she completed my class, but she seems to think I have a fetish for my students. She is driving herself insane with this idea. Now I've taken a job at the high school and you've shown up." Hamlet seemed more amused than a man in his position should be. "It's just a harmless coincidence. Perhaps she'll laugh about the whole thing with me when she knows the story, but I'll let her stew in her own jealousy a bit."

Ophelia decided to be bold. She placed her hand on Hamlet's leg; only a towel separated her finger from his skin. "To add to the humor of this whole situation, I must confess that I've been driving myself insane hoping that you *do* have a fetish for students." His hand covered hers and he seemed to be in contemplation. Then he squeezed her hand and removed it from his leg.

"Ophelia," he said, not meeting her eyes, "thank you for being so kind to me. The basket is lovely."

He didn't respond to her comment at all. She wondered if she'd said it aloud or just imagined saying it.

He stood and went to the door. "Well, my mother will be here soon. I really should get dressed."

She let out a deep growl of frustration once she was safely inside her car. So, Dr. Hamlet had a girlfriend. This was something Ophelia hadn't anticipated. But it didn't have to be a deterrent; they were clearly having trust issues. She contemplated her next move as she drove home. Perhaps Laertes was right. Maybe Hamlet was out of her league and she was playing a silly game--a game she was surprised to realize she wanted very badly to win.

Laertes was sitting on the front stoop when she pulled up. Ophelia attempted to walk past her younger brother without talking to him, but he grabbed her hand, staring ahead as he spoke. "So, were you successful today? Did you finally establish your superiority over a man?"

"Why so sullen, Laer?" she replied. "Why should you care what I do?"

She joined him on the cold cement, though her hips ached

almost instantly. The leaves were beginning to cover every inch of the overgrown lawn before them. The yard wasn't as neat and pruned as those of her neighbors, but Ophelia found the chaotic look beautiful. She wondered how long it would be until someone complained about it. Or had her neighbors finally realized how hard her father worked just to keep it looking this good?

After a moment of silence, Laertes answered. "I know you deserve autonomy over your own decisions and what you do with your body. But I don't trust Hamlet."

She wasn't expecting him to say that. She'd expected him to lecture her on her reputation.

Laertes turned to face her. "I think I need to do some digging. After my interview with him, I just got the feeling that his answers didn't make sense. Even as I wrote my feature, I felt as if his life story didn't add up. He puts on a great mask, and he's very charming, but I can tell it's all a show."

"Ah, yes, I forgot that you are the great human lie detector," Ophelia replied with more than a touch of sarcasm. Laertes rolled his eyes.

"Don't tease. I'm being serious. His story about leaving his position and taking his father's post just doesn't add up. Really, who does that? It's not like principals are kings of their school and the position must remain within the bloodline. There has to be something more behind his coming here. Heck, there could be something more behind the death of his father."

Ophelia regarded her brother with a raised eyebrow. "You realize you're a reporter for *The Shakespeare Chronicle*, right? You sound like you're some great investigative reporter for *The Boston Globe* or *The Washington Post*. Get ahold of yourself, Laer."

Laertes heaved a sigh of frustration. "Every great reporter has to start somewhere. You may mock me, but I trust my gut on this. Dr. Hamlet is hiding something. I feel I should visit his old college and do some digging, but I haven't got a clue where to begin, nor what I might turn up. I just know he's a liar, but about what? That, I must admit, I do not yet know."

Ophelia softened her tone. It was true he had a way of

reading people, and his hunches were usually proven correct. Maybe he was right to mistrust Hamlet. "I think I could help you with a major lead, something for you to look into. But nothing comes without a price."

Laertes perked up. "Name it. This could be my first major investigative piece, and a way to prove to you that Dr. Hamlet is not someone you want to be involved with."

"Hmmm." Ophelia took her time considering what this information might be worth. "You will have to do the grocery shopping for the rest of the month."

"I can't even drive! How would that be possible?"

"Hamlet asked if he could trust me before telling me, so it must be important. So, if you want the lead, you will find a way to get the groceries taken care of. Perhaps we could make a basket for your bike, though you'd have to make quite a few trips. You're resourceful. I'm sure you'll find a way." Ophelia watched as her brother contemplated and cursed her. "How did you intend to investigate his old haunts without transportation, anyway? I hope you didn't think I would help you. Providing you with this information is betrayal enough. If Dr. Hamlet finds out you're asking around about him and that I'm involved, it will ruin all of my attempts to be with him."

"Why should you care if you betray him? Why are you so determined to make him fall for you? Why not just focus on making him fall in general?" Laertes sighed. "I don't understand your goal. It's not like you love him."

"You still haven't answered me about transportation."

Laertes grumbled and she was relieved that the diversion worked. If she were being honest, she didn't know why she wanted to have Hamlet so badly. It wasn't like anyone had put her up to the challenge of seducing him. This was a self-imposed torment.

"I haven't thought that part through. I wasn't even sure I would really take this investigation on. I just have this nagging gut feeling, and the longer I waited for you to come home, the more convinced I became that it was important. What if he did something bad while working at Shakespeare Community and took his father's position out of convenience?"

"Like what? What terrible thing do you think he got away with? And who runs from criminal activity to their hometown, to a position that would put them in the public's eye? It doesn't make sense."

"Maybe he was stealing student work and publishing it as his own! Maybe he had an affair with someone he shouldn't have!" Laertes stood up and began pacing as he thought. "Maybe he had inappropriate relations with a student."

The last statement struck a chord with Ophelia. If Hamlet's ex-girlfriend was accusing him of having a fetish for students, perhaps there had been sexual misconduct.

"Well, do you want the information or not? We have to pick up dad soon, and I'd like us to sort this out while he isn't around. He's already angry about my behavior the other night."

"OK, fine, yes. Tell me what you know. I'll find a way to get the groceries done, and I'll find a way to investigate this all on my own."

Ophelia smiled, but part of her felt wrong, like she didn't want to betray Hamlet. Why should she care if she betrayed his trust? Laertes was right; she wanted to seduce him. It wasn't as if she actually loved him or wanted anything real with him. But she had to admit that she was enjoying the chase. She didn't want it to end. But Laertes had piqued her interest enough that she, too, wanted to know if Dr. Hamlet had hidden secrets. And she might be able to use whatever Laertes dug up to her advantage.

Her brother stopped pacing and stared at her expectantly.

"OK, OK, don't be so impatient. Here is what I know: when I arrived at Hamlet's house, there was a yellow Volkswagen Beetle in the driveway. When Dr. Hamlet opened the door, he greeted me in a towel." Ophelia smirked at Laertes' obvious disgust. "Stop imagining our principal in a towel and focus," she teased. "While I was there, a woman came down the stairs.

Hamlet introduced her as Arabella. After she left, he asked me if I could be trusted. He told me that he and Arabella were seeing each other, and that Arabella was a terribly jealous woman. He said she was a former student of his and that she constantly accused him of having affairs with students on campus."

"What if she's right?"

"I don't know. He had a great laugh over her thinking I was his new lover. If he *did* have affairs with students, I can say that he had every opportunity to have his way with me, but he didn't. Just sounds to me like Arabella is a jealous girlfriend and an insecure woman."

Laertes started pacing again. "So, Arabella, the girlfriend with the yellow bug. Not much of a lead, but more than I had an hour ago. Listen, I don't think you should go to his house alone again. It might not be safe. What if he assaults you?"

"You can't assault the willing, Laer. Besides, don't you think you're being dramatic? He already had me alone and did nothing."

She realized she had been sitting on the stoop for a long time. Her bottom felt sore and she was clinging to her sweater for warmth. She stood and checked the time on her phone. They would be late to pick up their father.

"Are you coming along to pick up dad or not? We should have left ten minutes ago."

"Of course," Laertes said, walking toward the car ahead of her. "Did you forget? We're going to practice parallel parking, and I get to drive home today. Also, Dad said he'll take us to Bard's BBQ on the way home."

"Great. I get to sit in the back and get car sick while you accelerate and brake like a madman. Then, after my stomach's all stirred-up, I have to attempt to digest something off of Bard's menu. Sounds wonderful."

19

Macbeth

High-pitched buzzing, like a swarm of bees, was all Macbeth could hear. There was an immense pressure behind his eyes, and the stadium lights made him feel as if his brain might be bleeding. He was standing in formation waiting for the drum major to lead the way. Juliet was shifting from side to side; she always did this before the halftime performance, a way to banish her nerves. He used to find it endearing, but tonight he had the urge to tell her to knock it the hell off. He knew the migraine was causing this intense feeling of agitation. He would love to be able to just walk off the field, but he was a section leader. Every trumpet player looked to him to lead the way. Besides, his family was in the stands. A lecture from his father would not make his head ache less.

As he led the trumpets through the "Shakespeare Pride Song," Macbeth reflected on all of his extracurriculars. Being a leader should make him feel proud. He had accomplished more than all of his classmates. He was head of the school newspaper, a section leader of the marching band, the treasurer of student council, a top performer in the chess club, and the president of the debate team. But he didn't feel any sense of happiness at his involvement in these activities; they were not his choice. His father was the only one who felt pride in his achievements. It was like his parents had given birth to him so that he could do the things they'd never done. They'd never considered what he wanted for his life.

Macbeth remembered getting his first chess set at four years old. His father's face had beamed with excitement. He remembered watching his father methodically set up the board and admire all the pieces. He'd wanted to pretend the kind and queen were riding about the board on horseback, but his father had slapped his wrist and begun teaching him the structure of the game.

The song ended and Macbeth led his section off the field, surprised that he was able to go through the motions without consciously thinking about them. It was as if his muscles had memorized each step and no longer needed his brain to direct them. Normally after a halftime performance, Macbeth and Juliet would sit in the band bleachers, lean into each other and wait for their cue to play once more. But tonight, he didn't think he could tolerate her body pressing against his. He slipped off without saying a thing to her or anyone else. He didn't feel he owed her an excuse for departing, and part of him was sad to acknowledge this new feeling. It was as if an earthquake had occurred when Juliet had gone to that party, and now a great divide lay between them.

In the locker room, he could hear the announcer call the halftime kick off. He pressed his clammy palms firmly against his eyes, thanking God he was alone. He turned off all but the light in the shower room and began to strip off the heavy woolen marching band uniform. He went to the showers and turned only the cold water on; he hoped the shock of it would distract him from the pounding pain behind his eyes.

With a towel around his waist, Macbeth returned to his locker and found Lady sitting on the bench. The sight of her caused him to stumble.

"This is a locker room for boys, Lady. Wouldn't you rather wait for me outside?"

She patted the bench beside her and Macbeth obliged. They sat shoulder to shoulder.

"Why so irritable, Macbeth? I saw you skulk off the field.

Even Juliet came to me and expressed her concern. She said you 'weren't yourself tonight.' " Macbeth grunted at the mention of Juliet and Lady gave a knowing smile. "Ah, is it Juliet who has you down? Perhaps you are already tired of hearing her endless chatter about her new love life? Perhaps you are feeling jealous or simply shocked at how quickly she replaced you as the main man in her life?"

"It's a headache, Lady," Macbeth answered through gritted teeth.

He'd noticed a boldness about her ever since their argument over his grades and whether or not he'd become valedictorian. She seemed so sure of the path to their future, all while he secretly wished he could escape his current trajectory. Perhaps he'd been the foolish one all along. He and Juliet had made fun of Lady and her devotion to duties as his betrothed. They had called her a shadow. But Macbeth now saw that he had been the one who lived in the shadow of reality. He hid in the shadows of his mind, dreaming that he could escape the pressures of his family, escape Lady, and lead a fantasy life with Juliet.

"Macbeth, look at me. Forget about your headache," she said, as if Macbeth were lying, as if she knew the pain in his head was just a symptom of the heartache he felt for Juliet.

Maybe she was right. He had been rather irritable since his "diner date" with Juliet. After ordering milkshakes, she had filled him in on her budding love for Romeo. His stomach had hurt so much that night he'd vowed to never slurp the sugary treat again.

Lady must have known his mind was wandering. She placed her hand on his chin and turned him to look at her. "It's time you realized that *I* am to be your wife, not Juliet, and with that comes all my comfort and loyalty. I think I have long since proven my loyalty, but allow me now to show you the comfort I can provide."

Lady's hand left his chin and ran down his bare chest. Goosebumps spread where she touched. Macbeth couldn't comprehend what was happening, but it was clear that Lady had a plan for them. She wasn't a shadow but a viper, waiting for her moment to strike and paralyze. Her touch took away his headache and left him breathless.

"You see, Macbeth, this arrangement doesn't have to be a punishment for us. Perhaps now that your muse has shown her true colors, you can see that we can be a powerful combination. Perhaps now you will see that your parents have chosen a worthy match for you."

"I've never heard you talk like this or act like this." He wondered how she had kept this side of herself hidden for so long.

"You never bothered to look at or listen to me. But I'm hoping you will fully notice me now," Lady said matter-of-factly.

"Yes. I think I'm beginning to see the parts of you I never bothered to look for before." Macbeth leaned in and kissed her.

He'd never imagined his first kiss would be with Lady. It now seemed odd that he hadn't ever given her a chance romantically. He had treated her like he did everything else his parents pushed upon him: he'd gone through the motions and followed the rules. He'd learned early on, with his first chess set, that things in life were to be used according to the rules, so he'd the same with Lady, not seeing that she was the queen and could move freely.

"How foolish I've been, to discount the possibility that we could be rightly matched."

"Foolish and shortsighted," Lady pointed out, unafraid to offend him. "Macbeth, our futures were locked and intertwined the moment our parents determined it. We must trust the traditions of our ancestors and use them to our advantage. We can find enjoyment in each other. I am your intended, so it is I alone who am truly committed to you. Your success is now my success. Do you see?"

"My eyes are wide open now." Macbeth pulled her close and pressed his head against her chest. "Nothing will ever blind me to your power again."

∞∞∞

The smell radiating from the kitchen was intoxicating: a blend of spices, vegetables, and rice. Lady had joined Macbeth's mother as she normally did on a Saturday, a way to prepare for her eventual annexation into the home. Though their marriage was determined, Lady still had a few months to prove her worthiness to his mother. Should she fail, the arrangement would be terminated and Lady would become a disgrace to her family.

Macbeth had known from the moment they were introduced that Lady would do everything in her power to bring pride to her family, much the way Macbeth did everything he could to succeed academically. Reputation and family pride was everything in their culture, so a lot of pressure was placed on the children. He wondered if he and Lady would carry on these family traditions and values with their own children. Most Korean families no longer practiced the old traditions, but his father was adamant that the family structure would be maintained the same way it had been for his ancestors.

Macbeth thought back to the day his parents had told him of Lady. He had been merely thirteen, still struggling with the changes a boy goes through in becoming a man: painful growth spurts, soiled sheets, pimples that would pop up in horrifying places, and a voice that randomly screeched. All of it caused Macbeth much embarrassment. He was hardly considering romantic relationships during that stage. Mostly he considered where to best place the hole he wanted to crawl into.

He recalled how his father had made the announcement over dinner: a worthy match had been found for him, a girl from a respectable Korean home. Macbeth remembered dropping his fork, and the high-pitched ring it had made when it hit his plate. His was the only Korean family in the town of Shakespeare that he was aware of. He hadn't expected his father to be able to make an arrangement. Then his father had called him away from the table; his mother had not joined them. The two men of the house went to the room that had been arranged for Macbeth's studies. On the computer, Macbeth's father brought up an email with Lady's picture. Macbeth had felt nothing at the sight of her long, straight black hair, charcoal eyes, and small-framed body.

His father had noticed his neutral reaction and said, "Do not worry, Macbeth. Western ideas of love may cloud your mind, but you will see that a wise match is better than foolish lust."

Juliet had looked at him in horror when he'd told her about the match the next day. He'd often wondered if her horror had been due to his family's values, or if she'd been upset that they would never be together. Of course, he'd spent many years fantasizing that it was the latter. When Lady's family finally made the move to the United States a year later, he'd ridden his bike to Juliet's house to inform her. They'd sat on her lawn, under her father's watchful eye, wondering what the first meeting would be like. It was as uncomfortable as they'd imagined, and after that day, Lady had followed Macbeth everywhere. Juliet had said she'd become his shadow.

Now, Macbeth felt foolish for never taking his commitment to Lady seriously. He had treated her like an afterthought. She would become his wife no matter what. Why bother getting to know her?

As he now reflected, he felt that Lady was right. Juliet had been a distraction, and he felt angry toward her. Juliet was the one who'd started calling Lady a shadow, teasing that she was attached with an invisible string, joking about the way she looked at her. It had infected his mind and blinded him to the gift his family and his culture's traditions had provided him. How could he consider her his best friend when all she seemed to do was scoff at his traditions and the wife his father had carefully chosen for him?

Macbeth realized he had turned several pages of *The Lit-*

tle Prince without actually absorbing it. It was difficult enough translating the French text as he read, but today his mind had additional distractions, and it was even more aggravating that Juliet was at the core of it. He slammed the book down and went to find his father. Passing through the kitchen, he went to the garage where his father repaired electronics, which was his way of supporting the family.

"Appa, we need to talk. I need to make a declaration, and I hope to receive your blessing."

His father's voice sounded grave. "This sounds like it's of great importance to you. But keep in mind, my blessing is mine to give, and it may take me time to consider your declaration."

Macbeth felt as if an invisible fist had his throat in its clutches. The steadfast wisdom of his father was another thing he had taken for granted. "I have been foolish and unappreciative of the sacrifices you've made to provide me with better opportunities than you had growing up in Korea. I see now what a gift my education is, and in addition, what a gift Lady is. I request your permission to marry her immediately. I do not want to wait any longer; she must be by my side both day and night. I see that she can be a great asset to me as I finish my courses and prepare for college. Her future is interlocked with mine, and I know that she will push me to reach greatness."

Macbeth waited, his heart pounding so loud he worried his father could hear it.

A smile spread across his father's face and he spread his arms wide. "This is a proud moment." As they embraced his father continued. "I was beginning to worry that coming here had turned you away from our sacred ways of life, that there were too many worldly temptations. Today, you have made me satisfied. I give you my blessing!"

His father wiped the tears from Macbeth's eyes. Macbeth hadn't realized he was crying, and out of joy for what life held for him. For too long he'd felt his destiny was a punishment, but Lady had turned it all around.

"Does Lady know of your intentions to have the kunbere

ceremony before graduation?" his father asked.

"No, I just decided this morning," he admitted.

"Do not worry about it. I know she will be happy. We will have something to celebrate tonight at dinner. Your mother is sure to be joyful, which means a lucky night for me." His father winked.

Juliet danced through the recesses of Macbeth's mind all through dinner. He wondered if he should call her later and tell her about his decision, but every time he looked in Lady's eyes, he knew the answer was no. Juliet wouldn't understand his decision, and would likely try to talk him out of it. *Should I give her one more chance to confess her love for me?* he wondered, and realized he'd been tracing a J in his curry.

20

Claudio

Football practice was amazing that morning. Claudio felt strong, fast, and energetic. It was like the universe was coming together to give him everything he wanted. When he'd seen the school paper the previous week, he'd been mortified. He'd wanted to find Puck and break every limb in his body. Then Hero had approached him with The Shakespeare Chronicle in hand. She'd been smiling, and the whole world had shifted for him. Claudio only wished he had told her how he felt sooner.

After showering, Claudio walked to class with DJ, as they always did. DJ was chattering about how he and Juliet had broken up over the weekend. Claudio tried his best to be attentive.

"I'm sorry about Juliet," he cut in, "but it didn't seem like you guys really had that fire. Ya know what I'm saying? Like, Hero and I can't be separated. We can't keep our hands off each other when we're alone. You were never like that with Juliet. She has the same lunch period as us, and you don't even sit with her."

DJ started walking ahead of him and Claudio could tell he'd struck a nerve.

"Awesome. I'm trying to tell you about my break-up, and all you can do is think about Hero," DJ said. "I'm not asking you to compare what you have with Hero to my relationship with Juliet."

Claudio immediately felt sorry for what he'd said. DJ was right. He'd always had a different way of talking about girls and thinking of them. Why wouldn't his relationships be different, too?

"Hey, DJ, wait up!" Claudio called.

They entered the classroom and found their seats.

Claudio dropped his voice so his classmates wouldn't overhear. "You're right. I wasn't being sensitive. I was just saying that you and Juliet didn't seem that into each other from the start. I never saw you guys together and you rarely talked about her."

"Maybe you didn't realize I cared about her because you were too busy thinking about sticking it in Hero all the time."

DJ was stacking his books like he was going to change seats. Claudio reached across the aisle and put his hand on his arm. "DJ, wait. You're right. I've been totally self-centered. But you are still my best friend."

"Easy to verbalize, harder to practice." DJ's voice was disconnected and steely. He wouldn't even meet Claudio's eyes.

The morning bell was about to ring, and Mrs. Jones would promptly begin class. Claudio needed to make amends fast. DJ was his closest confidant, and he needed him more than ever.

"Damn," he said standing up. "I can't believe you're gonna make me do this." He raised his voice so everyone could hear him. "DJ, you are the best friend anyone could have. I love you like a brother, and I am sorry I hurt your feelings. If you stand up now, I will hug you tighter than I hug Hero."

Laughter spread through the room. Even Mrs. Jones had a smile on her face. Claudio stood with his arms open and DJ, whose face was a deep shade of red, stood up and hugged him.

"Bro," DJ said as they hugged, "you are an embarrassing individual, but I love you anyway. Apology accepted."

Bianca, a cheerleader on Hero's squad, said, "I wonder if Hero knows she's sharing you with a man."

Laughter erupted once more, but this time Mrs. Jones was less pleased.

She pushed away from her desk and placed herself at the front of the classroom. "Thank you for the display of affection, boys. So nice to see your softer sides. But it's time to begin class."

∞ ∞ ∞ ∞

"You're not sitting with Hero today?" DJ asked as Claudio tried to squeeze onto the bench next to him.

Claudio had realized how neglectful he had been of DJ. From the moment Hero had approached him, they had been inseparable. They ate lunch together, spent time after school together, and went home only to text each other until they could no longer fend off sleep. He used to do those things with DJ.

"I told her I wanted to spend some time with you. She's cool about it. Bianca was sitting with her and told her about our bromance. But, like I said, she gets it." Claudio wanted to talk in private, without any other students hearing. "Skip school with me. We'll say we're going to the garden to eat, but we'll ditch."

"Man, we have practice after school. Coach will hear about it if we don't show up for classes and then go to practice. I don't want to get benched for the next game."

"Let's skip that, too. Come on, we clearly have some catching up to do." Claudio attempted to persuade him further. "You can tell me more about your break-up with Juliet." DJ's resolve was weakening, so he tried another tactic. "Let these hounds have your lunch," he said, gesturing to the other guys at the table, "and we'll hit up a drive thru, my treat. We could take it to the woods and hang out in our old fort."

"Damn. You know I can't resist a drive thru, and now you're throwing in our old hangout spot? You've successfully twisted my arm. I hope you're happy."

Claudio shouted across the table, "Yo, Don Pedro, help us out with Coach tonight. We aren't going to make practice."

Don Pedro cocked his eyebrow, clearly disapproving.

145

"That's gonna be a hard no from me. I'm not getting wrapped up in whatever shenanigans you two have planned. It's not worth sitting out a game."

Benedick chimed into the conversation. "I'll do it IF you deliver a note to Beatrice for me. I'll tell Coach you got a phone call, seemed upset, and had to leave, and that DJ went to support you."

"Yes!" Claudio nudged DJ with his elbow. "You got the note ready, or are we going to have to sit here while you write it?"

Benedick rifled through his bookbag and presented the note. "Written and sealed with my tears."

The two boys stood up and Claudio took the note. "I'll give it to her tomorrow morning, you have my word. But if she doesn't want to take it, there's nothing I can do."

Benedick nodded in agreement.

Goosebumps sprang up on Claudio's arms as he stepped into the cool autumn air. He loved days like this, when the sun was shining but the air felt crisp. He drove with DJ sitting shotgun to their favorite fast-food spot, then headed to their second favorite spot: a patch of forested area near their homes. He and DJ had always gone there as kids to get away from the watchful eyes of their parents. Sometimes they would just sit around talking and having a laugh. Other times they would become silly and pretend they were on a survival mission, or shooting nature shows.

He thought back to one such event as he pulled off the road onto a gravel turn around area, where he parked.

"Hey, DJ, remember when we used my dad's old camera and pretended to make a nature show about lizards? You flipped that rock, picked up a salamander, and it immediately bit you."

Both boys chuckled.

After exiting the car, they walked just under a mile to the clearing they'd made when they first explored the area. It was hardly a clearing anymore; it was overgrown with young oak trees and evergreen saplings.

DJ pointed out their tree. "Wow, look at how worn down our initials are now."

Claudio went over to the tree and touched the spot where they'd both carved their mark. He traced the letters before sitting with his back against the tree. He was happy to have his friend by his side. Then he opened the grease-soaked bag of fast food and divided it up. The burger he'd ordered was already cold, but it still tasted better than the slop they served in the cafeteria. He savored each salty bite.

DJ wiped his mouth before speaking. "It's nice to be out here. We haven't done this since my mom passed."

"Yeah." Claudio sighed, struggling with giving his friend comforting words. "I've been a neglectful friend lately and we needed this."

He paused, but nothing comforting came to his mind. They heard the chattering of squirrels and the occasional plop of a liberated acorn.

"So, you want to try telling me about your break-up with Juliet again?" Claudio finally said. "Honestly, though--and I'm not trying to hurt your feelings--I'm still surprised you two started dating in the first place. Like, I knew your families were close and you spent time together, but you never talked about her like that. I always thought of her as your cousin or a stepsister. I thought you did, too."

"It's OK," DJ said before looking Claudio in the eye. "You were right. She really didn't mean that much to me. I guess we were dating because it made our parents happy, and I'm kind of relieved that we don't have to pretend we want it as bad as they want it for us." DJ paused, stuffing some French fries in his mouth. "Go on, talk about Hero. I know you want to."

"I think she's ready, and I want to make it special for her."

"Ready for what?"

"You know..." Claudio thought it was obvious, but DJ looked genuinely confused. "She's ready to have sex."

DJ pounded his chest and coughed up a French fry.

"Don't act that surprised!" Claudio said. "She and I have

147

had crushes on each other for a while. There's a lot of pent-up energy. Ya know?"

"I guess. So now you're gonna get into her even more." DJ laughed at his own joke and Claudio punched him in the arm. "Ow!" DJ rubbed it. "To be honest, I'm surprised you haven't had sex yet. I really thought you would have by now, considering you spend every moment with each other. I was kind of feeling mad that you didn't tell me all the details."

"Well, I didn't want to do it right away. I wanted to show her that I want more than just her body. Besides, I've been trying to plan it so that it's perfect. I want it to be the best night of her life."

DJ threw a fry at Claudio, who attempted to catch it in his mouth.

"So, Casanova, you want to tell me what you have planned?" DJ asked.

Claudio told him everything. Even though DJ was also a virgin and couldn't offer much advice, it felt good to have him as a sound board. He left the woods feeling less nervous about the date he had planned for the following night.

$$\infty\infty\infty$$

The following day, after first period, Claudio tracked down Beatrice to deliver Benedick's note as he'd promised. She seemed disgusted by the folded-up paper, but took it and shoved it in her notebook. Claudio was struck by how different she looked lately. It was as if she'd dropped an entire dress size since the beginning of the year. She'd always been on the plump side compared to girls like Hero, who had a more athletic build, but he had to admit she looked good. Had it not been for the dark circles under her eyes, Claudio would think she was doing better than she'd ever been with Benedick. He considered asking Hero about how Beatrice was doing later. Hopefully Hero wouldn't think he was trying to dig up dirt to help Ben.

The rest of the day he fidgeted; he tapped his pencil until his teachers told him to stop, then he moved on to chewing the end of it, or using the sharp tip to poke his finger pads. Tonight was his date with Hero. He would take her to The Globe Diner for dinner and bring her back to his house. There he had a bag waiting with everything he needed to set up a picnic under the stars: a blanket, two cups, a bottle of merlot that he'd swiped from his parents' cabinet, and most importantly, a condom, which he had tucked into a side pocket. He worried it would fall out while he was removing the blanket, and he didn't want Hero to feel that she had to have sex, but he wanted it close by in case she did.

Claudio was pretty sure she wanted him. She was sending signals, or so he thought. She would hold on to his belt buckle when they made out, and once when he became aroused, she'd slid her hand over the top of it. Even if the night ended up just being a picnic, it would be romantic. He had set up the fire pit so that they could enjoy the warmth, and he thought the cool weather would at least draw their bodies closer, if only for the warmth.

After school he ran upstairs to clean up for the date. He used a large amount of shower gel, which smelled like a mix of pine and citrus. When he stepped out, he studied himself in the mirror, flexing and wishing he'd spent more time in the weight room. He touched the pimple that had popped up on his shoulder; there was nothing he could do about the blemish. Hopefully she wouldn't notice.

Hero sat next to him at the diner instead of across from him. He liked that. He wanted to be close to her, too. She rested her head on his shoulder and told him he smelled nice. Claudio felt full of pride at having her next to him. He put his arm around her waist and stroked her hip as she talked about her day. When they got back to his house, she seemed happy to lay out under the stars, like she knew where it was going to lead and wanted him just as badly.

He was almost ready to pack up the starry picnic when

it happened. She leaned in for a kiss, placed her hand inside his shirt, and he didn't fight his desire. He turned his brain off and let his heart lead the way. Being with her like this filled him with euphoria. When it was over, she pulled the blanket over herself and told him that she loved him.

Claudio rested his forehead against hers and whispered, "Stay with me forever."

* * *

The night before had been Claudio's highest point, but that morning was his lowest. Hero had texted that she was staying home from school, that she felt too ashamed. He didn't understand. Was she regretting last night already? Why?

DJ's text came next. "What the hell, man? It's everywhere!"

"What are you talking about? What's everywhere?" Claudio texted back.

"Just get to school now so we can talk before practice."

Another text came in from his coach. "Emergency meeting in the locker room. We will not practice this morning."

His phone buzzed again, and Claudio had a bad feeling in the pit of his stomach. Why would Hero be ashamed, and what was the emergency meeting about?

Ping, another message from Ophelia. It had a weblink followed by, "Even I am not this depraved."

His hand shook as he clicked the link. It took him to a video on a chat platform called Webshare. The video made him want to pull his hair out. He was looking at his and Hero's nude bodies. He threw the phone across the room. His pillow absorbed his frustration as he punched it, and when he could no longer fight it, the pillow absorbed his tears. He couldn't understand how it had happened, why it had happened, or who would do this. Now he understood why Hero couldn't come to school. But he wouldn't stay home. No. He needed to man up and figure out why this had happened.

He picked up the phone he had just thrown. It had a chip in the case, but was otherwise OK.

He sent Hero a text. "I just found out about the video. I don't know what is going on, but I vow to get to the bottom of this. I'm so sorry. I will fix this, trust me."

She didn't respond and Claudio couldn't blame her. Slamming every door in the house didn't make him feel any better, but he tried it anyway. He just had to find a way to make this better, to go back to having Hero in his arms.

He had to get outside for fresh air. He walked toward the fire pit, still full of black charcoals from last night. Standing there, he scanned his surroundings. Could a neighbor have heard them and taped them? His neighbors were DJ's family, the Ramoses, and Ms. Desdemona, who operated a family counseling center in town. He couldn't imagine either having a motive to film his intimate moments, let alone post it to the internet. Perhaps Bianca and Katharina could see them from their grandmother's house, but that didn't make sense. Sure, Katharina could have a vicious bite, but only when provoked, and Bianca was one of Hero's best friends.

He looked to the treehouse that sat back against the tree line. Could someone have hidden there? It didn't make sense. They would've had to know about Claudio's plans for that night, and the only person he'd told was DJ. Maybe DJ had betrayed his trust and told someone about their conversation, but who would want to hurt him? His mind raced. He had to get to school.

Storming into the locker room, he found DJ. Without acting, he pulled DJ off the bench by his shirt. Adrenaline coursed through him and he tried not to yell. "Tell me you have nothing to do with this."

"Calm down. I'm just as upset as you. We need to stay rational so we can figure this out together." DJ's voice was steady. "So think. How could I have done this?"

Claudio released DJ, who plopped back onto the bench. His shirt was crumpled where Claudio had grabbed it. Claudio sat on the bench across from him.

"I don't know, DJ. You're the only one I told. You must

have told someone else. Nothing else makes sense right now."

"Well, someone else must have known. I didn't tell anyone. Could Hero have told someone about the date?"

Claudio responded through gritted teeth, "It was a surprise picnic. Remember?"

"OK, stay calm. I'm just trying to help you figure this out. I watched the video this morning and the angle looks like someone put a camera in a tree, or maybe used a drone. I don't think anyone was standing in the woods or somehow seeing you from the street. Doesn't look like it came from a neighboring house, either."

Claudio buried his head in his hands. His voice barely a whimper. "I just don't understand how this could be happening. Promise me you didn't do this to me. Just promise me and I will believe you."

"You are my best friend. You know I don't even have a working camera on my phone. Come on, I know you're shaken. I'm here for you."

DJ moved next to Claudio, putting his hand on Claudio's back and rubbing in small circles. Claudio had so many questions swirling in his mind, but didn't have time to ask. Coach had arrived along with other members of the football team. Everyone had their eyes on Claudio.

After being told he was suspended from the team, Claudio stormed out of the locker room.

On his way out he heard Don Pedro say, "This is why I've been saying girls aren't worth it. Stay focused and keep your head in the game."

Claudio was caught off guard by the lack of compassion. He'd thought Don Pedro was more than just a teammate. He had considered him a friend. DJ was the only one to come after him, but Claudio told him he needed space. He went straight to the office.

"Get my parents on the phone right now," he demanded, and Ms. Hultz seemed alarmed. "I think I need a lawyer."

He wasn't sure if his parents had heard the news yet. News

traveled quickly in a small town, so it was likely that they were just finding out. Claudio hoped he could tell them before they saw the video. As he waited for Ms. Hultz to dial his parents, he wondered why. Why would someone do this? What would they get out of it?

21

Romeo

The video of Claudio and Hero was everywhere. Romeo had seen it too, but he hadn't watched it with the same fascination and depravity of his classmates. He wasn't sure why he'd watched it at all. His cousin, Mercutio, had sent him the link and once he'd opened it, he couldn't avert his eyes. It was clear the private moment was not meant to be seen by all, and that Claudio and Hero were unaware they were being filmed. What he saw on the screen was two people in love, two people seeking a deeper connection, not two people making porn or putting on a show.

Romeo rarely went to his father for help, but he saw Claudio storm out of the locker room and heard him demand a lawyer, so he waited outside the office. When Claudio reappeared, he stood in the main lobby with his back against the wall and his head hung low. Romeo approached him.

"I'm sorry for what you're going through," he offered, hoping it sounded genuine.

"What could you possibly know about it?" Claudio seemed to strain as he spoke; perhaps he was fending off a panic attack.

"Look, you're right. I've never had anything like this happen to me. No one in this town has. But I know what it's like to be in love, and I know how violated I would feel if that moment was broadcast to the public. I want to offer you and Hero help, if you want it. I could contact my father if you wished. I know most people look down on his occupation, but I think his experience could be valuable."

Claudio looked up and spoke like a beaten man. "Yes, please. Yes. I'm being punished for something I didn't do, and I hate to think that Hero is suffering the same repercussions. This is a damn disaster. I think you might be right that your dad is the best person to handle this. He's used to representing the accused, and right now I feel like everyone wants to hang this on me."

Romeo nodded and pulled out his phone. Claudio leaned against the wall and slid down to a seated position as they waited for a response. He gently hit his head against the painted cement wall. Romeo's phone chimed. He could feel Claudio's eyes burning through him as he read the message.

"Well, turns out he's seen the video. He already knew what my text was referring to. He said I should arrange a dinner with your parents tonight to discuss how to proceed," Romeo related. "He also said you should leave school immediately to avoid saying anything that could be used against you."

He didn't tell Claudio that his father said he was proud that Romeo knew to come to him. Claudio stood up and thanked him with a handshake. Romeo then headed straight for Juliet's locker. He wondered if she knew about the video yet. It was doubtful that anyone had sent her the link. Romeo couldn't help but selfishly wonder how this was affecting her. When he reached the hallway, she was closing her locker and zipping up her backpack.

"Juliet," he called out. She looked up and smiled. *There's no way she knows about the video. She wouldn't be this cheery.* When she approached, he wanted to embrace her and kiss her, but knew it wasn't wise. They couldn't be public with their relationship just yet, and now Romeo had involved himself in a larger scandal. *One thing at a time*, he warned himself.

"Hey. Are you still planning to come tomorrow night?" she asked, referring to Friday night youth group.

"I wouldn't miss it," he said as they both started walking

toward her classroom. But he had bigger things to talk about. "Did you hear about Hero and Claudio?"

"No. Did they already break up? I hope not. They seemed so well matched. She's in my trigonometry class and it's like she's riding through life on a cloud lately."

"It may be worse," Romeo replied. "Somehow a video of them having--well, sex--leaked onto the internet. I'm sure most of the school has seen it."

"What!" Juliet grabbed his arm, her mouth agape. Her lip trembled when she began to speak again. "How could that have happened? That explains why everyone seems to be huddled in groups this morning. Macbeth blew me off, too, which makes sense now. His mind was likely focused on organizing the news team to discuss how to cover it."

They stopped outside her classroom, "It's awful, isn't it?" Romeo asked. "I can't imagine what they're both going through. I saw Claudio this morning. He seems torn apart, like that cloud he'd been floating on dissipated without warning. I asked my father to help his family; he was kicked off the football team this morning."

Juliet leaned in and spoke softly. "That's what I love about you. You see someone in need and you step in so selflessly.

Romeo hoped no one was watching as he ran a strand of her silken hair through his fingers. He felt so relieved that she wasn't disappointed that he'd turned to his father. God, how he wanted to kiss her. She had said "love." She'd said "love" for a second time, and he wanted to focus on nothing else.

"I love that you see who I truly am at my core." He paused, his chest consumed by an intense ache. "Juliet, I wish I could kiss you."

"I feel the same."

The bell rang and Juliet walked into her classroom. Romeo watched her take her seat before turning to leave. His teachers didn't care if he were late. It was like they feared his father would take legal action if they tried to punish him, or they'd recognized that Romeo didn't need an education to become a success in life. He would have access to more money than most of his classmates would earn through a lifetime of work.

Romeo didn't care about being late, either. He'd never really focused in school. It wasn't that he didn't enjoy learning; it was just that he didn't know what he should do with his life. He'd lacked a passion, until he'd met Juliet. Since meeting her, he'd spent numerous hours imagining what their life could be. He had a trust fund that his grandmother had created, which would become his in a mere three months when he turned eighteen. With that money, he and Juliet could leave town and buy a modest home of their own. If he left his family, he would leave their wealth, too. So, he would have to find work. The trust fund wouldn't last forever. But he could use some of it to learn a trade. Maybe he would learn how to fix cars; he loved all the cars his father had had over the years. Juliet could stay home, if she wanted, to raise their children; Romeo imagined they would have a house full of them. If she wanted to work, he would support that, too. They hadn't discussed any of those things yet; his imagination ran wild with all the possibilities.

He was glad that Juliet didn't seem upset over the video of Claudio and Hero. He had spent many hours longing for her to touch him. He wanted to assure her that he could protect her, that no shame could touch their love, but in the pit of his stomach he knew that their relationship came with great difficulties. He pushed those dark thoughts aside.

22

Laertes

Articles were due by the end of the day; no extensions would be granted. Laertes was working hard to meet that deadline and was now adding his finishing touches. This time he'd interviewed Mr. Craw, the school's counselor. Mostly his article covered the resources that Mr. Craw offered. Laertes hadn't known the sex video would come out earlier that week, but he hoped that students might read his article and reach out to Mr. Craw if they felt affected by the incident.

He placed the portrait he'd taken of Mr. Craw in the upper left corner of the article, with words wrapped tightly against it. He was proud of the portrait; Mr. Craw's eyes were earnest and the lines on his face showed a life filled with joy. Laertes envied that. Giving the article one last look over, he attached the completed piece and sent it to Macbeth. He then took a well-deserved stretch, twisting from side to side until his back cracked.

"Darling, my darling, I see you have finished." Puck's voice was deep but sing-songy.

"Yes, and I'm ready to head to lunch. It's not an exciting article, but it's timely. I can only hope that those affected by this video leak realize they have someone they can talk to and trust."

"Wow, you're such a good soul. I wonder how Ophelia became the jaded one. But that's a tale for another time." Puck gave Laertes a "come hither" look. "But really, Honey, it's time to come get dirty with me, don't you think? Get a little more jaded yourself?"

Laertes shot Puck a look. "What do you need now? Your last endeavor worked out at first, but their romance ended in quite a disgrace. Don't you feel slightly responsible? I know I feel some of the blame." Laertes moved over and sat next to Puck anyway.

"Laertes, my dear, you really do have a pure heart. But no, I'm not like you. I didn't have anything to do with that video or their disgrace. So there is no 'responsibility' to feel."

Puck's eye twitched ever so slightly as he spoke, and when he finished speaking, it stopped. Any other student wouldn't have noticed, but Laertes had trained himself to read faces. Could Puck have been involved in that video? Had he staged it in order to have fresh gossip? Or maybe he felt the same culpability that Laertes felt but didn't want to admit responsibility.

Puck continued talking. "Working with you the other day taught me something, my wise, young friend."

"What's that?"

"That I need to start thinking of the big picture, about what I want to do with my life. I could turn this extracurricular into my career, and why not? I could move from high school gossip columnist to writing for a celebrity magazine. How amazing would that be? And look at me." Puck stood up and twirled. He was wearing a sequined cardigan and black slim fit jeans. "I was made to mingle with the stars; I could move my fine black booty out to Hollywood and get some real juice flowing. But, if I want to do that, I need to start following your example and build myself a proper portfolio."

Laertes smiled. "Well, in this instance, I'm happy to have some influence on your life."

"So help me. I'm the one who brought Hero and Claudio together. No, strike that, *we* did that. Now let's try to do them a little justice."

Laertes couldn't help but breathe a sigh of relief at hearing Puck say that. Puck's eye wasn't twitching because he'd had a hand in the video's leak; he *did* feel guilty about the possibility that their article had led to Claudio's and Hero's lives being ruined.

Puck sounded excited. "I've started writing an article about what happened, the fallout, and who the possible suspects are. It's more of an investigative piece. I just need help putting all of my ideas together. It's not my normal smut, and as you well know, I'm on a tight deadline."

Laertes perked up when Puck mentioned his article being an investigative piece. He knew how he could make this work to his advantage.

"OK," Laertes said, and Puck pumped his fist triumphantly in the air, perhaps a bit too soon. Laertes pulled him back to his seat by his shimmering cardigan. "I do have a condition, a favor I will need as payment for my help, if you will."

"I like you. You always surprise me with your cunning. You're quiet, but crafty." Puck laughed.

"The favor is simple: I need a ride. I have an investigative piece of my own that I'd like to work on, and it requires some travel."

"Oh, my, where on earth do you need to go?"

Laertes hesitated. He didn't want to give Puck too much information and have him get involved, but if he wanted a ride, he had to give Puck the location. "Shakespeare Community College. You don't have to help in my investigation. I plan to do that entirely on my own. You could drop me off or go explore the school yourself while I do some digging."

"You want to tell me what you're investigating at Shakespeare Community? Maybe you need a partner in this."

"I'm keeping this one private until I find what I need."

"Well, I suppose I could use the time to explore the college wildlife." Puck extended his hand. "You drive a hard bargain, sweetie, but you have a deal."

Laertes took his hand and beamed. *Ophelia is going to mess herself*, he thought. "So," he said as he pulled up Puck's article, "let's see what you have so far." Laertes' heart sank when he read the headline: "Who Was Behind the Camera?" This wasn't the redemption article he'd expected.

Puck must have noticed the change in Laertes' energy. "All I've done is compose the rumors that are already swirling around the school. I'm not accusing anyone who hasn't already been accused. We are clear of guilt on this one."

Laertes scanned the article. Puck had listed Claudio and Hero, proposing that they'd hoped to exploit the other to gain a higher social status. He'd listed members of the football team and the cheer team, arguing that they had a personal grudge against Hero or Claudio. Those accusations included Ophelia. If his sister hadn't been so obsessed with Dr. Hamlet, Laertes might actually agree with the assertion. His sister loved to stir the pot. But this time he knew she was blameless.

Laertes sat engrossed, reading the suspect line up and their possible motives. He had to admit that Puck had a compelling article. Macbeth would be pleased with all of the papers it would sell.

Puck was growing impatient. "Well, what do you think? It feels a little messy. I need you to help me polish it up. I want it to be perfect before sending it to be scrutinized by Macbeth."

"I think you've accused too many students. We need to eliminate the ones with weaker motives and help our classmates have a serious debate. For example, you included Katharina with the motive that she's the school Scrooge and loves ruining everyone's happiness. While that's a rumor that I've heard, too, you and I both know we could absolve her by asking Bianca about her sister's whereabouts. They're always together."

"OK, I see what you're saying. Let's sort out the petty gossip and get to the real meat." Puck put his arm around Laertes and kissed his cheek. "See, this is why I need you. I'm not used to thinking about the validity of gossip. I just report what's being said. You are going to help me to take my work to the next level." Puck squeezed Laertes again and Laertes braced himself for another kiss. "I'm so thankful for you, my friend. And remember, if you change your mind about your little investigation, I'd be happy to add my flair."

Laertes worked through his lunch break and met Puck again after school. By the time they submitted the article to Macbeth, they'd accused five students. Claudio was the most obvious accusation. He would have done it to show off Hero like a trophy. Then they'd presented Hero. The article suggested she was tired of being in the shadow of Ophelia. Then they'd accused two football players, DJ, who wanted to destroy the relationship so he could have his best friend back, and Don Pedro, who wanted the lovebirds to break-up so Claudio would focus on the game. Finally, the article presented Ophelia. They'd suggested she was jealous of all the new attention Hero was receiving, that she couldn't stand to share the spotlight. Laertes struggled with allowing Puck to include her, but he couldn't deny that rumors of Ophelia's guilt were going around. Laertes couldn't clear her name without sharing the bigger game Ophelia was playing at, so in a way, he felt he was protecting his sister by allowing her name to be included. At least, he hoped she would see it that way.

A strong vibration against his chest woke Laertes. He'd fallen asleep with his phone resting there. He'd been texting himself places to check out and people he should try to talk to while at Shakespeare Community College. It was eight in the morning. Normally Laertes would spend Saturdays sleeping until his father complained, but today Puck was fulfilling his end of the bargain. Laertes chuckled, imagining Puck dropping him off for his first day of college. He would probably wear a floral dress with a cardigan and act like a doting mother. He amused himself with the thought before popping out of bed. Puck had agreed to pick him up at eight thirty, so Laertes had just enough time to make breakfast and get dressed.

His father was already in the kitchen having coffee when

Laertes went down to grab a toaster tart. "Who are you, and what have you done with my son?" Polonius asked with a slight smile. "The real Laertes would never leave his room before ten. So tell me, what has possessed my son?"

Dr. Hamlet had taken possession of Laertes' mind. Ever since he'd captured Dr. Hamlet's portrait, he couldn't shake the nagging feeling that something wasn't right, and he aimed to get to the root of it. Dr. Hamlet wasn't a man to be trusted. Laertes wanted to tell his father the truth, but he wasn't sure what his dad would say. Would he try to dissuade him?

"Well, dad, I'm not sure how you will react to this--" Laertes began.

"Oh." His father became very serious. "Should I be worried? Did something happen with Ophelia?"

"No, no, no! It's nothing bad. Maybe you'll be happy."

"Come out with it already." His father's impatience was beginning to show.

Laertes gave a half-truth. He didn't like lying to his father, or anyone, for that matter. "I'm going to Shakespeare Community this morning with Puck."

His father nearly choked on his coffee. "I don't understand. Is this a date? Why--"

Laertes cut him off. He hadn't anticipated his father thinking that. "No! Dad! No. Puck asked me to help him pull together a writing portfolio. He's finally begun to think seriously about his future. I was surprised that he asked me for help since I'm an underclassman, but he noticed my work ethic."

"Well, I've raised you and Ophelia to set goals and dream big," his father admitted.

If you only knew the big goals Ophelia has, you might not be so proud of how you raised us, Laertes thought, but he couldn't bring himself to expose Ophelia. Besides, his father would just attribute Ophelia's man-eating to their mother.

A car horn interrupted the conversation. Puck was, to Laertes' surprise, very prompt. Laertes shoved a big bite of cherry toaster tart into his mouth and waved to his father, hoping Polonius wouldn't ask any more questions. If Puck came in the house, he might expose Laertes' true motives for visiting SCC.

He got in the passenger seat, which had a purple shag cover on it. Laertes hoped Puck hadn't done anything inappropriate on this seat. Shag seemed hard to clean. Puck was listening to a local heavy metal station and had the music loud, so Laertes didn't bother trying to start a conversation. Instead, he looked out the window and considered what questions he might ask the head of the Language Arts Department. He was surprised he'd been able to secure a meeting, but Dr. Drake had said he was always happy to help a new journalist find his way.

After parking, Puck finally regarded Laertes. "Meet at the car no later than noon. I can't spend an entire day here."

Laertes didn't argue. He set an alarm on his phone and exited the car. Puck wandered off without explanation and Laertes wondered where he was headed and how he would find his way. He sat on the curb and studied the map he'd printed of the campus grounds. It took several minutes for him to feel oriented. Puck had parked in front of a building used for dorms. Laertes circled the lot on the map. He didn't want to be late getting back to the car. He couldn't trust Puck not to leave him stranded.

Laertes walked in the direction of Verona Hall, where department offices were found. It was a pleasant day, so the fact that the building was two blocks from where Puck had parked didn't bother Laertes. Once inside the building, he picked up his walking pace. He had five minutes to reach the third floor and find Dr. Drake. He was slightly out of breath when he entered the office. An assistant was typing away and paused to help him.

A moment later, Dr. Drake came into the waiting area and greeted Laertes with a warm smile and firm handshake. He led him down a gray hallway that had been formed by cubicles. Finally, they entered Dr. Drake's office. Laertes was surprised to see the office lacked a desk. Instead, there were two plaid armchairs next to a side table and several bookshelves. Laertes felt like he was in someone's library; he was comfortable among the books.

Dr. Drake motioned for him to take a seat. "So, Laertes. Your email was vague, but I gathered you'd like to get some information about SCC so you can utilize it for an article you're writing. I've got to tell you, I love the idea of advertising the programs we offer here to the students at Shakespeare High. Will you be making this a regular feature? I could help with contacting other department heads. Are you interested in attending SCC yourself? We have a wonderful program for writers."

Laertes squeezed his hands, which were stuffed inside his pockets, wondering how his idols mustered the nerve to ask tough questions. *Now or never.* "I apologize for being unclear in my intentions. Yes, I am gathering information for an article, but I actually wanted to ask you about a former member of your department."

Dr. Drake shifted in his seat, his legs now facing away from Laertes and his arms folded in his lap.

Laertes noted his body language and started questioning anyway. "You see, our new principal used to work here. I'm sure you remember Dr. Hamlet. I wrote an article about him recently. It was very popular, but he didn't provide much background information. The students are quite interested in knowing more about his college life. So I thought I'd meet with former colleagues." Dr. Drake was now tapping his finger against the arm of his chair, but Laertes pressed on. "Perhaps you could help me understand why he decided to leave SCC?"

Dr. Drake moved from tapping to picking the lint off his pants. He didn't look up as he spoke. "Laertes, you have the potential to be a good journalist. You're already digging beneath the surface; that's a sign of your determination. I admire that." He sighed. "But I'm afraid you won't get much help on campus. There are things that can't be disclosed due to legalities."

"Perhaps you could tell me what classes he taught while employed here. Surely that information can be shared."

"I'm sorry, Laertes. I have to cut our meeting short. But I

do hope you consider attending our school. We need more students with your spunk."

Dr. Drake stood, still avoiding Laertes' eye, and opened the door for him to leave. Laertes was surprised that Dr. Drake couldn't discuss Hamlet at all. He fumbled with his wallet and offered Dr. Drake an index card where he had his contact information written.

"If you think of anything that you can share with me, I would appreciate it."

Laertes felt defeated as he left Verona Hall. *Now what?* he wondered. *If Dr. Drake is legally bound to secrecy, who can I talk to?* The staff were clearly not going to provide him any information. Then he remembered Ophelia's tip. It was his only lead, and maybe his only hope. He checked his watch. With the meeting cut short, he still had two hours. He found a bench and consulted his map once more. Campus suddenly became active as students exited buildings and splintered off in different directions. Laertes tried to ignore the hoards so he could focus on his map. He found every parking lot and circled it. His only objective was to find that yellow bug. He didn't have Arabella's last name, so it was the only way he could think of to find her. Besides, he couldn't imagine that many students owned such a garish vehicle.

It was exciting to be on campus in the fall. Laertes felt as if he were walking through a glossy campus brochure. Students walked about in their SCC hoodies, balancing coffee in one hand and books in the other. The leaves were falling, and the old buildings looked beautiful in the soft glow of the sun. He had checked three parking areas so far and had not seen any sign of the yellow bug. It could be a lost venture. She could pull into a parking lot that Laertes had already checked, or maybe she didn't have classes until the evening. *Another dead end.*

He sat at an empty picnic table set along the student quad and tried to come up with a new plan. As he contemplated his next move, he spotted Puck. He was leaning against a tree with a broad grin on his face, talking with a boy in SCC sweats and a long sleeve tee. *Of course Puck would use his time on campus for flirting.* He didn't want to spy on Puck, and it was getting close to noon. Laertes consulted the map and decided to check one more parking lot before heading to Puck's car.

The parking area next to London Tower Dormitory was full of old beaten down vehicles. There was no yellow Volkswagen in sight; it would have stuck out like a sore thumb. With shoulders drooped, Laertes accepted his defeat and headed toward Puck's car. As he neared the parking area, he saw Puck coming from a side path. He also spotted what he had been seeking: the yellow Volkswagen. His heart leapt as he picked up his pace.

"This has been a good trip. I'm glad you blackmailed me into coming," Puck called to him.

"Is there any way I can get you to stay longer?" Laertes asked.

"Not a chance, boyfriend!" Puck replied as he unlocked his door. "I got what I came for, and you had plenty of time to complete your little investigation."

"I just need to speak with the person who owns that car," Laertes pleaded.

"Oh, Lord! Did you scratch it? You should just pretend it never happened."

"No, it's part of my investigation. This person could provide key intel."

"Look, we aren't about to have a stake out; I can't spend my entire Saturday here! Just leave a note with your phone number and arrange a meeting. I'm ready to get home. Believe it or not, I like to prepare for exams."

Laertes slapped his forehead. "Why didn't I think of that?!"

He scribbled a note on the back of one of his index cards, which had his contact information--one day he'd have real business cards--and tucked it under the driver side windshield wiper.

Before walking away, Laertes whispered, "Please, contact me. Please."

$\infty\infty\infty$

The door to Ophelia's room slowly inched open with the force of Laertes' knock.

"Come in, if you must," she called.

"I got a ride to Shakespeare Community today," he said, leaning into her room.

Ophelia sat up and looked at Laertes in amazement. "Are you going to tell me what you found? You must have found something. Why else would you come to gloat?"

"Well, I'm not exactly here to gloat. Just to offer words of caution. I spoke with the head of the Language Arts Department."

Ophelia raised her eyebrow and Laertes hoped she was genuinely impressed.

"Go on, spit it out. You have groceries to buy, remember?" she taunted.

"Well, he wouldn't answer my questions, and alluded to legal action that is forcing him to remain quiet when it comes to Dr. Hamlet."

"So?"

He threw his hands up as he stepped into her room. "Well, there must be some scandal that occurred. Otherwise, why the silence? There's a reason Hamlet left that job to come to Shakespeare High, and I aim to get the truth."

"Wow, that's riveting stuff." Her sarcasm grated on Laertes' nerves.

"Oh, and your tip paid off. I found the yellow car."

"Oh, now this is exciting. Did you speak with Arabella? What did you learn?"

"Well, nothing. She wasn't in the car. I left a note and now I have to wait to see if she responds."

"Well, Laer, I wish you well. I also wish you would get on your bike and fetch some food. I'd like to make lasagna tonight and time is wasting." She swept her hand through the air as if clearing a cloud of dust. "Move along."

23

Beatrice

Pulling up to Hero's house was a reality check. The lawn was not its normal lush green; it was overgrown, and leaves covered most of the lawn and walkway. The house looked dark; curtains were drawn. The outside of the house was just as depressing as the inside. Beatrice was glad that Bianca had asked her to help bring Hero some cheer. Beatrice had been caught up in her own relationship drama, but Hero needed them right now. She carried an armful of schoolwork for Hero, and Bianca had a gift bag filled with cards that the cheer squad had made. The girls made their way to the front door and rang the bell. Hero was expecting them.

A moment later Hero's mom opened the door. Seeing her was a shock. She was normally so perky and well dressed. Every girl on the squad looked up to her. This morning, her skin looked ashen, her jeans and sweater were crinkled as if they'd been pulled from a laundry pile or slept in, and her hair was oily and limp. She told the girls they could head up to Hero's bedroom before making her way to the couch. Beatrice and Bianca shared a glance before making their way upstairs.

Hero was perched on her window seat with a notebook in hand. She snapped the notebook shut and set it behind her as they walked in. Bianca immediately went to Hero and embraced her. Hero looked at Beatrice while locked in Bianca's hug and feigned a smile.

"I brought your missed schoolwork," Beatrice said, setting the books and herself at the end of Hero's bed.

Bianca sat next to Hero. "This whole situation is terrible. Tell us how you've been. We all miss you so much."

Hero sighed deeply and looked at the floor as she spoke. "It's the most humiliating thing I've ever experienced. My parents are ashamed, too. Although, it's hard to tell if my mom is more ashamed that her daughter was kicked off the cheer squad, or that her daughter has a sex tape that's been viewed by the entire town."

Beatrice struggled to find words to comfort her friend. "I just don't understand how this happened. Have you talked with Claudio at all?"

"I don't know if I can trust Claudio. He texted me that he was consulting with Mr. Montague, but how can I be sure he wasn't the one who planned this? He seemed so sincere, but maybe I was just a trophy he wanted to gloat about." She put her head in her hands and began crying. "I was genuine in how I felt about him. I thought he loved me, too, but maybe I'm just a fool. I feel sick over this whole thing."

"Do you really think Claudio would do that?" Beatrice asked. Claudio and Benedick had been friends for a long time. Benedick had dropped hints about Claudio's crush on Hero well before Puck's little article had brought them together. Beatrice just couldn't accept that Claudio would plan something like this.

Hero's words were sharp accusations. "He was the one who planned the date. He took the lead that night. Who else would have known to set up a camera? It's the only thing that makes sense. And if it's true, then I'd be happy to see him dead."

Bianca gasped and grabbed Hero's hand. "You can't mean that."

Hero pulled her hand back into her lap. "If he did this, he's ruined my life, and I'm in an eye for an eye mood these days." Hero directed her next comment to Beatrice. "I wonder if Benedick knows anything. Are you two back together?"

"If Benedick knew that Claudio was planning to do something like that, he would kill Claudio himself! He may be an idiot, but he wouldn't allow you to be violated like that. At his core he is a man of honor." Beatrice paused and softened her voice. "He wrote me a note and Claudio gave it to me before this situation happened. It was a sweet note. He said I looked more beautiful than ever and that he wanted us to be together again. My defenses are weakening, if I'm being honest, but we're not back together and I haven't returned his communications."

"Maybe Benedick could help me. He could find out if Claudio was really behind this and help me get revenge if he did."

Beatrice didn't fully comprehend what was being asked of her. "I'm sure Benedick would do anything I ask. He is so desperate to have me back."

Bianca's head was shaking as she looked between the girls. "Is revenge really what you want? It could end up making you feel worse. And what if Claudio isn't behind this? Keep an open heart, Hero. Don't let this harden you." She attempted to joke. "You don't want to end up like Katharina, do you?"

Hero rested her head on Bianca's shoulders. "My heart is hardening. I wish I could curse the world like your sister does." She pulled her phone out of her pocket. "Do you know I've gotten messages from guys saying they would love to taste me like Claudio did, or that I have beautiful breasts? I also received a few messages telling me to repent and that I'm a whore. I don't know how they're getting my phone number. I can't imagine that anyone will take me seriously again."

Tears erupted from Hero's eyes and Beatrice joined Bianca in embracing her. Hero took spasmodic breaths and did her best to keep talking. "I feel so alone in this. My parents seem content to let me waste away in my room. My dad can't even look at me. They treat me like I'm a failed project that they don't know how to dispose of. I feel like they need me to disappear so they can move on with their lives."

"Hero, they're your parents. I'm sure they still love you.

Everything is just fresh right now. Give it time." Beatrice tried to offer soothing words, but she understood how her friend was feeling.

When her own parents were going through a divorce, she'd felt like an object they didn't know what to do with, like everything would be easier if Beatrice just went away. Even now, she wondered if her parents would have remained married and in love if they'd never given birth to her.

Hero whimpered and leaned into her. "I just wish this had never happened. I want the shame to go away, but how? It seems like an impossibility."

The girls continued to try to soothe Hero's pain. Before they left, they gave her the bag full of cards. She seemed grateful for the letters, and both Bianca and Beatrice hoped it would lift her spirits.

Once in the car, Bianca wasted no time in questioning Beatrice. "Are you really going to get back together with Benedick? I'm happy if you are. I can't tell you how bad I've felt about the whole thing."

"Look, you don't need to feel bad. It was just a game of spin the bottle. If I'm honest, I'm sorry for being so upset about it all. It was about more than the kiss. Benedick wasn't prioritizing our relationship. He was taking me for granted, and we were always bickering. I think this time apart was a good thing in the end. Maybe he will have a greater appreciation of me, and I can have more patience with his silly antics."

"That's so mature of you. I know Benedick has been hurting."

Beatrice rolled down the window. She needed the cool air to wash all the sadness off her. Her stomach growled and she felt a wave of pain, like her stomach was eating itself. She hoped that Bianca hadn't heard the gurgling over the breeze, but she did.

"You sound hungry over there," Bianca teased.

Beatrice let a lie roll off her tongue. "I was a little nervous about seeing Hero today. I couldn't bring myself to eat breakfast."

"I understand. I had to force myself to eat half a bagel. Katharina finished the other half. Perks of being a twin." Bianca grinned. "Would you like to stop at the Burger Hut and have lunch with me?"

"Thanks, but a Burger Hut burger on an empty stomach sounds like a bad idea, if you know what I mean."

Bianca laughed. "We could go to the diner instead. They serve breakfast all day."

Beatrice let a sliver of truth come out. "If I'm honest, I'm trying to watch what I eat. If I go to diner, I'll end up ordering a large stack of French toast and smothering it in maple syrup. It's best that I go home and eat the lunch I prepped last night."

"Well, that explains why your cheer uniform isn't fitting you as snugly. I could ask Katharina to take it in at the waist for you. She can sew in addition to her other artistic abilities."

"Good idea. I've been feeling like my skirt could fall around my ankles." Beatrice was relieved that they were a block from her house. She didn't want to keep talking about food or weight loss with Bianca.

Bianca pulled up to the curb and put the car in park, then reached for Beatrice's hand before she could open her door. "Beatrice, about what Hero said. I'm happy that you want to mend things with Ben, but I don't know that you should put Ben and Claudio at odds with each other. Emotions are high. Someone is bound to get hurt."

Beatrice rolled her eyes, turned, and smiled at her friend. She had no interest in debating the topic. Bianca had a way of bouncing between the bubbly cheerleader who just wanted to have fun to being the wise girl who was forced to grow up too soon.

Once inside her bedroom, she texted Benedick. "We should talk face to face. Can you come over?"

Benedick's response came twenty minutes later when he knocked on Beatrice's bedroom door. He stood there awkwardly waiting for her to invite him in. "I'm sorry I didn't text back. I was lying in my bed thinking of you when your text came. I just jumped up and came right over. I picked this on my way out the door." He revealed the orange gerbera daisy he'd been hiding behind his back.

"My favorite!" she stepped aside and let him enter her bedroom.

He sat on the corner of the bed and Beatrice sat on the opposite end with her back against the wall.

"I got your letter. Claudio gave it to me." Benedick turned to her expectantly, but her words stuck in her throat.

"I hope you know I meant every word. I can't apologize enough. You were right to say I was taking you for granted. I was. I thought you'd never leave my side." He started to blubber as tears escaped. "I was never worthy of your loyalty. Your needs came second to my own. But--"

Beatrice moved closer and put her hand on his shoulder. He leaned into her chest and let the tears flow. She'd known this moment of repentance would come, but hadn't expected to feel so sorry for winning the fight.

"It's not all your fault. I didn't speak up for myself when we were together. I just let myself get swept along in what you wanted, and when I finally did speak up, it was too late. I was already angry at that point--angry at all the words I left unsaid."

Pulling back, Benedick's face went from pain to confusion, then he contorted with laughter. Beatrice's mouth fell open and she followed where Benedick was pointing. His tears had left two trails starting at her breasts and running the length of her shirt. She fell back on the bed; her laughter made her stomach ache all the more. After a few moments they were both gasping for air.

Benedick positioned himself on top of her. "We really should get this shirt off of you. I'm afraid I've ruined your outfit."

She gently pushed him onto his back and got on top of him. Without words she pulled her shirt over her head and tossed it aside. "Looks like you soaked my bra, too."

Beatrice reveled in Benedick's response to her body. This was what all the calorie counting had been about. She hadn't planned to lose her virginity, but it felt right. She tried not to overthink it. Afterwards, they lay side by side. Beatrice propped herself up on her side and looked Benedick in the eyes.

"Ben, if I wanted you to hurt someone, would you?"

They exchanged apprehensive glances before he spoke. "Did someone do something to you? I wouldn't just hurt them; I'd murder them."

She kissed him, knowing that he meant it. "What if it wasn't me they hurt, but someone close to me? Would you do something about it?"

He put his hand around the back of her neck and looked her in the eyes. "For you, I would do anything." Their eyes remained fixed as silence sat between them. "What is this? Is it a test?" He got out of bed and began gathering his clothes.

"Would you fight Claudio?"

He stumbled over his pants. "What! Never. Wait, did he hurt you?"

"No, but Hero believes he's the one who filmed them having sex. That he ruined her reputation to boost his own, and she's lost so much. I hate seeing her in so much pain. Her own parents seem to have abandoned her."

"Do you really think he would do that? He's had a crush on her since she moved to town. If all he wanted was to put a notch on his bedpost, he could have slept with Ophelia years ago."

Beatrice was now dressing, but wished she had put this conversation off a little bit longer. It felt like they were on the precipice of an argument.

"Look, Hero believes it, and I believe her. It makes sense. Who else could have filmed them? If I had the strength, I would get revenge myself, but what could I do but wish harm his way?"

"I know Claudio. He is devastated by this. He loves Hero. I don't think--"

Beatrice interrupted, "Oh, you men speak empty promises so easily. Why don't you leave, Benedick? I'm tired."

There it was. Her words hung in the air and she looked at him expectantly. She needed him to soothe the anger that had welled up. It felt out of her control. She didn't want him to go; she wanted him to stay and fight. An awareness draped over her. This was how she had always behaved, like a dog who growled when what it really wanted was to be pet. Half dressed, she collapsed to her knees and wept.

"Beatrice, what do you mean, we speak empty promises? Please, love, don't get upset."

"You said you would do anything for me, did you not? But when I asked you to help get revenge on Claudio, you refused. I thought I was the most important thing to you, but I guess it will always be 'bros before hoes,' right? That's what you guys say. So why don't you leave and go back to your bros, and I'll just return to crying into my pillow like I was before you got here."

She cursed herself inside. All she had to do was say "I'm sorry that I'm acting out," but she couldn't. Benedick was right; this was a test. She reached for her shirt.

Standing over her, he pleaded. "Don't do this, Beatrice. I love you, and if you want me to turn against a friend, then I will. If that's what you truly want. But please, take some time to be sure before I go against Claudio. It would bring me great pain to turn my back on a friend. But it's you I want to spend my life with. I know where my priorities lie."

She wiped her dripping nose on the shirt that never made it on her body. It was still wet with Benedick's tears. Tossing it to the side, she rose onto her knees and hugged him around the waist. "You really do love me."

24

Juliet

Juliet checked her phone one more time before going to school. Macbeth still hadn't responded to her message. She'd told him about her plan to use him as an alibi so she could attend homecoming with Romeo. Was Macbeth upset with her? He was scared of her father, so maybe he was upset that Juliet would put him in a position where he might have to lie to him. An apology was in order.

It was too late to undo it. Juliet had already fought with her parents over going on a blind date. Her mother was still hopeful that she would reconcile with DJ. Once she'd convinced them this wouldn't happen, her father had said he didn't want Juliet to go on a date with anyone that he hadn't had a chance to vet first. She recalled throwing her hands up in bewilderment, and had actually shouted at her father, telling him that he was being unfair. The bewildered look on his face stuck with her. He'd seen the situation getting further from his control. She had stomped to her room. She wasn't proud of her behavior, but it was effective.

Later that night, her mother had come in and hugged her tightly. "It's just a dance, but if you should want to continue seeing this boy, you will have to bring him home to meet your father."

Juliet hugged back. "That's all I'm asking. It's just a dance. Besides, I don't even know who Macbeth will set me up with."

Her mother pulled away and had a grin on her face. "What if it's Dunkin, the short chubby boy who marches behind you in band? I think he plays French horn?" Juliet feigned horror and her mom laughed.

She and her mom had a good time guessing who the mystery date could be. Juliet wished she could tell her mom who she was really going with. Maybe her mom would advocate for her with her father, but what if she didn't?

Once at school, Juliet decided to seek out Macbeth before the morning bell rang. The newspapers were already out, so she grabbed one before leaving the lobby. The front page stopped her in her tracks and she crumpled to the floor as she read, unaware of the other students' sideways looks as they made their way to their lockers. "A Surprising But Predictable Engagement," the headline read.

"Everything OK, Miss Capulet?" Polonius's voice pulled her from her trance.

"Sorry, just reading the first page before class," Juliet called back as she stood and headed straight for the bathroom.

She braced herself on the sink, pulling air forcefully into her lungs. *He didn't tell me*, drummed through her mind. Her best friend, engaged, a January wedding date set, and she hadn't had a clue. Why the rush to get married? The plan was always for Lady and Macbeth to marry after college, and Juliet was sure he would've found a way to get out of the engagement by then. At least, that was what she'd thought he wanted.

Katharina entered the bathroom. "Are you going to be sick? If so, tell me so I can leave. Seeing people vomit makes me vomit."

Juliet turned and pushed past Katharina.

She heard Katharina call after her, "I thought I was supposed to be the rude one! Sheesh!"

She bumped into Ophelia as she rounded the corner and managed to utter an apology.

Ophelia seemed bright and even more radiant this morning. "Juliet! I'm actually glad we bumped into each other."

Juliet's head cocked to the side. Great. Now she was acting like a dog hearing the word "treat." "I'm sorry, I really am in a hurry. Could we talk about this later in French class?"

"Sure. I was just hoping we could study together before Thursday's exam."

Juliet's heart was pumping fast. She felt dizzy and she needed space. "Sure, let's do that," she gasped as she scampered away.

A chilly gust of wind whipped her wheat-colored hair. She hadn't realized she had left the building. Her feet had a plan of their own. The phone in her backpack was buzzing. Probably Romeo. She ignored it and continued walking, her feet leading her toward the community park.

It was a few blocks away from the school. Juliet couldn't think straight. She just knew she had to get to the park. When she rounded the corner, she noticed someone from her church walking their dog. *Damn it all to hell,* she thought, which immediately made her feel remorseful for wishing damnation on a good person. Pulling the hood on her sweatshirt over her head made her feel more secure. She continued to walk toward the playground.

The red tunnel on the jungle gym was slightly moldy, but she just needed to get inside. This used to be her favorite place in the park when she was a kid; ever the shy one, she'd liked to sit in the tunnel and watch the other children play. Now, it was a tight squeeze. She couldn't sit upright, though she tried. Instead, she lay on her back, propping her head on her backpack and pulling her knees to her chest, and wished she could go back to being that little girl.

Her phone buzzed again but she continued to ignore it. She thought back to the last time she and Macbeth had hung out. In hindsight, she realized he'd been shifting in his seat a lot. He hadn't made jokes or laughed. He hadn't shared what was going on in his life. It was all her fault. She'd blathered on and on about Romeo, barely giving Macbeth a chance to get a word in. She had acted as if her own life was the only thing of importance.

She had always found comfort in prayer and her faith. Normally the words came easily, as if she were having conversations with a close friend, but today she couldn't string together a coherent thought. Was it possible that God had abandoned her, too? Had she become like the prodigal child, leaving all she had ever known for Romeo? She felt torn in half. Her tears came in sobs between strained breaths. She wasn't sure how long she cried, but eventually she succumbed to rest.

∞∞∞

"I think there's someone in the tunnel," a deep voice called, startling Juliet awake.

The thumping in her chest seemed to echo in the plastic tunnel. She saw a uniformed policeman walking toward her while another seemed to be searching the park.

"Juliet, is that you?" the officer called.

Her mind raced to assemble an escape plan, but the officer was coming toward her in a light jog. "Add it to my many mistakes," she whispered under her breath before wiggling out of her hiding place. Her face burned with embarrassment.

"She's here!" the officer shouted to his partner. "Radio it in!" He climbed the steps of the play gym and got down on his knee as she perched on the edge of the tunnel. "Are you alright? Did anyone hurt you?"

"I'm... I... No, no one has hurt me. It's... Well, I guess I made a bad choice today. I got upset at school and came here. I'm sorry to cause a fuss." She was shaking, though she wasn't sure if it was from the chilly fall weather or her frayed nerves.

"Here, have my jacket." She wrapped herself in the officer's warmth. "How long have you been in there?"

She stumbled on a step and the officer caught her arm. "I don't know. What time is it?" She felt the urge to climb back in and refuse to come out. The officer's jacket offered warmth, but couldn't shield her wounded parts.

"Don't be embarrassed. I'm glad you're okay. I know your father and mother will be relieved. Let's just get you home." The officer opened the backdoor of his car and Juliet got in.

An older officer sat in the driver's seat and studied her through the rearview mirror. Juliet averted her eyes and noticed the clock on the dash. It was two thirty-two. How had she slept that long?

On the ride home, caged in the back of a police cruiser, she considered how careless she had been. Of course when she hadn't arrived at her first period class, her teacher would've reported her absence. Whenever Juliet missed school, her mom always contacted them, so the office would rightfully question her absence and reach out to her mom. She must have caused them so much panic. What about Romeo? No doubt he would've been worried when she wasn't at her locker. He'd probably gone to her classroom and noticed she was missing. Juliet thought about how many times her phone had buzzed after she left. She'd never even looked, but she could imagine her parents and Romeo desperately trying to find her. She began weeping.

The older officer addressed her. "I guess I'd be weeping if I had to face my father after skipping school. Even more so if I had your father." She continued to cry and he softened his tone. "Look, we've all made mistakes in life. Yours is hardly the worst. Your dad will be angry, no doubt, but I know if you're honest with him, things will work out. He's a fair man. This I know."

Honest. That word stuck in her mind as the car pulled into the driveway.

Her parents were sitting on the front porch; her mom's cheeks were red and smeared with makeup from crying, and her father had his Bible out. Juliet's heart dropped into her stomach when Pastor Ramos came out of her house with two teacups. When he reached the car, the officers exited and didn't open the door for her. She watched helplessly from the backseat, unable to hear the conversation Pastor Ramos and the officers were having.

It was Pastor Ramos who finally liberated her. "I think it's best that you come with me," he said with a very solemn tone.

He guided her to her mother's garden. Her mom had placed a bench swing there, so that she could sit and enjoy her crosswords and morning prayers in the peace of her garden. The swing creaked as they sat facing the porch, where her parents were hugging as the officers spoke to them. A slight shaking from her mother's shoulders let Juliet know that she was once again crying.

"You really had your parents in a frenzy today. They called me to pray with them. I must admit, I was quite worried myself. I even called DJ to ask if he knew where you could be." Silence sat between them for a time. Pastor Ramos continued, "Do you want to talk about it?"

She knew she would need Pastor Ramos to help mitigate the situation. Still, she struggled with being honest. Could she trust her own pastor with the truth? Was this her opportunity to confess and begin everything anew? On the one hand, her parents might understand feeling upset that her best friend got engaged without her knowing. But she had already told her parents that Macbeth was setting her up on a date. If he was willing to do that, how could he not tell her he was getting engaged? It wouldn't make sense, and her dad built his life around finding holes in people's stories.

Pastor Ramos spoke again. "Juliet, I'm here to help you. I want you to tell me why you left school. If it's a problem you're having with DJ, don't let that stop you from opening up. I realized rather quickly that, we--your parents and I--put a lot of pressure on the two of you. That was wrong of us. But I didn't come here as DJ's father. I came here as your pastor, and I want to help."

Juliet saw a second path next to honesty and decided to see where it led. "No, it's not DJ. It feels silly and hard to explain, but I was thinking of Hero and became overcome with empathy. The situation is heartbreaking."

A dark shadow seemed to fill Pastor Ramos's eyes when

Juliet mentioned Hero. "Oh," he said. "I hadn't realized that the news had already reached the school." He noticed the confusion on her face. "Oh, that doesn't make sense. You wouldn't have known."

Juliet felt knocked off course. "What are you talking about?"

"I'm sorry, Juliet. I spoke out of turn. Excuse me a moment."

The sick feeling in her stomach intensified as Pastor Ramos returned to her parents. She stared at her hands, which were drenched in sweat. What was Pastor Ramos referring to? What news could there be about Hero? Maybe they'd figured out who was behind the camera.

"Juliet." It was her mother's voice. She looked up to meet her eyes. "Pastor Ramos told me you were thinking of Hero this morning." Her mom sat down and pulled her close to her, holding her head against her chest. "Oh, honey. My sweet Juliet. You are always caring and worrying about others. It makes sense that you would go to the playground. The officer said you looked as if you had been crying when he found you. Oh, sweetheart. We should have talked to you about what happened with Hero and Claudio. We thought avoiding the topic would help shield you from the pain. Seems ridiculous now that we let you hear all about it from your classmates instead. We aren't as perfect as we try to be."

"Mom," Juliet said as she pulled away from her embrace, "why did Pastor Ramos say he hadn't realized the news reached the school?" Her mom opened her arms again, but Juliet stayed where she was and held her mom's gaze. She was tired of her parents sugarcoating things. "Mom, please. Just tell me what's going on."

Her mom put her arms down. "I guess we shouldn't make the same mistake twice. We will handle this tragedy as a family. We can take comfort in knowing that your father will seek justice."

Juliet was surprised by the urge to shake her mother, to

end this delicate dance. "Mom, please!"

"Hero was found this morning in her room."

"What do you mean? Isn't that where she was supposed to be?"

"Oh, this is so difficult to say." Her mom was stroking the cross around her neck.

Juliet tightened her hands into fists. "Don't treat me like a child. Just tell me."

"Hero hung herself. The time of death is still unknown. She left a note. Perhaps in your empathy, you knew she was in more pain than anyone else realized. You always had a gift for knowing people's hearts."

There was a ringing in Juliet's ears before everything went black. When she awoke, she was on the couch in her living room. She could hear her father and Pastor Ramos speaking in hushed tones. Her mother came into the room with a bowl of ice water and a towel.

"Oh, Juliet!" Her skin seemed to jump from her bones at the sight of Juliet sitting up. "She's awake!" her mother called into the kitchen. "Juliet, don't sit up. You've had quite a shock."

Her father came in and immediately started talking as he sat on the edge of the couch. He left little space between his words as he rattled off his revelations. "I want you to know that I forgive you for this morning. I understand that you were feeling some big emotions. We don't have to speak of it again if you don't want to, but this morning made me realize that you do need someone to talk to. Especially now, with what Hero has done to herself. Pastor Ramos has recommended a therapist. I think it's a good idea. Your mother will make you an appointment. I think it's important that you stay home from school tomorrow. No doubt there will be upsetting rumors swirling around."

Juliet didn't want to stay home, and she didn't want to talk to a stranger. She wanted to see Romeo. She wanted him to hold her and tell her everything would be OK. "I want to go to school. I should be there, to pray with friends and help where I can. Student council will no doubt want to organize something to honor Hero."

"We're your parents. Let us do what we're meant to do and take care of you. We know what is best." Juliet bit her lip as she listened to her father, suppressing her scream. "Your mom has made iced tea. Why don't you take a glass to your room and get some rest while we discuss a few things?"

Juliet tried not to stomp like a petulant child, but her steps were heavy as she moved to her room. If her parents wanted to do what was best, they would allow her to make her own choices, or at least involve her in the process of deciding what was best. She wasn't a child anymore. She would legally be an adult before the end of the school year, yet she was being sent to her room, shielded from adult conversations. Conversations about her! She took her school bag to her room with her, relieved that her parents didn't confiscate her phone. She needed to reach out to Romeo, let him know she was safe and see if the news about Hero had indeed reached the school.

There were so many missed calls and message notifications to sort through; she ignored everything except those from Romeo.

"Juliet, are you sick? I waited for you at your locker, and you weren't at your homeroom."

"Juliet. Let me know that you're OK. I'm thinking of you."

"I'll drive by after school today. Could you be by your window so I can see you're OK?"

"Just drove past your house and saw a cop car. What is going on? Can you call me?"

That was his last text.

She wondered how many times he'd driven past her house, hoping to see her. If only she could call him... But it was too risky. Her parents would hear her talking, and they might decide it was best that she spend this time in prayer or reading her Bible. Juliet didn't want to talk to God about this. According to God, Hero was burning in Hell for taking her own life. Juliet couldn't take comfort in that.

She composed a text to Romeo and hit send. She hoped he wasn't too worried about her, and wondered if he also knew about Hero. "I am so sorry about today. I saw that Macbeth was engaged and I freaked out. I didn't think it through; I just left. Forgive me?"

Hearing her father's footsteps coming, she quickly hid her phone in her pillowcase. She hoped he was going to his own room, but she rested her head on her pillow and pretended to sleep just in case.

The door cracked open. "Juliet," her father whispered. She rolled over and rubbed her eyes. "Good, I see you're resting. Strong emotions can be draining, I'm feeling pretty exhausted myself."

Her father sat on the bed and she propped herself up on her pillow, hoping any vibrations from text messages would be absorbed between the plush head support and the mattress. Her father's shoulders were slumped, and she wasn't sure what to do. Because he was a district attorney, she'd grown up always on her best behavior. Her mother had taught her to think about how her actions would affect her father's image, that she should be a source of pride to the family, not an embarrassment. How does one comfort their father when they are the source of the pain?

Finally, he met her expectant gaze and began what Juliet assumed would be a long lecture. "When the school called this morning for an absence excuse, your mother rightfully went into a panic and called me at work. I had just gotten word about Hero, but I left immediately and went to the school because I knew that was where my daughter should be."

"I'm sorry to have worried you both."

"I always felt like you and I had a special bond." He grabbed a lock of her hair, always loving to run his fingers through it. "In my mind, I thought I'd raised a daughter who knew she could trust me and come to me with anything. I guess, before today, I'd been too involved in my work to notice the gulf that is growing between us." She placed her hand over his and he let go of her hair. "I'm sorry. Maybe you don't like when I do that anymore." He placed his hands over his eyes and cried. Juliet hadn't seen her father cry since he'd laid his mother to rest.

Juliet felt a pain that was entirely new, as if a wound were slowly opening in her chest, one that could be easily healed if only she would ask for help. She and her father were growing apart, but she couldn't make him understand. He wanted her to go back to being the little girl who bounced on his knee and thought he was a warrior of God. But she was changing in ways she didn't understand.

Now it was her turn to stroke his blond curls. It soothed him and the crying stopped. He sat up as if he had awoken from a trance. "Well, anyway, I came to tell you that the school sent out an automated message. Classes will be cancelled tomorrow for all students. It seems the news of Hero's suicide has finally been released. It was a wise decision on your new principal's part. He will need the time to rally the staff and figure out how to handle this tragedy." Juliet didn't know what to say. "Your mom is making some pot pie. That woman knows how to soothe a man after a weary day." He patted his stomach and stood up.

"Daddy?" He stopped just before opening the door.

"What is it?"

"Do you think you'll always love me, the way you did when you used to proudly carry me around on your shoulders?" His eyebrows furrowed as he regarded her. "I made a mistake today, and I know I'm going to make many more in my life. I'm sorry for the pain it's going to cause you and mom."

He sat on the bed once more and pulled her into his arms. "Just do your best to honor your family and do right by God."

After a tight squeeze, he left. Juliet was aware that he hadn't answered her question. Perhaps it was wrong to expect unconditional love. Her father was right. A gulf had opened between them.

25

Hamlet

Early Tuesday morning, Hamlet walked into a nearly silent building. Ms. Hultz was in the gray conference room brewing coffee. For a moment, he wished he had a vase of flowers so the room wouldn't feel so heavy and sterile.

He cleared his throat before entering, hoping he wouldn't startle his hard-working secretary. "Ms. Hultz, you are an angel. Thank you for coming in early to prepare this room. It will be a busy day."

She turned toward him and he thought she looked just as gray as her surroundings. "Just doing my job," she sighed. "It was a good idea to cancel classes today. We all need to come together to grieve and decide how to move forward."

Dr. Hamlet opened his arms and offered a hug. It felt like the right thing to do, and she seemed grateful for the gesture. He patted her lightly on the back.

"Did you know Hero well?" he asked. "I must admit, I've barely had a chance to build relationships with the students at this school, but you know them all and their families. This must be hard for you."

"Hero was a quiet girl, but very talented. I was happy to see her in love. It's just such a--" She swallowed hard. "It's a shame."

Hamlet released her from his embrace. "You're right; we have to face this together and find a way forward as a school.

189

Were you able to arrange all my meetings for today? There's so much to do."

Ms. Hultz pulled a page off the printer and presented it. "Your schedule for today. Coffee will be ready in a few minutes. You're going to need it."

When his uncle had suggested he take the vacancy left by his father's untimely death, Hamlet had had no idea he would have to deal with sex tapes and suicides. Why did his uncle ever think he would make a good principal? He read over the day's agenda and slid to the floor. He wanted to feel like he had when he was a child, without a care, visiting his father. He'd loved to hide under his father's desk while he worked. His dad would give him a book and a flashlight, and occasionally would slip him a sticky honey lozenge from a drawer. For a moment he felt like the heavy load wasn't on his shoulders, that his father would be able to take care of it all. *How did he run this school all those years? He made it seem so joyful and effortless.*

"What's this?" he said aloud as he reached for something white that appeared to be taped to the bottom of the desk. Hamlet had difficulty peeling the tape off. He had to slide the top drawer out to release what he now realized was an envelope. A knock interrupted him before he could see its contents. He nearly cracked his head open as he quickly stood up and tucked the letter under his agenda.

Ms. Holtz poked her head in. "Most of the staff have assembled in the auditorium. I just wanted to let you know."

"Ah, yes. I was just reviewing my notes. Thank you."

The staff of Shakespeare High were dispersed in clusters around the auditorium, and Hamlet beckoned them to join him near the stage, where he was perched on the edge. There was much chatter as the staff moved into a tight group. Hamlet turned on his mic and tested it, and a hush fell upon the room. He opened his folder to look at his notes and discovered the envelope's edge peeking out, begging for his attention. He remained focused on the task at hand.

"I do not have to remind you of what brings us together

today. We have all felt the merciless shift in energy that comes with the loss of someone so young. As you know, this Friday was meant to be the homecoming game against Grimm B high school, followed by a dance for the student body. With the support of the student council, whom I was able to meet with yesterday after school, along with the district superintendents, a decision has been made to cancel the event."

Hamlet paused and let the teachers have a moment to talk among themselves. It would have been useless to try to hush them after delivering the news. When they fell silent again, he resumed.

"I know many of you were looking forward to the festivities. However, we felt it's best to use this time to come together as a community to offer one another comfort and support. On Friday evening, rather than hosting a football game, the stadium will be used to hold a candlelight vigil to honor Hero, her family, her friends, and all who have been affected by her death. Parents will be informed after we finish this meeting."

Hamlet allowed the teachers another moment to discuss the announcement before continuing. "As a district, we recognize the importance of this decades-long tradition. The student council has proposed an event that we hope will become a new staple in our community in addition to future homecoming festivities. This event will be called 'Under The Harvest Moon.' With your support, we will organize a carnival to be held in our stadium, a crowning of a Harvest king and queen, and a dance for students in our gymnasium. The governing student body will have a planning meeting this Monday, October 12, which is open to all students and staff to organize ideas. This will require many volunteers, and ten personal learning hours will be rewarded to staff who help with the event.

"We must pull together to move forward. I will be meeting with local law enforcement in a few moments, so I regret that I do not have time to open things up for discussion. Please send me any comments or concerns via email. I will be working late into the evening in order to provide as many responses as possible. I am ever appreciative of your cooperation. Now, I will turn things over to our school counselor, Mr. Craw, who will lead us in a moment of silence. I hope you will make use of him and the resources available to you and the students during this difficult time."

Hamlet breathed a sigh of relief as he moved off the stage. He felt the staff was receptive to the changes that were happening in light of Hero's suicide. After the moment of silence, he stood outside the auditorium a moment, not ready to move on to the next task. Before him was a glass display filled with trophies and mementos from past years. His father's picture was among the portraits of past leadership.

"Give me your strength," he whispered before heading to his next meeting. He realized how much time he'd spent shut up in his office and knew that was not how his father had run the school. He vowed to make a point of walking about during student transitions, to build relationships with both students and staff. This was his new life, and it was about time that he applied himself fully. He could not only fill his father's shoes, but create a legacy of his own.

∞∞∞∞

The envelope Hamlet had found sat in the pocket of the folder, and after a long day of fielding parent phone calls and sitting through meetings, he'd forgotten all about it. He emerged from his office and shut off all the lights. Ms. Hultz had gone home hours ago. The sun was already lowering in the sky, casting deep purple and pink hues on the horizon. Hamlet once again thought about why his uncle would suggest he take a position for which he had no experience. Perhaps his uncle saw more in him than he saw in himself. Perhaps he'd always called him "boy" to encourage him to man up. Whatever the reason, Hamlet felt he could become a strong leader like his father. As he left, he thought he saw his father watching him from the window of his office, but instead of fear, he felt comfort. His father would always be with him.

26

Don Pedro

"You're in a foul mood today," Don Pedro said to Katharina accusingly, as if he hadn't been in a funk himself. He'd actually let his anger get the best of him at school today and found himself being sent to the guidance counselor's office. In his mind, the whole ordeal wasn't his fault, it was Puck's. Puck had been gossiping before the start of Geometry about how it was possible Hero had killed herself over the guilt of creating the video. Without thinking about the implications, he had stood up and called Puck a ludicrous fairy. That part he wished he could take back, because of course it was seen as homophobic. Don Pedro had been referring to Puck's role as the school mascot, which was a woodland fairy, of sorts. Wasn't it?

Katharina sat picking the pepperonis off her pizza, which irritated him. *Why did she agree to pepperoni pizza if she doesn't like it?* It was too quiet in the parlor today. Don Pedro swirled the ice around his glass of soda, hoping the noise would be louder than Katharina's breathing.

"You haven't been so pleasant yourself," she retorted.

"Lovely," he said sarcastically. "I'm glad I wasted my money to come here and fight with you."

"Are we having an argument? I thought we were simply labeling each other's demeanor."

A week ago, Don Pedro couldn't seem to get enough of Katharina. But with everything that had happened between

Claudio and Hero, he couldn't help but see her as a distraction to his desire to get drafted and leave this town. Look at what falling in love had brought Claudio. He had nothing now. Half the team believed he was responsible for Hero's death, and wouldn't play a game with him even if he hadn't been removed from the team. Don Pedro didn't know if Claudio was guilty or not, but it was disrupting his ability to play the game he loved, so he was angry with Claudio all the same.

Katharina softened her tone. "I don't want to argue. Why don't we just share what's bothering us?"

Don Pedro said nothing. He felt like they were about to enter a marriage counseling session.

"OK," she began. "I guess I'll be the one to start. I'm tired. I spent my night listening to Bianca cry over Hero, and it makes me feel helpless. And--I know this is selfish--but I've been working hard to design a new set of crowns for homecoming, and now I need to rethink them to match the harvest theme, but my brain is a muddled mess. I'm wondering if I should just abandon the project altogether."

Don Pedro stared at his drink, still stirring it with his straw. It was captivating watching the ice spin and little droplets of water form on the outside of the cup. He couldn't really explain why he was feeling so unaffected by Katharina's attempts to connect with him. It was like his heart had hardened over and he couldn't get back the magic he'd once felt exuding from her.

"Well, I guess nothing is bothering you, then. Must just be me."

She folded the pizza in half and shoved it in her mouth. Don Pedro didn't want to give her sloppy and aggressive eating the reaction she was obviously seeking. He'd seen this petty behavior play out between his parents too many times to be lured in.

"Katharina I'm sorry you haven't been sleeping," he said. "I suppose I haven't been sleeping much myself. Look, I don't think I can have a heart to heart with you. Not right now, and maybe not ever again." Her eyes widened and she bit her lip. "Don't cry, Katharina. It won't be good for your reputation." He hated himself for being so cold, but maybe his callousness would be enough to keep her from trying to resuscitate what was so obviously dead. "I think our timing is just off. This tragedy has overshadowed our lives and I don't think I can go back."

She grabbed a napkin and headed for the bathroom. Don Pedro went to the counter, paid the bill, and grabbed some to-go boxes. He considered just leaving, but knew it would be wrong not to offer Katharinaher a ride home. He wasn't entirely cold-hearted, and she hadn't done anything to warrant how he was feeling.

No one could really understand how stuck he felt. With the homecoming game canceled and Claudio kicked off the team, Don Pedro felt he had lost his only shot of getting drafted and leaving town. The team was a mess. They'd never make it to the county playoffs, and without a homecoming game, Don Pedro doubted scouts would bother coming to any game at Shakespeare High. He couldn't afford to go to college without taking huge loans out, and his parents certainly hadn't set money aside for him. Instead, he would be stuck stocking shelves at the grocery store, and it crushed his spirit.

He went back to the booth and started portioning out pizza slices. Katharina came back; it was clear she'd been crying.

"Take it all," she said, "I've lost my appetite."

"Can I give you a ride home, or would you rather call Bianca?"

"Give me a ride home, please," she mumbled. "I don't want to give Bianca another reason to cry tonight."

The radio was turned off, as it had been for days in Don Pedro's car. He was in no mood for singing. Besides, the sound of Katharina grinding her teeth provided an appropriate soundscape for the drive, and seemed to fit the overall mood of his life.

When he pulled up to the curb in front of her house, he

tried to make her understand. A part of him felt he owed her that. "Look, I'm a nobody now. I don't have a snowball's chance in Hell at making it to the NFL. My dreams have been ripped out from under me by a fool-hearted boy and a selfish suicide."

Katharina slapped him and Don Pedro grabbed her wrist harder than he'd intended.

"I'm trying to tell you that you're better off without me. You'll go to some fancy art school and be famous someday, if you don't have me dragging you down. And while you're living your dreams, I'll still be here stocking canned peaches."

She didn't respond, just slammed his car door so hard Don Pedro worried the glass might shatter. "Sheesh!" he said aloud. "Lord knows I can't afford that. Although, I don't know that God is really looking out for me lately."

He watched her stomp to the front door and disappear inside before breathing a sigh of relief. It was over. He didn't have to worry about paying for dates, didn't have to think about sleeping with her and risking getting her pregnant, didn't have to wonder if she would want some fancy engagement ring, and didn't feel trapped by love anymore. He wouldn't suffer like Claudio.

27

Laertes

There were many things Laertes could be focusing on: his exams, gathering donations for the Harvest Festival (a task Ophelia had assigned), writing his staff spotlight for The Shakespeare Chronicle, or preparing his camera equipment to photograph the upcoming vigil for Hero. With all these tasks, he had plenty to keep him busy, but instead, he found his mind on Dr. Hamlet with laser-like focus. He felt in his core that something was off about him. Once again he found himself staring at the portrait he had taken of Hamlet and wondering what secrets he was hiding behind his dark brown eyes and dimpled smile.

Going from an almost tenured college professor to a principal just didn't make sense. It certainly wasn't a pay upgrade, and the workload would be doubled; was Dr. Hamlet really that dedicated to continuing his father's work? His actions said no. Hamlet spent most of his working hours locked up in his office, while his dad had spent them in the classrooms and in the halls. He would pop in and join after school clubs, and worked to elevate the community with evening adult learning programs.

Laertes was disappointed that Arabella, the girl with the yellow "bug," had never reached out to him. She was his only hope of finding out answers to his burning questions. For a moment, Laertes wondered if he was obsessing simply because Ophelia had made it her mission to try to seduce Dr. Hamlet. He felt protective of her, so he was using the one thing he was good at to intervene: journalism.

Laertes racked his brain for an angle; he wasn't ready to throw the towel in yet. Lying back on his bed, he searched for another way to gather information on Hamlet. He couldn't go to Hamlet's family. That was a family with deep secrets, a long history of closed doors, and unexplained wealth. Hamlet hadn't made any close relationships with the staff at Shakespeare High, so there was no one to probe within the school. In fact, his father seemed to be the only person Hamlet had attempted to build a relationship with, and Laertes felt it was purely out of necessity on Hamlet's part.

Like the sun emerging through dark clouds, it occurred to him that he could search for a college forum. Most students posted in forums for social and academic purposes. He could find a thread or start a thread asking for information. Laertes popped up and went downstairs to find the laptop. Ophelia was already on it wearing headphones and typing away. He waved to get her attention. "Could I have a turn on the computer? I need to study for my algebra test," he lied.

She sneered but unplugged her headphones. "Fine. I could use some exercise anyway. Without cheer practice, I fear I'm going to transform into a hideous couch potato."

"Perhaps becoming a couch potato would do you some good. Keep you out of trouble," Laertes suggested, and Ophelia hit him on the arm. "Ow!"

"See? If I don't maintain my fitness, I won't be able to punch you with vigor, and you really deserve a good beating from time to time, Laer."

Laertes repeated her words, mocking her tone as he rubbed his arm. She went up to her room and he got comfortable in front of the computer. He went to a popular forum site, created a fake profile, and searched topics. There were plenty related to Shakespeare Community College, and Laertes found a thread specifically for English majors. He typed out a post and then deleted it, repeating this cycle until it felt plausible.

"My brother took a class with Dr. Hamlet a few years ago

and said it was one of the few experiences that really helped him grow as a writer. I'm disappointed to see that Dr. Hamlet is no longer on staff. Does anyone know where he went or why he left?"

Laertes hit "post" and decided he would let his mind rest on the topic. After all, he really did have studying to do. He heard the front door close. A moment later, his dad collapsed on the couch next to him. "Long day?" Laertes asked rhetorically.

"Something smells good. I assume you two ate already." His dad got up from the couch and moved toward the kitchen. Laertes noticed that his limp was becoming more pronounced, though he never complained. *Curse my selfish mother for placing it all on his shoulders.*

"Yum," his dad called, "fish tacos. We haven't had this in a while. I thought Ophelia hated fish."

Laertes moved into the kitchen as his dad made a plate. "She does, but she has me doing the grocery shopping lately, so she'll have to make do." He smiled and his dad chuckled while wagging his finger. "She had a veggie-packed taco, so we don't have to worry about her getting hangry and lashing out at us later."

His dad's tone became serious. "How has she been?"

"She seems fine. Why do you ask?" He wondered if his father knew of her pursuit of Dr. Hamlet.

"It's hard to lose a friend--" Of course that was what his dad was referring to. Laertes' head had been so clouded with Dr. Hamlet. "--and it's even harder when that friend chooses to take their own life. I feel terrible that I haven't taken time to talk with her since it happened. I just don't know what to say. Your mother was always better with these things. I saw Ophelia out running and thought it was a good way for her to work through her thoughts."

"This is Ophelia we're talking about. She's running because she wants to keep her figure. If she's taking this hard, she isn't letting on."

His father spoke between large bites of taco. "I don't think that's true. Your sister has her walls up, but under it all, she's a human like the rest of us. She's so much like your mom."

"I don't know if mom had normal feelings, either. Who leaves their own children without batting an eye?" Laertes considered retreating to his bedroom. He hated that his dad remained calm on the subject of his mother, as if he still loved her.

"I know it's hard to understand, but it wasn't an easy choice for your mom. I think, in a way, it was my fault for trying to tame her. She did love you both, but at the same time, this life brought her misery." Laertes listened to his father in disbelief. "I suppose when you become a father, you might have more compassion for the sacrifices parents make. I just hope you fall in love with someone who shares your goals and passions. That was my mistake."

Laertes couldn't bear to talk about her anymore. "Dad, what do you think of Dr. Hamlet? It's a big transition between how he runs the school and the way his dad did, don't you think?"

The taco shell shattered, dropping shreds of cabbage, fish, and tomatoes on the plate. His father searched for a fork while he responded. "Well, I think maybe he didn't realize how much self-sacrificing goes into public schools, and I'm sure it hasn't been an easy time for him. I mean, what principal is prepared to deal with a sex scandal and suicide? I think he's doing the best he can. I'm sure, given time, he will become a great principal like his father."

"You treat everyone with such empathy. I really admire that." His father beamed at the compliment. They both stopped talking as Ophelia entered the kitchen. "Wow, O, I didn't even hear you come in."

"How could you hear anything over dad's munching?" she teased. The run seemed to have put her in a better mood.

For a moment, Laertes just sat back and took it all in. This was his family, and as flawed as Ophelia was, she always had his back. Was she struggling with the death of her friend? His dad was right. She might plot and scheme for her own enjoyment, but that didn't mean she was above pain. He decided he would be more supportive of her, especially tomorrow when she was tasked with speaking at the vigil.

28

DJ

DJ was glad that school was finally over. As he pulled into the driveway and got out of his car, his attention was drawn to the jet-black shutters against the white painted bricks of his home. His mother had made those shutters, with their cross cutouts in the center and stark black paint. When she was diagnosed with ALS, a neurodegenerative disease, she'd decided she wanted to make their home a sanctuary. She understood that her body would slowly degrade, and it would become increasingly diffi-cult for her to leave home. DJ remembered how he and his father had painted the bricks white while his mom cut crosses into wooden shutters. When her right hand started to lose mobil-ity, DJ had taken over, helping to paint the shutters black. She was so proud of the way it had all turned out, and the way the family had come together to make it happen. It was as if she'd understood that the family needed a project to keep them from focusing on her deteriorating health. She'd died when her lungs no longer knew how to function. It had been a difficult thing for DJ to witness, and Claudio had been the only person he'd felt comfortable talking to during that time.

DJ felt so much guilt over everything that had happened, and he knew he should. He fell to his knees on the front lawn, his head hanging as the tears fell heavily. What would his mother think of the man he'd become? Too ashamed to live his truth, so overcome with jealousy that his actions had led to his friend's detainment and Hero's death. He'd just wanted to cause a rift between the lovers. He'd planned for Claudio to take the blame for streaming the video. He'd thought Hero would break up with him and that would be the end of it. Neither the immense shame and embarrassment Claudio and Hero would feel, nor the criminal implications, had ever crossed his mind. How much Claudio loved Hero had also been miscalculated. DJ had long ago written it off as a silly infatuation. He now realized he'd been blinded by his own love for Claudio and hadn't seen the truth. His best friend had found true love, and he'd destroyed it out of jealousy.

There was no backing away from this. He had two choices: come clean, or let Claudio continue to suffer. Puck had pulled DJ aside during lunch earlier in the week. He'd wanted to make sure DJ would keep his word to keep him out of this mess. Puck needn't worry about being complicit; if DJ confessed, he would say he stole the camera equipment and uploaded the videos on his own. His mind still searched for a way to make things better without revealing the truth.

He was startled when his father placed his hand on his back; he hadn't heard the door open or his father's footsteps over his own despair.

"Son?" DJ looked up at his father's outstretched hand. As he stood, his father wrapped his arms around him. "I know this is a tough time. I wish I could end everyone's suffering, but I am reminded that God has a plan, and I take comfort in his wisdom. I might not understand now, but one day I will see it all clearly." He released DJ from his embrace. "Come, have a glass of water. Claudio is already upstairs waiting for you."

When he got to his bedroom, he found Claudio sleeping on his bed. DJ quietly walked over to the wooden chair next to it and unlaced his shoes. Claudio seemed in misery, even while sleeping. The skin around his eyes was puffy and red, his face set in a frown. His friend had lost weight, too, probably from his overnight stay at the police station. He'd been detained on Monday, taken right from class. DJ imagined how brutal it must have been to learn of Hero's suicide while sitting at an interrogation table.

DJ himself hadn't learned about it until his dad had picked him up from school. He'd assumed his dad was picking him up to help find Juliet, only to find out she was safe at home and a bigger tragedy had occurred. He had cried heavy tears and was thankful that his father hadn't told him to toughen up. DJ had tried to call Claudio after getting home that night only to find out that he was in custody. His parents seemed frantic. Roman Montague had him released and sleeping in his own bed the next day.

DJ wished there was a way he could turn back time. Jealousy was something his father often preached about, how it took people down dark paths, but DJ had never taken it seriously. Now he had traveled down a dark path, and there was no light to help guide his steps as he tried to find a way back. He tried to move about his room quietly, but Claudio stirred and stretched.

"Hey, man. I hope you don't mind that I got here early. I had to get out of the house. My parents have spent most of the day trying to convince me not to go tonight. I couldn't listen to it."

Claudio rolled onto his side and propped himself up on his arm. DJ couldn't help but admire how handsome he looked, even in his current state.

"Why don't they want you to go?" DJ couldn't think of a reason Claudio shouldn't be there. It was his girlfriend who'd died, after all.

"Mr. Montague filled my parents in on a few details that I didn't know until last night. It's so upsetting. I've been dying to talk to you about it all." DJ sat on the bed and Claudio sat up, leaning against the headboard. "Benedick has been talking about beating me up if I go to the vigil. Apparently Beatrice and the girls on the cheer squad think I'm at fault for Hero's death."

DJ cursed under his breath. Another consequence he'd failed to anticipate.

"I can't blame them, because I'm the only one who makes sense. God, this hurts so much to say..." Claudio paused and his shoulders slumped.

DJ put his hand on his friend's shoulder. "What is it?"

"She thought I was behind it, too."

What have I done to the one I love so much! DJ felt every organ in his body violently shaking, knowing that he'd caused all this.

"She wrote in her--" Claudio swallowed hard, struggling with the words. "--in her note that she felt foolish for being seduced and being taken advantage of by me. That I had humiliated her and destroyed her reputation in order to put a notch on my bedpost. I wish she knew how much I loved her. I'll never have a chance to make this right. That's what kills me the most."

"I'm so sorry." DJ wished with all his being that he could take away the pain his friend was feeling. He wished he could switch places with Hero, so she could be here now with Claudio. Tears streamed down Claudio's face and DJ shifted to embrace him. Claudio trembled as his tears came in torrents.

"I want to tell people that I'm at fault," DJ whispered. "I can't stand to see you this way."

Claudio pulled back and sucked in air, seeming to consider what DJ had just said. "No, I can't let you do that. I know it wasn't you, and no one will believe you did it, either."

"Why not? Puck presented me as a possible culprit in his stupid article. I've heard other people suggest it. They would believe me." DJ's full confession sat poised on the tip of his tongue. He bit down, a metallic taste flooding his mouth.

"Don't be stupid. You might have known my plans for that night, but you lack motive and means." Claudio started crying again and spoke between breaths. "I could go to jail for manslaughter if what really happened that night doesn't come to light. I can't let you make false confessions and possibly derail real justice from being served. I want justice just as much as anyone else. I hate whoever did this." Claudio melted into the bed, burying his face in DJ's pillow as he cried.

DJ felt like he'd hit rock bottom. Claudio hated him. He might not know it yet, but DJ did. He was in a Hell of his own creation, watching the one he loved the most in despair, and knowing he was the cause of it all. What kind of monster would do that? *What kind of monster have I become? What did I expect to happen?* he wondered. *Did I really think the video would come out and somehow the end result would be Claudio realizing he wanted to be with me, that I was his soulmate? I'm a fool.*

DJ's dad always let himself into his room. The two boys sat up as he entered, although Claudio moved as if he carried a heavy boulder on his back.

"Boys, would you like some dinner before we go to the vigil? I made soup; I have always found that a hot bowl of soup helps fill the spirit with hope."

DJ looked to Claudio. "Come on, man. We've got to have a little more hope. Things can't get worse than this."

DJ's dad chimed in, "Trust me, boys. Trust that God has a plan. Trust that the truth will be illuminated. Perhaps all of the candles shining tonight will help guide us to the truth. We'll pray on it before we eat. Come on, join me."

The sentiment seemed to lift Claudio. He wiped his tears and the three men sat down for a steaming bowl of soup. DJ purposely drank it before the broth was cool; tilting the bowl to his lips, he let the hot liquid burn his throat. Comfort wasn't something he deserved, not even from a humble bowl of soup.

29

Juliet

The stadium was mostly empty. No surprise to Juliet. Her father thought being on time was late. Lights were still being placed on the stage, wires were being secured with tape, and someone was testing the sound system. Juliet could see Macbeth and Lady among the group setting up. Ignoring the acid that rose to her throat, she decided it was time to stop avoiding Mac; she had created the divide, and it would be up to her to build the bridge.

Lady approached Juliet before she could reach Macbeth. "I'm surprised you didn't volunteer to help set up," she accused, but Juliet was too astonished at how clear her English was to feel offended.

How silly that I attributed her silence to a lack of proficiency in English. All of those times I called her a shadow, she knew. I've never made her feel welcome; I've been nothing but a bully. A deep sorrow filled Juliet's heart. A true Christian would have embraced Lady. She hadn't chosen to be Mac's wife, and yet she'd taken on her duty without complaint. Juliet should have admired her resolve.

Lady gave her a knowing smile. "Guess you didn't realize shadows had voices."

Juliet wrung her hands, which had begun to sweat. Her voice cracked as she finally found the courage to reply. "I owe you both an apology and congratulations, it seems."

"I do not need you to feel sorry towards me. It is I who feels sorry for you. You thought, all those years, that you could steel Macbeth from his family and traditions. I watched you bask in the glow of his attention, waiting for my moment, and I knew it would come. Now it is you who will sit silently in the shadows."

A tear rolled down Juliet's cheek, but Lady showed no sympathy.

"I don't want you to go near him."

Juliet felt like a kicked dog. There was nothing to do or say to make up for how poorly she had treated Lady. She would not plead with Lady; it was clear she was made of steel. Before she turned back toward her parents, she looked up to see Macbeth watching her from the side of the stage, where he had been helping secure wires. The dimming sky made it difficult to read the emotions on his face. Was it sadness? Concern? Longing?

The bleachers were now peppered with mourners and those who'd come simply as members of a community that needed to make sense of the events that had led to this moment. Juliet scanned the growing crowd for Romeo. She didn't see him, so she joined her parents, who were sitting shoulder to shoulder on the bottom row of the metal benches beneath a fleece blanket. Her mother opened her arm to allow Juliet to huddle with them.

Her father was affixed to his phone and her mother nodded toward him. "Work. Even on a night like this."

"Must be serious. He usually shows better manners," Juliet responded.

Her mother leaned close and whispered, "Seems big. I spied the name 'Shylock' on one of his texts. I wouldn't be surprised if we have to leave this event early. I knew we should have taken separate cars."

Juliet felt the corners of her mouth pull as she tried to fight off the display of sadness. She needed the warmth of Romeo's love now more than ever, but her mother was right. If Shylock was involved, her father would be pulled into work. How could Juliet blame him? He'd spent most of his career trying to bring down Shylock's crime syndicate and the crooked lawyers who represented the family, including Roman Montague. She was grateful for the sound of Pastor Ramos's voice as he opened the event with a prayer. She let the frown show and the tears surface. There were too many things calling them forth tonight.

30

Romeo

The athletic field and bleachers were packed. All that could be seen were silhouettes lit by flames, which flickered and swayed in the breeze. The time was six thirty, but the sky was already becoming dark. Romeo hung near the exit gate with Claudio, DJ, and his cousins, Mercutio and Benvolio. His dad was to join them to offer Claudio protection. They were taking Benedick's threats seriously, although the police refused to do the same. It was obvious to Romeo that Claudio was not responsible for the video, but he understood how difficult it would be to prove his innocence. If he were Benedick or Beatrice, he might feel the same need for vengeance.

Romeo strained to search the crowd for Juliet. He missed her with every ounce of his being. She hadn't returned to school at all that week, and it was too risky to go to her house. He knew she felt like a prisoner in her own home.

As he scanned the growing crowd, his eyes landed on Puck, whose camera was swinging around his shoulders. Romeo seethed at the sight of him, swaying through the crowd, occasionally lifting his camera to snap a photo of people gathered to mourn. Romeo wasn't alone in feeling that Puck's gossip column had contributed to Hero's decision to take her own life, but Puck could walk through the crowd without fear while Claudio bore all the blame.

He texted his father: "Think we could sue the school

paper? It seems to me Claudio and Hero both suffered as a direct result of its gossip column." He tucked his phone back in his pocket; they could discuss it later. *This might cause a further rift between Macbeth and Juliet, but I think she will support me.*

The choir stopped singing and Ophelia took to the stage. Romeo stopped searching for Juliet and focused on Ophelia. He was curious what she would have to say about Hero's death and the events surrounding it. To his surprise, and probably to the surprise of many, Ophelia spoke of the stigma that comes with being young and sexual. He looked at Claudio from the corner of his eyes, and he seemed to be hanging on to Ophelia's words.

"We must ask ourselves what the true reason was that Hero felt she could not go on. She suffered because she was labeled a harlot, easy, promiscuous. No doubt many girls in the crowd fear what their reputations will become if they give in to their desires. Girls and women need to be able to own their feelings without fearing shameful labels, labels that their male peers do not need to take on. Girls must deal with a society that governs their bodies in a way that boys could never understand. We must use this moment to honor Hero by shining a light on the injustice that caused her so much suffering."

DJ's dad, Pastor Ramos, crossed the stage towards Ophelia. Someone must have decided to cut her short. Romeo was unable to hear the transition that was being made; he was distracted by the parting of the crowd before him. Juliet and her parents were heading towards the exit. His father's timing was impeccable. He felt a hand fall on his shoulder and smelled his dad's cologne. As Juliet's family passed, Mr. Capulet stared at Romeo and his father with obvious disgust.

Damn, Romeo thought. He would no longer be able to attend church with the anonymity that he had before. Mr. Capulet now knew he was a Montague, and if Juliet was right, he would do everything in his power to keep them apart.

"That man is such a sore loser," his father said, leaning in toward Romeo. "His poor daughter looked like she was a child being dragged away from a good horror film. I bet old man Capulet heard the word 'sex' and needed to rush that girl out of here right away."

Romeo felt the tension in every muscle of his body. Juliet was meant to break free from her parents so that they could have a few moments together. His father was probably right that her parents didn't want her exposed to a pro-sex speech.

His father leaned in and spoke again. "Any issues tonight with Claudio?"

Romeo cocked his head so his father could hear him over Pastor Ramos's prayers. "I'm not sure that anyone has noticed us. We've tried to stay on the outskirts."

"I'm thankful for the cover of this cloudy October night, but my balls are freezing."

Romeo cringed at his father's lack of tact and noticed that his friends had their heads bowed in prayer. He folded his hands and titled his head down, but his eyes didn't close. He felt in his gut that he needed to stay alert. He lifted his head slightly to scan the surrounding crowd and spotted Benedick; he was staring right at Claudio and Romeo with a look of disgust. Don Pedro was with him and seemed to be holding Benedick back. Romeo elbowed his father and nodded toward Benedick.

His father whispered, "Good catch, son. I think it's best we make our way out."

They didn't get a chance. In a flash, Romeo found himself acting as a human shield as multiple students rushed toward Claudio swinging fists and insults. It was his father who was able to push people aside and create the path needed for the boys to escape. Romeo, DJ, Benvolio, and Mercutio did the best they could to get Claudio to safety. People began picking up rocks and throwing them. One hit Claudio in the back of the head. He stumbled, but Romeo and Mercutio were able to grab him under the arm and keep him moving. Romeo felt a stinging sensation as a rock struck him in the arm. They got to Romeo's car and piled in. Romeo peeled out and saw that there was mass pandemonium in the stadium. In the rearview he could also see Puck racing toward his car, camera in hand. Romeo would break that camera if Puck planned to follow them to the hospital for a photo op.

"Do you have a towel?" Benvolio asked over the sound of DJ's wailing. "DJ, if you don't calm down, I'm going to have to slap you. We need everyone to remain calm."

"Here, have my sweater," Mercutio said, ripping his coat off so he could take off the wool sweater.

"I'm heading to the hospital," Romeo said, trying to keep his head about him.

Claudio tried to refuse. "I'll be OK."

"No, you won't," Benvolio said. "The gash is deep, and you're bleeding heavily. I'm amazed you didn't lose consciousness."

After helping Claudio get checked in at the hospital, Romeo called his father and let him know where they were. His father said he was gathering Claudio's parents and would be there soon. After hanging up, he checked his phone for communication from Juliet: nothing. He needed to drive by her house, if only to see the light in her window and know she was OK. Claudio was still in the waiting room. He was resting his head in DJ's lap while DJ applied pressure to his wound.

"Damn it!" Romeo called as he walked toward them. "Can't we get this man a room?"

Benvolio put his hands on Romeo's shoulders. "Take a breath, man. They said it would be a few minutes before they had a room set up." Romeo collapsed into a chair across from DJ and Claudio.

Claudio sighed. "I'm sorry. It seems that everyone who dares get close to me is meant to suffer."

Romeo felt Claudio's sadness. "None of this is your fault." He saw movement at the entrance; his father was walking toward them, Claudio's parents trailing behind. They clung to each other, clearly fearing the worst.

Romeo looked back at Claudio and DJ. "My dad is here now. I hope you won't mind me leaving. I have something personal that I need to deal with."

Claudio's parents rushed towards them and lowered to their knees in front of Claudio, fussing over him as if he were a small child. Romeo knew Claudio would be cared for and he could exit without feeling guilty. He headed toward the parking lot, but his father caught up to him.

"Romeo, wait. I'd like to talk to you before you leave."

"Can we talk outside? I feel like I'm going to flip out on the attendants if they don't get Claudio in a room. I mean, he's bleeding through that shirt."

The two made their way outside and Romeo propped himself up against a column. Every muscle in his body felt tired. "Romeo," his father began, "I just wanted to tell you how proud I am of how you acted tonight. You defended Claudio and got him to safety."

Romeo's face grew hot. He hadn't expected his father to offer him praise. "I was just doing what's right. I can't believe that Claudio's own friends have turned against him. They think they're getting justice for Hero, but they have no evidence against Claudio."

"You're starting to sound like a real Montague. Look, I want to cut to the chase. I have something that I want to give you. You were meant to receive it on your eighteenth birthday, along with access to your trust fund, but after tonight, I think this is the right time."

Romeo's father reached into his coat pocket and produced a manilla envelope. Romeo stood up straight.

"Your mother and I--"

Romeo was caught off guard. What did his mother have to do with any of this?

"--we had different views on how to raise you, and I admit that I was bullheaded. I wanted to raise you to follow in my footsteps, to maintain the family practice. Our family has been in the business of defense since the Roman Empire. I've always felt proud of that. Sure, when I was young I only cared about the money, but I hope you see that I do believe in innocence until proven guilty. I believe the accused deserve fair treatment."

Romeo was finding it hard not to fall into an argument over his father's statement. He knew his father defended people who were guilty beyond doubt, and he had done it for the money. It wasn't a secret that his father was on the payroll of Shylock's Mafia, either. But now wasn't the time to point that out. He bit his tongue and waited for the envelope to be offered to him.

His father rattled on. "Your mom wanted you to pave your own path. She didn't want me to direct your footsteps. Ultimately, I pushed her away. I was determined to make you a proper Montague. After all, you are my only son. Of course, I knew almost immediately that it was a mistake, and one I was too stubborn to take back."

Romeo couldn't help but loosen his tongue. "Wow. I never thought you'd take ownership."

"Well, I was a stubborn man, and I still am. It's what makes me a great lawyer. But you are half your mother, and you have the parts of her that made me fall in love in the first place."

Romeo couldn't believe his father actually loved anyone, but now wasn't the time for argument.

"Anyway, I don't want to get caught up in the past. My point is, you are becoming your own man despite my best efforts to make you into me. When your mom left, she made me promise one thing: that on your eighteenth birthday, I would allow you to choose what to do with your life. I was so confident that I would mold you that I agreed." His dad extended the envelope and Romeo ripped into it. "I've kept my promise, and I hope you see that I'm not a bad man, Romeo. It is my deep hope that you will join the family practice, but I finally see that your mom was right. You must make your own choices in life. I just want you to know that I'm proud of the choices you've made these last few days."

Romeo's hands shook and tears dropped onto the paper as he read it over and over. Romeo's father walked away without saying more, and perhaps there was nothing more that could be said. His father had finally given him the two things he'd wanted his whole childhood: his approval and his mother. The envelope held all of her contact information. His father would no longer keep them apart.

Romeo practically ran to his car, but once inside he felt torn. For so long he'd wanted to run away from the Montague name and everything it stood for. Having his mother's contact information would allow him to do that, but working with his dad had changed his view. Claudio had been punished and persecuted without a shred of evidence. His father was the only one brave enough to stand up for his legal rights. Perhaps Romeo could join the practice, and in doing so, heal the Montague reputation.

This was a turning point and he knew it. But which way to turn? Should he run away with Juliet and start over in a town that held less animosity toward the Montague name, or should he stay and work to restore his name and prove himself worthy of Juliet? He needed to talk to her. No matter what, she was his future.

31

Ophelia

Offended, angry, affronted: all of these words could describe how Ophelia felt the moment Pastor Ramos interrupted her speech. She'd spent countless hours thinking about how she could honor the memory of Hero, how she could try to turn this tragedy into a platform for change. She understood why her mother couldn't remain in this small town with small-minded people. They didn't get it. Shutting her down, quieting her message, wanting her to hide her opinion: this was exactly why Hero had killed herself.

Then there was all of the violence that had broken out, and during a prayer, no less. The people of this town wanted to act like they were righteous, but they were willing to throw rocks at someone who hadn't been proven guilty. The other girls on the cheer squad were quite adamant that Claudio was guilty, but Ophelia and Bianca remained doubtful. They'd been close to Hero. They'd seen how in love Hero and Claudio had been. Everyone wanted to rush to assign guilt, but they didn't really care about the truth. Just like they couldn't handle hearing the truth in Ophelia's speech. It was more proof that the people of this town were simple-minded.

Ophelia's thoughts were interrupted by her father. "I'm proud of you, Ophelia."

Her mouth fell open. "Why?"

"You stood up in front of everyone and dared to tell the

truth to a town clinging to its rules and traditions. That must have taken so much courage." Her father paused and Ophelia was still stunned that this moment was even happening between them. "I just wish your mother could have been here. She's missing out on watching you become an amazing, headstrong woman, just like her."

Ophelia bit her lip and choked back the tears. "Thank you, Daddy." Her dad opened his arms to hug her. *Daddy*. Saying that word flooded her with sentiment. She was reminded of how things had been when she was young, when her father was still her hero. Then her mother had shown her that he wasn't more than a doormat, so easily manipulated by love. When she pulled back, she considered the flaws in her mother's view. Always showing up for your family wasn't pathetic; it required strength. He wasn't manipulated by love. He was choosing to love even when it was hard.

"Are you coming home with Laer and me?" he asked, oblivious to the revelation Ophelia was having.

"The cheer squad has decided to remain on the field and hold our own vigil, since the sanctity of this night was disrupted. I can have one of the girls drive me home."

"Be safe and call me if you need anything." Her dad turned and started walking away.

"Wait," Ophelia called after him. "Dad, I'm sorry, I just realized I left my bookbag in the school. It has my house key and wallet inside."

A voice came from over Ophelia's shoulder, startling her. "Polonius, I was just coming to compliment your daughter on her brave speech." Her father beamed and Ophelia genuinely blushed at Hamlet's praise. "Forgive me for overhearing you, but Ophelia, if you need to get inside, I have to grab some items from my office before leaving. I can let you in." He smiled his dimpled smile and Ophelia's heart fluttered. "Polonius, would that be OK? I was just thinking I could save you the trip, since I have to go inside anyway."

Polonius clapped Hamlet on the shoulder. "That would

be appreciated. This week has been exhausting, I'm sure for you more than me." Dr. Hamlet nodded in agreement. Polonius turned his attention to Ophelia and gave her a serious look. "I'll see you at home. I trust you to make the right decisions."

As they got farther from the exiting crowd, Dr. Hamlet put his hand on the small of her back. Ophelia didn't want to seduce him. She wasn't in that mindset tonight. But it seemed her past attempts had already succeeded. She contemplated pulling away, but the warmth of him felt nice. He touched her with the confidence of a man. She liked that.

Dr. Hamlet unlocked the doors and Ophelia was overcome with how many memories had been created at this school. Perhaps the best memory would be created tonight. Just like that, a pang in her gut appeared like a warning. Ophelia brushed it off. Laertes had been filling her head with too many conspiracy theories. But the feeling of unease didn't alleviate. *I can always just grab my things and go. The game can end here and now. I have the power.*

32

Katharina

Katharina sat on the cold aluminum bleachers, watching every-one as they left. She was still in disbelief over everything that had occurred that night. A few rows ahead of Katharina sat a couple arguing. She listened with interest, wondering whose parents they were.

"I can't believe the way these kids behaved tonight. This generation has absolutely no respect!" The brown-haired woman waved her hands as if she were trying to conjure up some decency.

The man joined in. "I don't understand why that Claudio kid would even come here. It was cocky."

"I agree. Kids these days only think of themselves. They don't think about consequences," the woman spat.

Katharina rose from her seat and started walking down the stairs. She couldn't help but stop at the row where the couple sat. "It always amazes me when adults place the blame on youth. We are raised by your example. Don't you feel any responsibility?"

The man's mustache curled into his mouth as he ad-dressed her, and Katharina badly wanted to cut it off. "I bet you blame your parents for all of your behavior."

Katharina smirked. "My parents are dead." The man be-came tightlipped and the woman scoffed. "I used to feel sad about it, but watching you two has made me really grateful."

"Grateful?" the woman gasped. "What a horrible thing to say. You are exactly what I'm talking about. You see, Ronald, these children have no morals."

"I'm just grateful that I didn't have to watch them become old, bitter, and accusatory like you two. They died when they were young, still in love with the world and full of hope. They will always remain that way in my memory." Katharina walked toward the field knowing her message had probably fallen on deaf ears.

For a moment she yearned to join the prayer circle that the cheer squad had created, but she knew the circle would not welcome her the way they did Bianca. Instead, she walked to the car. She would wait for Bianca and give her time to grieve with her friends. As she leaned against the car, she noticed the lights in the main office were still on. She reflected on Shakespeare High. Everyone had pulled together to mourn an unexpected tragedy, but the way Katharina saw it, the school was always full of tragedy, the everyday tragedies that people were happy to ignore. No one would light a candle for her broken heart or all the trauma she was forced to keep bound up.

That thought made Katharina break down in choked sobs. There were some things she couldn't keep silent about anymore. She knew exactly who had filmed Claudio and Hero that night, but she'd worried she would cause more pain by revealing the truth, or maybe people wouldn't believe her. Instead, she'd stayed silent, hoping the truth would find its own way to the surface.

Katharina had woken that night and decided to climb into her grandmother's attic to look at the stars. The window in the attic gave her an excellent view of the night sky, but also the yards of her neighbors. Movement in Claudio's yard had caught her eye. At first she hadn't been able to tell who it was, but then she'd seen DJ cross into his own backyard, camera in hand.

After tonight, after the violence that had broken out, it seemed reckless not to tell someone. Maybe she could reach out to Juliet. She was the closest thing to a friend that Katharina had, but Juliet wasn't herself lately. Besides, Juliet had been friends with DJ since childhood. Where would her loyalties lie? With the truth, or with the pastor's son?

It became darker. The lights in the school had turned out. She crouched down so she could get a look at who was leaving. What she saw caused her to bear another secret. Dr. Hamlet walked out with Ophelia. Before they parted, Hamlet drew Ophelia into a hug, his hands around her hips, their bodies so close you couldn't see where one ended and the other began. Katharina stayed low, breathing shallowly until Ophelia returned to the field and Dr Hamlet left the parking lot.

Laughter escaped her lips, reverberating through the cold night air. She couldn't contain it, and part of her was horrified that it was happening. It became even more horrifying when she noticed her sister walking toward her with a clear look of dismay.

"What on earth are you doing? Stop laughing. The other girls are coming."

"I'm sorry," Katharina said while trying to catch her breath, but the laughter kept pouring out. She heard the car unlock and threw herself in.

"Really, Katharina, how can you be laughing on a night like this?" Bianca threw her half-melted candlestick at her sister, which startled Katharina enough to end the fits.

"I'm sorry. I shouldn't be laughing. But sometimes it feels like none of this is real. Like I'm stuck in someone's tragic play and I can't help but become amused by all of the drama."

"You're being absurd. I swear, it's amazing that we were formed in the same womb."

"You see, the very fact that we're twins is comedic. We couldn't be more opposite in our demeanor, and yet we're nearly identical." Bianca rolled her eyes and started the car. "I'm just saying, if you deconstruct it, it can be quite comedic."

They drove home in silence. Katharina watched Shakespeare High diminish in the side view mirror as they got farther away. She wondered what else she would bear witness to this year.

After all, it was only the beginning.

Acknowledgement

Shakespeare High: Act 1 is my first novel and required a strong support group to make come to fruition. I'd like to thank everyone in that support group; without you, I'd still be wallowing in my limiting self-beliefs.

First, I'd like to thank the friends who read Shakespeare High when it was still in its early stages. Diadra, Bekah, Karen, Heather, and Cassandra, I hope you know how much I valued your words of encouragement. There were many nights when I felt incapable of seeing this story through; I'm grateful that you didn't let me quit.

Thank you to everyone at Fiverr whose freelance work taught me how to improve my writing and whose words gave me the confidence I needed to persevere! JC McDowell, thanks to your advice my book matured and became more cohesive. Steamy shower scenes removed and more developed characters were a result of your commentary! I'd like to thank my proofreader, J.H. Fleming. You worked your grammar magic and gave Shakespeare High the coherence it needed. Thank you, N.O. Ramos! You were able to encapsulate Shakespeare High's essence; I'm so impressed!

Thank you to my husband for supporting all of my whims. You manage to keep me grounded while helping me soar and I am eternally grateful.

Finally, I'd like to thank my son Henry. I'm so glad that I get to be your mom. You remind me to play, to be present, and to laugh. I love you!

About The Author

Tiffany L Johnson

Tiffany L. Johnson is a woman of many talents and passions. Having been a storyteller for as long as she can remember, Johnson has always had a knack for creating fascinating tales and holding the attention of her audience. She was given the monicker "Storyteller" by her uncle at a young age, and even wrote her first book on her bedroom wall in crayon. Her Mother left a rather negative review.

Before pursuing her career as a novelist, Tiffany poured her talents into a variety of other areas in her life. From being an elementary school teacher, to a published poet, to a wife and mother, Johnson lives a full and happy life. She, her husband, their four-year-old son, and their rescue pup Steve enjoy a self-sustained life in Bucks County, Pennsylvania. On her homestead, Johnson raises chickens, pigs, and grows a plentiful garden. She's even been known to sing to her strawberries!

After being inspired to create "Shakespeare High" through meditation, Johnson got to work with plotting and writing her novel. She hopes to continue this series and expand her writing into other projects. When she's not creating masterpieces, Tiffany enjoys crocheting, yoga, belly dancing, and a vast variety of other things.

www.ingramcontent.com/pod-product-compliance
Lightning Source LLC
Chambersburg PA
CBHW051433170626
46809CB00006B/2437